TINA M EDWARDS is a1
of poetry and flash fiction. S
online writing platform that
particularly words that have b
She currently lives in the sou.
the inspiration for this book was found, walking its many fields,
paths and headlands. *The Secret of Creek Cottage* is her first novel.

www.tinamedwardswriter.com
https://twitter.com/bumbleandmoss

The Secret of
CREEK COTTAGE

Tina M Edwards

SilverWood

Published in 2020 by SilverWood Books

SilverWood Books Ltd
14 Small Street, Bristol, BS1 1DE, United Kingdom
www.silverwoodbooks.co.uk

ISBN 978-1-78132-977-1 (paperback)
ISBN 978-1-80042-006-9 (ebook)

British Library Cataloguing in Publication Data
A CIP catalogue record for this book is
available from the British Library

Page design and typesetting by SilverWood Books

For Sam & Molly,
never give up on your dreams.

Carol & Lor,
SB1. Where it all began.

&
for Rob.

*'The supernatural is the natural,
just not yet understood.'*

Elbert Hubbard

PROLOGUE

There was no doubt that the length of rope had achieved its purpose. It had been the ideal medium from which to make the noose that hung from the iron hook.

Backwards and forwards the body swung. Rhythmically, like the pendulum of an old grandfather clock. Accompanied not by a tick-tock, but by the sound of an eager Cornish wind that blew through the cottage. Unconsciousness had been quick. Death, as in the form of a corpse with no beating heart however, had taken a little longer. Its spirit now caught...somewhere between the real world and the unknown.

I

Present day

Kitty sniffed. There was that strange smell again; it reminded her of gone-off almonds. She must remember to mention it to Ben when he got home from work. Perhaps the drains needed looking at. She removed the bright pink washing-up gloves, a jokey, ostentatious farewell present from her best friend Lizzie, and put them on the wooden draining-board, looking out of the kitchen window as she did so. It was early morning and the sun was finally creeping up over the top of the woodland that surrounded the cottage. Later, when it was at its highest point, it would cast a dancing shimmer across the estuary. But it wasn't the only window of the cottage that had such wonderful views. She'd discovered within hours of moving into Creek Cottage that every window had views of the cove and estuary, even if you did need to be a contortionist to obtain them.

The small coastal village of Trunrowan could not be more different from the hustle and bustle of Bristol where she'd spent the best part of the past thirty-five years. Much as she occasionally missed being able to pop out on a whim to buy something completely unnecessary, she didn't miss the long hours working alongside her husband in his dental practice. The stressful nature of her job had taken its toll and was also a contributing factor, according to her GP, as to her not having yet fallen pregnant. She'd been assured there was no medical reason, so when she and Ben finally made the decision to leave Bristol to take on a renovation project in the form of a tumbledown cottage, as well as changing her career completely in the process, she embraced it wholeheartedly. Moving to Cornwall had been the perfect excuse to finally take up studying something she'd always had an interest in: herbal medicine.

It had taken six months of hard sweat, and a few tears along the way, to get Creek Cottage up to scratch and in a liveable condition. Their family and friends had thought them completely bonkers, taking on a renovation property that was over a hundred miles from Bristol, but funnily enough they were now eagerly organising which weekends they were coming to visit. Yes, it'd been a huge decision to relocate, but now they had, she hoped that the main reason for their move would soon materialise.

Kitty looked up at the kitchen clock Ben had insisted on bringing with him. She'd never liked the thing, it was far too grand, and even more so now it was in the cottage. If she got a move on, she'd have just enough time to catch the ferry across the estuary. She grabbed her coat from the back of the stable style door, pulling it shut behind her. She still couldn't get used to not needing to lock it. There were only a few cottages on this side of the estuary, and she would often go days without seeing anyone other than Ben and Marmalade their cat. She hurried down the shingle path to the small wooden gate at the bottom of the garden, which led directly onto the cove. The ferry was due to leave in five minutes.

Reaching the slipway just in time, Kitty hopped onto the ferry deck.

'Afternoon, Pete. Thought I wasn't going to make it then for a moment!' she said, smiling at the ferryman.

Pete nodded at her in acknowledgement. She was sure his face appeared to be covered in more and more white hair every time she saw him. All he needed now to complete the traditional sailor look was a pipe.

'Wasson? I saw ye running, young Kitty. Never did anyone any good. Running that is. Ye young 'uns 'ave all the time in the world. No need to run. Not like us old 'uns. We only 'as time for doing naught. But we ain't much use at running.'

Kitty grinned. Much as she'd become fond of Pete, he did talk in riddles most of the time.

'I'm surprising Ben. Thought we might go for a meal in The Ferry Boat Inn, what do you reckon?'

Pete nodded again, his beard almost touching his chest.

'Aye, ye can't go much wrong there, and the mackerel's fit at the moment. Am sure yer young man will see ye right with a glass of whatever tickles yer fancy.'

'Well, that's sorted then. Thanks for the tip-off.' Kitty handed over her two-pound coin for the journey. She loved the way he called her young 'un. In comparison to him, she guessed she was still relatively young. Fit as a fiddle he may well be, but an oil painting he certainly wasn't. More like a weathered sea goat.

'Last crossing tonight is nine. I also 'ave a date, with a pint of ale, and me missus is cooking up me favourite, so don't be late, otherwise ye be swimming back.' He chuckled at his own joke and then started coughing, wiping the back of his hand across his mouth.

Kitty stepped back instinctively. She'd become well versed over the years in dodging patients coughing and spluttering, but today she had no face mask to offer her protection. Thankfully the ferry came to an abrupt halt and she hurriedly stepped onto the quay.

'Thanks Pete, see you later,' she called behind her, while Pete waved, still coughing up a storm.

II

1916

They were now almost two years into what people were calling the Great War. Some Great War! How could you call a war great when all that was happening was the killing of innocent young men? In Loveday's eyes there was nothing great about that.

She remembered the day Will told her he was signing up for the cause, she'd practically begged him on hands and knees not to go along to the village hall. She'd banged things, huffed and puffed, and even denied him his marital rights, despite the fact they were trying for a cheel. Generally, she tried her hardest to be as difficult as possible.

'Loveday, ye is being as stubborn as a mule. Ye do realise don't ye, that I won't have a choice in the matter soon?' Will had said in exasperation.

'Aye, but ye do 'ave a choice at the moment. If ye is to be called up, it won't be yet. How will the village manage with no boats out at sea each day, what will we all eat, how will we manage for money? How will I survive alone in this godforsaken, damp, flea-ridden cottage!' she'd screeched at him.

'It's not flea-ridden and never will be, not with the amount of cleaning ye does. Ye is being bleddy ridiculous. The boats will continue to fish as they always do, things will just be a little harder on the elders that's all, but...they will manage, Loveday.'

Will had tried his hardest to remain positive and calm.

'Well, ye go ahead and get yerself killed then, but don't expect me to be 'ere waiting for ye should ye return,' she'd spat, continuing to bang pots and pans as loudly as she could.

'What's that supposed to mean?' Will asked, finally rising to the bait.

'Ye knows we 'as been trying for a cheel for ages, but 'ow's that going to happen if ye ain't 'ere?' She'd stopped banging pots and had plonked herself down on the back doorstep, rubbing her floured hands onto her apron. Not being one for showing emotion, Will had placed his hand on her shoulder and gave it a pat.

'I 'opes to be 'ome occasionally, Love. I really wont 'ave no choice in the matter, so let's try and make the best of what time we do 'ave left together, shall we?'

Those were to be his final words on the subject, and he'd bent down and kissed the top of her head, taking a deep breath in as he did so.

She smiled, remembering him telling her how good she'd smelled, and how there was no time for those types of thoughts, much as he knew she desperately wanted a cheel; he had other things to be getting on with.

For one, he'd promised George Weaver up at Bramble Farm that he would help out with the milking. If he didn't go right that minute the cows were sure to be sore and swollen and he couldn't afford for the work be given to someone else. Will had returned on furlough only twice since leaving Trunrowan two years ago, but as far as Loveday was aware, he was still alive out there somewhere. She'd received a handful of letters, which she read every day; it made her feel close to him. What little she did know, was that he was in France and still serving as part of the 7th Battalion of the Duke of Cornwall's Light Infantry. Even though she hated him for joining up, deep down she was immensely proud. Not that she would ever let on to him, of course.

Loveday looked out of the cottage's back door and up into the night sky. There were stars dotted everywhere, some shining brightly, others tiny specks, trillions of miles away. When she was a cheel her ma called the stars moon dust, left by those who travelled the night sky while she slept. Her ma always had a story or two to tell her. She hoped she'd remember them all by the time she had children of her own.

Tonight the clouds were moving northwards and in an hour or two the full moon would be at its fullest. Then she would make her way to the bottom of the garden and across the cove, eventually taking the path that would lead into the ancient wood.

It had been an off-the-cuff remark in Granby's, the village store, one morning where she'd been nattering to her friend, Mabel Weaver, that had started her on her current journey. Loveday had collected her rations and had carefully covered over her bicycle's basket, when old Mrs Cromp had come out of the store and thrust a piece of crumpled paper into her hand. She didn't say anything at the time, just smiled in a knowing sort of way, which totally baffled Loveday, until she smoothed out the piece of paper and read the message. Taking a deep breath, she pushed the paper into her pinny pocket, straddled the bike, and pedaled as fast as she could all the way down Chillyhill Lane and back to the sanctuary of Rowan Cottage.

Once home, she placed the crumpled piece of paper onto the kitchen table and sat herself down, trying to catch her breath. When she'd finally managed to control her breathing, she smoothed out the paper and whispered the words under her breath.

Deep in the ancient wood is a woodcutter's cottage.
On the first evening of the next full moon,
you are welcome to join us in our gathering.

What could it mean? And what sort of gathering was it? She didn't know of the woodcutter's cottage; perhaps she'd never ventured deep enough into the ancient woodland. She did know though, that Mrs Cromp was somewhat of a mystery. People in the village said she was cunning folk and in the main stayed clear. No one would knowingly associate with these people unless they were in desperate need of healing, or perhaps a potion for a stubborn ailment. But take as she found, Loveday had felt an instant kinship to the woman.

Mrs Cromp was a rotund lady with a ruddy complexion. Her silvery hair was worn high in a bun on top of her head, where a dark-red velvet scarf secured it in place. Long strands of wispy locks framed her face and gave her a distinct, dishevelled look. As to her age, well that was anyone's guess; she'd been around for as long as Loveday could remember, tending to keep on the outskirts and rarely coming into the heart of the village. And she had always looked the same. She could often be seen foraging for wild flowers from the cliff top overlooking the estuary, in winter as well as summer. At other times, she'd be scouring the high tideline in the cove, gathering seaweed and shells, head down, walking slowly and methodically, day or night. But mostly she kept herself to herself and didn't venture into the village unless necessary. Today however must have been one of those days.

Loveday's stomach was beginning to flutter, as though she'd swallowed a jam jar full of butterflies. If her memory served her right, there'd been no one else in the store when she'd quite outspokenly mentioned to Mabel that she was still without a cheel and how desperately she wanted one. Mrs Cromp must've been in the shop somewhere, Loveday had just not been aware of it. It was certainly possible as there were all sorts of boxes and shelves in the store that she could have been behind. Perhaps the invitation was to do with her comment?

Umm, but that still didn't get over the fact that Will was away at war. She wasn't naive enough to think it could happen without the seed of a man. She knew the ways of the birds and bees well enough.

The next full moon would be on Thursday and today was Monday, so there wasn't much time to ponder over the finer details. What she needed to do was go along and find out for herself exactly what the note meant. She wasn't sure how she'd managed to talk herself into potentially venturing into the ancient wood, but she did know that she would take any scrap of advice, no matter how small, to help her conceive a cheel. Regardless of what it entailed. She'd speak to Mabel as soon as she could and see what her thoughts on the matter were.

III

Will rubbed his eyes. He still couldn't focus. He rubbed them again, harder this time. Damn it, they still weren't right after that bleddy last bombardment of artillery shells, thankfully delivering only tear gas and not something more deadly. If only he'd secured his gas mask under his chin. Schoolboy error and he should've known better.

His eyes were always worse when he'd just woken up, not that he did much sleeping in the shithole of a trench that was classed as home. When they landed at Boulogne last summer, he'd never dreamed that his life would be like this. An existence, nothing more, nothing less. His thoughts and feelings had been stripped bare, twisted and pulled from his insides, then somehow rammed back in, distorted. Seeing and smelling the horrors of war was like living on the edge of a deep, dark precipice continuously. Day and night.

Eventually, his eyes began to focus enough for him to safely heave himself up from the sodden wooden crate which had served as his bed for the night.

'Good morning, Wilbur,' came the irritating voice of Private Garraway.

Bleddy Wilbur, how many times did he have to tell that man, it wasn't his name? He decided to ignore him and began walking down the trench towards the latrine. He was in no mood for pleasantries, all he wanted to do was go about his daily business in peace and quiet.

Private Garraway – or 'Hock' as he was known amongst the battalion – followed behind Will humming loudly, squelching in the mud.

'Not sleep well then, Wilbur?'

Will stopped abruptly and turned sharply, squaring up to Hock.

'Do ye ever bleddy shut up?' he spat out, doing his best to keep his fists tight at his side. 'No, I did not bleddy sleep well, and I don't want to make small talk when I 'ave just woken up from the little sleep I did get. Now, why don't ye fuck off. Preferably as far away from this trench as possible!'

Will could feel his face reddening with frustration, and he lunged forward. Hock stepped back, as Will, struggling to keep his footing in the mud, reached out with both hands to steady himself, shoving Hock as he did so. Down they both went with an almighty thud.

Being in such close quarters it was only seconds before both of them had various bodies in between them, ensuring that the altercation went no further. There wasn't enough room to swing a cat in the trench, let alone accommodate a full-on brawl. A few moments later a voice boomed out from behind the rabble.

'Gridley, Garraway, get yerselves over here, right now!'

Bleddy hell, Will thought to himself. All he had had to do was keep it together for a few seconds and ignore the little weasel, but no, he couldn't even manage that, and now he was up against the Sergeant. And his latrine visit was going to have to wait a little longer…

That morning's events were just one of many other similar occurrences that had begun happening on a regular basis. Will wasn't the only one struggling with the damp wet weather: morale was at an all-time low. At least back in Cornwall he could've dried himself off in front of a nice open fire and warmed himself with a drop of ale. Here the stench of rotting flesh was unbearable and there was little liquor to drink as a reprieve. Unlike many of the other men, at least he was used to rancid smells from the fish when he'd worked the boats, but this putridness was like something he'd never encountered before. It was almost as if the devil himself had decided to bunk down with them. And to add even more misery to the dire situation, it had been raining continuously for days. He knew it was a double-edged sword, for when it did eventually stop, the bombardment from the Germans would start up again and they'd be sent out of the trenches and up to Delville Wood in an attempt to secure its foothold.

Delville Wood reminded him of back home with its thick tangle of beech and hornbeam trees. Loveday always delighted in collecting the winged seeds each autumn from the hornbeam, stringing them together with pieces of coloured cotton and adding scraps of pretty material as she did so. Trunrowan's harvest festival just wouldn't be the same without them. Will wondered if she'd continued making them over the past two summers he'd not been there. He made a mental note to try and remember to ask her.

Each morning, he would allow himself a moment of reminiscing. Not for long but just long enough so he didn't forget what his beautiful Loveday looked like. He wished he could bury his face in her long auburn hair, smell the sea salt that lingered in its curls. If he breathed deep enough he almost could. And if he closed his eyes, he could see her sparkling green eyes darting from side to side, enticing him, beckoning...

'7th Battalion, get yer kit together, we're off!' A loud holler broke his thoughts and Will scrambled to grab his rifle and gas mask.

'Use the dense hazel thickets for cover, stay close to the edge of the wood, this one is for our taking boys. NOW let's get to it,' shouted Sergeant Foster from the end of the trench, as Will and the rest of his battalion made the straightest line they could muster in the squalor. Thoughts of Loveday were now firmly erased from his mind. He needed to survive. He *would* survive this godforsaken hell hole. God help any Hun that came his way today because he was itching for a fight and this damn war to be over. He waited his turn to go over the top and, as he wiped his face with the back of his hand, he realised it was still raining.

IV

Present day

Ben came out of the practice door and looked up to clear blue sky. There wasn't a cloud in sight, even though he could feel a gentle onshore breeze. You really couldn't beat Cornwall in the warmer months; there was nowhere else quite like it. He would even admit to not being particularly bothered by the rain and wind when it came, and Trunrowan certainly had more than its fair share of wet and windy weather. There was something quite magical sitting on the sand in the cove and watching the raging clouds billowing over the headland.

As he continued walking down Fore Street he spotted Kitty, the late afternoon sun catching her skin. He'd never seen her look so healthy. Coastal life certainly agreed with her. She was wearing his favourite yellow dress, the one with bright pink flowers dotted all over it, which complimented her short dark hair and freckles. He smiled to himself; it was a dress she would not have been seen dead in when back in Bristol.

'Hi, babes. Good day?' Kitty stood on tiptoe to kiss him.

'Well this is a lovely surprise. Not bad thanks, only ten patients all day. You know, I still can't get used to the slow pace of it all.'

'Ten, is that all? You must be beside yourself with boredom.' She laughed.

'And most of those were holidaymakers – I really don't know what all the locals do when they have toothache because they certainly don't come and see me.'

Holding hands, they walked down the cobbled street towards the quayside, past all the quaint shops that were rammed to the hilt with people buying holiday souvenirs and copious amounts of Cornish fudge.

'Well, given the state of most of the locals' teeth,' she whispered, looking around as she did so, 'I would imagine they don't go to the dentist. They probably tie a piece of string around their rotten teeth and attach it to a doorknob!'

'Harsh, Kitty Gridley. Do you know, I think you could be on to something there. Anyhow, what have I done to deserve this surprise welcome?' he asked, slipping his arm around her waist and pulling her towards him.

'Well, I thought, seeing as I have the most wonderful and gorgeous husband in Trunrowan… Why ever not?'

'You, young lady, are definitely after something. This all seems a little fishy to me,' he said as they strolled past the empty lobster pots lined up on the side of the quay.

Kitty raised her eyebrows at him. She knew his sense of humour too well.

Ben knew her too well too, he guessed she was buttering him up for something. But regardless, it would be nice to spend an evening out together.

Their lovemaking that night had been slow and sensual, an intimacy they had not shared for a while. Ben knew that Kitty was desperate for a child and, at times, sex felt purely functional. But tonight had been different. They'd spent a lovely couple of hours talking, laughing and enjoying great food, washed down with a few rather large glasses of wine so that for once, Ben didn't mind that Kitty had an ulterior motive.

Now, lying with Kitty nestled contentedly under his arm, he watched her rhythmical breathing, and sighed. A deep contented sigh, noticing the full moon beginning to rise and glisten through the bedroom window as it skimmed the top of the woodland. Without it the sky was as dark as could be with no street lights to pollute it.

Of course it was the same sky he'd always looked at, but tonight it felt special. It served to remind him how very lucky they were and just how much their lives had changed for the better.

Kitty stirred, groaning a little. Ben felt a sudden rise in warmth from her naked body. He carefully moved his arm thinking he might be disturbing her but she groaned again, only louder this time, tossing her body from side to side. Ben moved further across the bed to give her some more room, hoping she might settle again but instead she let out a loud piercing scream. Sitting bolt upright, she began shaking uncontrollably.

'Hey, it's OK, calm down you've had a bad dream.' Ben pulled her towards him but she resisted.

'Get off me!' She pushed him away with her flailing arms. 'Get off me!'

'Kitty, calm down. It's me, Ben. You've had a bad dream, that's all. Take some deep breaths. That's it, babes, slowly in and out, nice and slow.' He was well rehearsed in panic attacks happening in the dental surgery, but it was a whole different matter when it was happening to someone he loved.

Kitty's breathing eventually settled but her eyes were still shut. What on earth could she have been dreaming about to have woken in such a sudden, frantic manner? Gently, he lifted her head and looked at her startled face.

'Hey, there now, it's not so bad after all, is it? Look, it's a full moon too, especially for you.' Kitty opened her eyes and they both looked towards the bedroom window. Kitty attempted the smile Ben had been seeking and he gave her a reassuring squeeze.

'So, all is well, Mrs Gridley.'

He winked at his vulnerable and dishevelled-looking wife, who was now pulling the bed sheets up around her as she lay back down.

'Was my lovemaking actually that bad?' he asked and they both broke into a giggle. Kitty rested her head on Ben's chest. She wasn't normally one for having bad dreams. She could sleep for England and was rarely disturbed by anything, even less so now they were in Cornwall. He would talk to her in the morning and see if she could remember what it was all about.

V

Loveday perched on a milking stool in the large kitchen of
Bramble Farm, legs crossed like a pixie on a toadstool.

'There ye go.' Mabel handed Loveday a cup of nettle tea and
passed her a large chunk of homemade fruit cake.

'Oooo, thanks, just what the doctor ordered – yer ma's fruit
cake is the best this side of Bodmin.' Loveday said as she sunk her
teeth into the juicy cake.

'Yer right, Loveday, it is indeed. I ain't never gonna match
Ma's cooking skills. I just ain't cut out for it.'

Loveday, unable to reply with her mouth still full of cake,
attempted to raise her eyebrows in acknowledgement.

'So, what ye gonna do then about this meeting in Rowan
Wood tonight? Ye going?' Mabel continued.

Loveday licked her lips as the last mouthful was lovingly
swallowed. 'Well, I 'ave to really, don't I? I can't be seen to look
a gift horse in the mouth. I mean, who'd have thought it, old

Mrs Cromp thinking of little old me and me problems?'

Mabel pulled a face. 'Umm... Well ye go careful, she's probably after yer guts or perhaps she needs some of yer luscious auburn locks for one of 'er spells!'

Loveday shrugged.

'I'm being serious, Loveday. Ye knows she's cunning folk and I'm sure she's not up to anything sinister or naught but...'

'It'll be fine, Mabel. Why don't ye come with me?'

Mabel recoiled in horror.

'Sorry, Love, but yer on yer own for this one. 'Opefully she'll give ye a potion and you'll escape her hidden claws...alive.'

They both giggled.

'But I ain't gonna get with cheel with no man around, am I? Magic potion or no magic potion!' Loveday uncoiled her legs from underneath her and hopped off the stool. 'Look, I 'ave to go now. I promised I'd help Daisy with her post round this afternoon but I'll make sure I check in with ye 'morrow morning. Let's hope this weather holds out and we gets a clear sky tonight.' And taking a last gulp of her nettle tea, she left Bramble Farm and made her way up over the back field to meet Daisy.

It was a glorious day and she was sure that tonight's full moon would not be obscured. It was on days like this she would think of Will and wish he was with her. They had spent lots of time in this field and the one over yonder when they were younger, courting, lazing in the long meadow grass, talking and kissing when they were sure that George Weaver wasn't out and about. She would pack a basket full of bread and cheese and if she was lucky enough, she'd sneak some ale from her pa's flagons he kept in the outhouse. A tiny bit from each flagon so as not to arouse suspicion. Will often said it was like drinking a totally new ale with them all mixed together. If he could remember little snippets of their life together, she was sure it would give him the strength needed to make it back home.

Gosh, she was panting a little, she hadn't realised how warm it was and blast! She had forgotten her sun hat too. She stopped at the top of the field and rested her hands on her knees, bending over slightly to catch her breath.

'Afternoon, Loveday!' the cheery voice behind her said.

Loveday stood up to be greeted by the blonde bombshell that was Daisy. Daisy was not only blonde *and* curvaceous, but also had the biggest personality to go with it and was a truly lovely person. Loveday watched her jump off her Post Office standard-issue bike and run towards her with arms outstretched as if she was about to lift her up in the air. Instead she received the biggest hug ever, in the way that only Daisy hugged.

'Any room on Betsy for a worn-out me?'

Everyone knew that Daisy's bike, her pride and joy, went by the name of Betsy.

'Nah, she's only just managing to keep going with me on 'er. Sometimes I thinks the only reason them wheels keep going round is 'cause I'm pedalling so 'ard.'

'Don't worry, I've got me breath back now – do we 'ave many letters to deliver?'

Daisy patted the pannier bags that hung either side of her bike.

'We've enough. I've some from the boys on the front and I think there is one for ye in there somewhere.' She winked at Loveday.

'So if yer ready for some more exercise, we'd best get going. You'll be pleased to know I've already done up yonder so it's downhill all the way now.' And with a quick mount back onto Betsy, Daisy rumbled down the lane with her legs sticking out, singing at the top of her voice. She was going to have to run after her, now wishing she'd not volunteered to help.

The deliveries in the village and to the few outlaying cottages took most of what was left of the hot sunny afternoon. Trunrowan was sheltered from extremes of bad weather most of the time, but on hot summer days it really could get quite unbearable. When finally they had finished, both of them welcomed Granby's village shop as the final stop.

'There, much easier with double the pairs of 'ands,' Daisy said, handing Loveday a cold bottle of homemade ginger beer that Mrs Granby had given her in exchange for the pannier bags.

Loveday shook her head. Sometimes it was quite draining making sense of the riddles that came out of Daisy's mouth.

'Glad I could 'elp,' Loveday replied, gulping back the welcome cold drink.

'Think you've earned this 'un then,' and Daisy handed over a small brown envelope. Loveday snatched it a little too quickly.

'Ye not gonna read it now then?' Daisy asked, sitting on the low stone wall opposite Granby's.

'Nah, but I'm going 'ome now so will read it there.'

Loveday finished the last drops of her ginger beer and handed the bottle back to Daisy.

Daisy took it reluctantly.

Loveday could see the look of disappointment on her face and felt a pang of sadness, especially as she did such a good job of ensuring everyone received letters from their loved ones. As there was no one special in Daisy's life, there were no letters for her but she always took great pleasure in seeing others happy.

'Look…if yer passing by the cottage 'morrow, why don't ye pop in and we can catch up over a cup of something? Perhaps I'll 'ave some news from Will to share with ye then, once I've read his letter.'

Loveday knew it had been the right thing to say when she saw a smile erupt on Daisy's face. She suspected Daisy got quite lonely at times, but at least she was spared the constant worry of losing a loved one.

'Oh yes, that would be nice, if yer sure? I'll see ye 'morrow then,' Daisy replied and Loveday blew her a kiss, bidding her farewell.

Loveday literally had no energy left to run home, despite her refreshment. Instead she walked as fast as she could, resisting the temptation to take Will's letter out of her dress pocket and read it. Finally she was back at the cottage and, as she pushed the stiff wooden back door open into the kitchen, she was greeted by the sight of her straw hat gracing the kitchen table. 'Not much use there,' she muttered to herself, as George their big fluffy ginger cat, slithered in between her legs purring for attention. He'd have to wait.

Loveday impatiently pulled at the brown envelope as a single sheet of paper fell onto the floor. Will's large and distinctive handwriting was the most comforting thing she'd seen in a while... Then she noticed the black lines that had been struck through various parts of his handwriting. Great. More time spent trying to decipher what Will had originally written. Still, he was alive, well, at least when he had written the letter.

Loveday,

I hope this letter finds you well and things in the village are not too awful.

Life here in ▮▮▮▮ *is wet and miserable. The days are long and boring except when we are* ▮▮▮▮▮▮▮▮ *there have been many* ▮▮▮▮▮▮▮▮ *but our unit has* ▮▮▮▮▮▮▮

Thank you for your last letter and for the knitted socks and soap, they are much appreciated. You are obviously getting very good at knitting as this time they actually cover my feet and not just my toes! Good practice for when we have a little one of our own.

My dear, dear Love, I long to smell the sea air and feel the sea salt on my skin and of course see you my love, you are always ▮▮▮▮▮▮

With all my love
Will xx

Loveday instinctively lifted the letter to her lips as tears began to trickle down her cheeks. She quickly wiped them away. No time for sentiment is what her ma would say if she saw her now. She had to stay strong and keep on going, after all, the country was at war and everyone had their part to play, be it keeping the home warm, hauling the fish in or delivering the post. *They* had to stay strong and so must she.

Carefully she placed the letter on top of Will's other letters and re-tied them with a piece of purple velvet ribbon, pushing them to the back of the kitchen dresser drawer. She shut the drawer firmly. Now what was the time? She had to focus and get ready for her meeting with old Mrs Cromp.

Glancing out of the kitchen window at the setting sun, she reckoned she had about an hour, maybe more, until the moon took centre stage. Good, just enough time to cool off in the sea and cleanse her hot, sweaty body. Picking up the basket she kept by the back door, she headed off down the shingle path to the cove at the bottom of the garden, patting George's head as she passed him.

George stuck his tail and bottom in the air with disdain and sauntered off to find a nice comfy spot in the vegetable patch. Poor puss, she'd still not fed him.

VI

Present day

Despite lying awake for the most of the night, Ben had got up with the larks and was reading yesterday's newspaper at the kitchen table when Kitty appeared in the doorway, looking sheepish.

'Morning, Mrs Gridley. Sleep well?' It was more of a rhetorical question; he knew the answer. Kitty pulled a face at him.

'OK, OK, stupid question. Sorry! Let's start again.' He got up and clicked on the kettle. Kitty plonked herself down on a chair and hugged her knees into her chest, her knee-length yellow bed socks with faces of monkeys stared back at him. He smiled.

'Morning, Mrs Gridley. How's that hot handsome husband of yours doing?' They both laughed.

'Toast?' Ben asked as he handed Kitty her morning cuppa.

'Yes please… Umm sorry about last night. I feel a bit of a twit to be honest. Don't think I've had a nightmare like that since I was a child.'

'Well, I think we can safely say that you are actually still somewhat of a child.' Ben's eyes wandered to the monkey faces. 'But, you were quite shaken up, I have to say. Do you remember what the dream was about?'

Kitty shrugged, looking over both shoulders as she did so.

Ben frowned. What was going on in that head of hers?

'Now you look as though you've seen a ghost!' he said, watching the colour drain from her pretty face. He put the toast rack in the middle of the table and continued grabbing cutlery and pots of various homemade jams and jellies from the pine dresser, while Kitty rested her head on her knees.

'I'm just tired, Ben. I think I may go back to bed. You know I'm no good to anyone when I've been deprived of sleep.'

Ben watched Kitty fidgeting on the chair, she was certainly looking agitated. He wouldn't push it; he knew that in good time she would eventually share her concerns with him.

'Probably a good idea, love. I've only got a handful of patients booked in this morning and then I thought I'd take Pete up on his offer and sail out with him to Creek Point. See what delights I can bring back for our supper... That's if you're sure you don't want me to stay home with you?'

Kitty had already got up and was heading towards the staircase.

'Permission granted but you go careful – we all know you don't have sea legs!'

Ben sighed. He really did need to get out of the cottage and away from the surgery for a while, and a change of scenery was as good as a rest, or so the old saying went, regardless of his wobbly legs.

Once upstairs in the bedroom, Kitty felt the coldness and anxiety that she'd felt in the kitchen dissipate. She peered out of the window that overlooked the cottage garden and shingle path that led to the cove. She watched Ben in his smart suit and shiny shoes head off towards the garden gate, his large haversack slung over one of his shoulders. Hopefully it held his jeans and a warm jumper for his trip later. She wondered if he'd packed some suitable footwear, those shiny shoes would have him slipping over the deck within seconds. She thought about opening the window and shouting down to him to remind him, but stopped herself. Oh well, he was a big boy, she was sure he'd done so.

She watched until she could no longer see him and then clambered back into bed, grateful for the luxurious feather duvet that her mother had given them as a 'cottage warming' present when they'd left Bristol. She pulled it up around her neck, snuggling down into the soft pillows. She felt exhausted, like when you'd had too much to drink the night before, but she'd only had a couple of glasses of wine. The dream had obviously taken a lot more out of her than she had realised. She daren't tell Ben that it had been so vivid. The image of the body swaying back and forth, hanging from a meat hook in the kitchen ceiling, *their* kitchen ceiling, quite rightly had woken her. What she needed now was a few hours extra sleep to refresh her and then perhaps she'd make a start on clearing out the shed at the bottom of the garden; she'd been meaning to give it a proper tidy since they'd moved in. It was the perfect space for her new practice and the practical side of her herbal medicine degree; making botanical essences from the Cornish flora that surrounded Creek Cottage.

Slowly she felt her body relax and eagerly awaited the lull of sleep, but it didn't come. Instead, there was an almighty clap of thunder directly overhead and she heard their cat howl. Marmalade hated thunder, rain, or anything other than the heat of the sun or the warmth from the fire. He had settled in well, all things considered, and at least she didn't have to deal with the thought of finding him run over on a road somewhere. Here in Trunrowan, the most likely thing to happen to him was possibly coughing up a fur ball.

Kitty sighed and rolled over so that she could look out of the window just as the rain began to hit the pane of glass obscuring the beautiful view that was normally visible, and another clap of thunder sounded out across the estuary as it moved closer.

Darn that blasted cat. What the hell was he howling at now? She'd have to get up and see to him. She was surprised he hadn't run up to the bedroom at the first rumble; he was normally very good at forecasting weather changes, often way before anything happened.

Kitty put her dressing gown back on and stood at the top of the stone stairs.

'Marmalade, come on… Puss, puss.'

She waited; there was nothing but an audible hiss and whine from below.

'Marmalade! Come on please, if I have to come and get you I'm not going to be very happy!' Slowly she began to walk down the stairs.

'MARMALADE!' And just as Kitty was about to shout again, a larger than life ball of ginger fluff whizzed past her up the stairs, hissing as it did so.

Oh for god's sake, what on earth was wrong with the blasted thing? She hovered for a second or two contemplating whether to go back to bed or check downstairs just to make sure one of the farm cats hadn't decided to come in from the storm and help itself to Marmalade's food. Perhaps that was what was putting him in such a foul mood.

She continued down the steps and into the kitchen, no cat to be seen but the wind and rain had somehow managed to blow open one of the kitchen windows and it banged back and forth with the momentum of the wind. Strange, she had been sure it was shut earlier. No wonder it felt so cold.

She reached across the old Belfast sink to catch the handle of the window but kept missing it. Ah finally! She caught the handle and pulled it shut, ensuring the catch was secured firmly. Now she was not only tired, but also wet and cold.

Another clap of thunder in the distance rumbled and a few seconds later the encroaching darkness was replaced by a flash of lightening. Out of the corner of her eye she thought she saw Marmalade dash across the kitchen, a swift moment of movement and at the same time experienced the coldness and anxiety she had felt earlier.

Blimey, she must be really knackered; perhaps she was coming down with something. Marmalade would just have to fend for himself now because she was definitely going back to bed and she was going to shut the bedroom door so he couldn't disturb her.

Climbing up the stone steps once again, she wearily made her way into the bedroom and was greeted by the sight of Marmalade curled up at the bottom of the bed, happily snoozing. Kitty felt a shiver creep over her. She was sure she'd seen him downstairs in the kitchen only a few moments ago.

Sleep Kitty, she told herself. Sleep. Before you really do start losing the plot.

VII

1916

Loveday enjoyed her daily swims in the sea. Having the cove at the bottom of the garden was like stepping into a huge private bath, well, apart from being accompanied by seaweed and the occasional crab. The salt from the sea was a miracle worker, be it a sore or a nasty cold. Her ma had always sung about the benefits of a daily dip, its ritual passed down through the generations.

Tonight she floated on her back looking up at the full moon. As she let the gentle waves ebb and flow over her naked body, she allowed herself to think of Will...until she was joined by a lone gull who kept pecking at her hair. Reluctantly, she swam back to shore and squeezed out her hair, rubbing herself down vigorously with the large towel she'd packed in her basket.

Once she'd pulled her clothes back on, she hung the towel on the cottage gate. The moon cast a beautiful shimmer on the waves that whispered over the shingle in the cove. Now she understood why she had been instructed to visit Mrs Cromp when the moon was at its fullest; it was so that she could find her way there. Even though she knew most of the land around Rowan Cottage, she rarely ventured deep into the ancient wood.

Finally she set off. Despite the moon's brightness, the darkness surprised her. She wrapped her shawl tighter around her as she felt the temperature drop and, watching her footing, she carefully followed the narrow, meandering path deeper into the wood. The smell of the damp earth hinted at past memories she couldn't quite recall. Walks when she was a child perhaps? Cobnut foraging? Whatever it was, it gave her a well-needed sense of warmth and security.

She should have brought a lantern. She cursed herself, then decided to sing, the sound of her own voice intended to distract from her rising sense of nervousness.

'Stick to the path. Don't veer off,' she sang under her breath. 'Stick to the path, ye will soon be there.' But following the path was becoming increasingly more difficult as the deeper into the wood she ventured, the denser the treetops became and less of the moon's rays filtered through.

An owl's hoot called out from above. Loveday hoped it wasn't a warning call and convinced herself it was to reassure her she was on the right path. Surely it couldn't be much further; she must have been walking for at least half an hour, maybe more.

Just as her eyes were beginning to dangerously fail her, she made out a small clearing in the distance. Thankfully the path widened and the trees that had surrounded her all the way up from the cove now became more and more sparse, allowing her to strengthen her stride with more confidence.

She'd only once before ventured this deeply into the ancient wood, that she could remember, and that had been with her pa when she was a young 'un. They'd been collecting pieces of rowan wood to sell at market; the wood was adept at stirring and preventing milk from curdling. Some of the cunning folk would made small wooden figures or charms from rowan to sell at the market. Carrying them about oneself was said to keep aches and pains at bay. Her ma swore by the rowan, saying it was nothing short of a miracle cure.

The owl that had been hooting earlier emerged from a nearby tree, swooping down in front of her, his wings silent, momentarily creating a gentle waft of cold air. She had finally arrived. Slightly hidden by some low-lying bushes was what looked like a rickety wooden hut. Loveday twitched her nose as she caught a faint smell of wood smoke and, looking up, she watched a wisp of smoke curling its way through the tree branches and into the moonlit sky above.

Smoke was a good sign. Mrs Cromp must be in. Loveday took a deep breath, stood as tall as her tiny frame would allow, and knocked on the wooden door. Almost immediately the door opened and she stepped back hurriedly as a large black cat strolled out, hissing as it passed.

'Go on, shoo!' came a gravelly voice from inside.

Loveday hoped the comment wasn't meant for her.

'Shoo, out with ye! Pesky bleddy cat.' The voice was closer this time. 'I said shoo. Go find some mice or summut, not that ye be in danger of starving any time soon!' Another black cat scurried past Loveday, even larger than the first.

'Hello…? Mrs Cromp, is that ye?' Loveday stepped forward, hovering, unsure as to whether she should venture in. She could hear the voice clearly but couldn't see who it belonged to.

'Yes, yes, come in me dear and shut the door behind ye, or else we'll 'ave the whole of the bleddy woods' wildlife brought in to us.'

Loveday did as instructed and stepped into a small dimly lit room. In the centre was an open fire with a good flame burning, heating an old tin pan that was precariously balancing above it. Around the fire were four other people. How they were all going to fit in the room she didn't know but she was ushered in anyway.

'Go in, go in, don't dither, girl. That's it, shut the door. Now then, come and sit down and warm yerself up.' Mrs Cromp patted a tiny space on the floor in front of the fire where a colourful cushion awaited her.

She felt as though the small gathering had been waiting for her as she made her way to the cushion, smiling at faces she didn't recognise. There were two other young women of a similar age to herself who smiled at her, their hair tied up almost identical to Mrs Cromp's. She wondered if they could be her children? No, she was far too old for that to be possible. Grandchildren then...or great grandchildren? A much older woman was sitting on a chair next to them and nodded at Loveday but made no attempt to smile. Even in the dim candlelight, Loveday could feel the woman's green cat-like eyes boring into her as she sat down on the cushion and crossed her legs to enable a little more space around her. She was feeling a little claustrophobic. She had never done well in small spaces.

Next to the fire and sat in a rocking chair was a rather tubby looking man. He had a kind face and stood up as she sat down, then bowed. A flamboyant bow, like the ones that medieval court jesters did. He was dressed in vibrant coloured clothes, adorned with jangly bells on the outsides of his trousers and shirt sleeves and she knew instantly that he was a Droll Teller.

Apart from the rocking chair and a table that was covered with an array of dried flowers and herbs, the room was sparsely furnished. She wondered where Mrs Cromp was sitting and hoped she had not taken her seat.

'Drink this, it will warm yer cockles, ye looks like ye could be doing with a decent meal inside ye!' Mrs Cromp ladled some broth from the balancing tin pan and filled a pewter jug, handing it to Loveday.

Loveday drank thirstily, hesitating only for a brief moment as she remembered Mabel's earlier words of warning. She tussled with the notion of being poisoned by the broth or refreshed, but her thirst got the better of her. Mrs Cromp looked harmless enough close up, although it was very dimly lit in the cottage.

As if reading her thoughts, Mrs Cromp smiled. 'Don't worry, me dear. It won't 'arm ye. Just a nice warm broth made from nature's larder.'

Loveday had already drained the jug and was feeling surprisingly refreshed. The broth had left a pleasant tingling sensation in her mouth.

'Thank ye, it were very tasty.' She handed back the pewter jug.

'Aye, it is indeed. Well, I be a bit surprised ye did turn up me dear if truth be told, but am glad ye did,' Mrs Cromp said as she added more kindling to the fire.

'Let's sit a while and listen to some music and tales from Gribble Gummo.' The woman with the cat eyes said.

Loveday assumed that the Droll Teller must be called Gribble Gummo. The name suited the flamboyant man, and she watched him take a small fiddle out of a carpeted bag that was on the floor by the side of the rocking chair.

'I think I be a bit curious as to why ye asked me 'ere?' Loveday said quietly. She waited patiently for an answer that she had pondered over ever since the note was passed to her by Mrs Cromp outside the village shop, but nothing was forthcoming.

The music stopped and the only noise was the crackling from the fire. It had begun to burn fiercely with the added kindling and the warmth in the small room was making Loveday feel relaxed. Mrs Cromp sat herself down next to Gribble Gummo and placed her hands in her lap.

Now she was closer to Loveday and in the fire's glow, Loveday could see the leathered skin of her face. She looked old, much older than the last time they'd met, but how could that be? She still wore what Loveday presumed was the same red hair-scarf on her head, which miraculously somehow managed to hold back the masses of grey hair underneath it. And despite the wrinkled skin, her cheeks glowed with a redness that somehow leant to an energy that emanated from inside the old woman.

Her small eyes were also green, like the woman with the cat eyes, but the colour was more akin to deep green emeralds. They twinkled with the glow of the fire, bright and alert like those of a much younger woman. She absolutely fascinated Loveday.

'Stop staring, love. I ain't naught special to look at. I be the same as ye and ye be the same as I.' Mrs Cromp said as Gribble Gummo began to play his fiddle again.

Loveday felt as though she was being hypnotised. She could feel herself blushing and was thankful for the warmth of the fire to camouflage it.

'But ye be right in that I did ask ye 'ere for a reason and of course ye wants to know why…so I will tell ye. But not until later when we've paid Gribble Gummo the respect 'e deserves.'

'Well, let's begin then…but first I don't mind if ye tops up me jug to 'elp wet me voice.' Gribble Gummo stopped playing his fiddle and handed his empty jug to Mrs Cromp who took it and shuffled to the nearby table, pouring a large quantity of yellow liquid into the jug. It was at that point, Loveday realised it was going to be a very long night.

The next few hours were taken up with tales of smugglers hiding in nearby caves. Piskies who curdled milk. Giants who crushed whole villages and dragons whose breath burnt whole fleets of fishing boats. There were mermaids who followed boats into shore and witches who danced on the moor of Bodmin.

Loveday listened carefully. She was totally transfixed by Gribble Gummo and his storytelling. Some tales he said were true and had been passed from village to village as warnings. Others were from years gone by and no one knew if they were really true, or figments of imagination. Mrs Cromp kept Gribble well fed throughout; passing him homemade pasties and the yellow ale, until Loveday thought he would burst. She and the other women were occasionally offered drinks but no food. It would seem that Gribble's payment for his storytelling was in kind, for which he seemed perfectly happy. No wonder he was so tubby if all of his storytelling was met with food and drink.

Loveday's favourite story so far was a tale from a village that Gribble called Madron, not too far from Trunrowan. Gribble spoke of this tale with quiet enthusiasm for he said he personally knew it to be true and Mrs Cromp kept nodding in agreement. The three other women also seemed particularly interested in this story and it soon became apparent why.

'There goes a tale that dates back many, many moons. Maybe even thousands of moon years, right back to the beginning of our ancestors. The tale is of a village not far from these shores, 'igh up where ye can just about see the twinkle of the sea and where upon its land are magic stones.' Gribble paused, ensuring everyone's attention was fully on him.

'Not the stones that ye and I know of, but four stones that not even a strong man could move on his own. Now, these stones were special, *are* special. They hold magic powers within the hewn granite. People from around these parts calls the holed stone, the Crick Stone.' Gribble reached for his jug and took a big gulp, wiping his mouth with the back of his hand and continued.

'There are tales of farmers and fisherfolk, who 'ave come from far and wide to visit the stones and to cure their aches and pains. But there is a stone amongst them that is more special than the others. It has a 'ole carved out of it, just big enough for a person to crawl through. There are tales of barren women who visit the stone with the 'ole…and become pregnant!'

At this point the room became so quiet that Loveday was sure she would hear a mouse squeaking; even Gribble's bells had stopped jangling. Try as she might, Loveday could not help but let out a small gasp.

'But whoever visits them must first leave a gift for the guardian who protects the stones. It is believed they be the Piskies.'

Gribble had found some space on the floor, his back arched as though imitating a performing animal of some kind.

Loveday was sure at this point they were all under his spell and would have done anything he asked of them, but within the time it took to blink, he was back sitting in the rocking chair slurping from his jug and rubbing his eyes.

'I think it be time I rested me 'ead. It's way too late for old Gribble Gummo.' He chuckled as Mrs Cromp stood up and begun ushering them all out of the way. Gribble then wobbled off to what Loveday could only presume was his bed for the night; obviously the worse for far too much drink. When Mrs Cromp came back from helping Gribble to his bed, she sat in the rocking chair and took Loveday's hand.

'Ye thinks ye is barren don't ye, me love?'

Loveday, feeling it would be rude to pull her hand away, shifted uncomfortably.

'But ye ain't. Ye just needs a little 'elp that's all. And I can 'elp ye with that...if ye wants me 'elp of course, for I knows that ye would love and cherish a cheel of yer own.'

Loveday let out a small gasp. How on earth did Mrs Cromp know how she was feeling?

'Do I?' Loveday replied, not really knowing what else to say, especially as the room was still full of the three other women who were also now staring at her, waiting for her answer.

'My dear! Ye are versed with the ways of marriage, I presume?' Mrs Cromp said quizzically.

She could feel her face getting hot again. 'Oh! Gosh, yeah, of course I be. It's just that Will, me husband, is fighting for King and Country and with all the 'elp in Trunrowan, it ain't gonna 'appen without 'im!' Loveday was feeling a little uncomfortable with all this nonsense talk. Silence filled the room again, apart from the occasional sound of snoring from Gribble Gummo's room.

Mrs Cromp began rocking the chair, pushing her feet hard off the floor until Loveday thought she would fly off the back of it.

'Where there's a will, there's a way me love, but it depends on 'ow much ye wants this cheel. You may 'ave gathered by now, if ye didn't know before, that I comes from a long family of what people calls, cunning folk. I knows people do talk and it's true I do 'ave some...powers shall we call 'em. They've been bestowed upon me by me own ma and her ma before her. They is to be used for 'elping folk and 'ealing, but never for any dark magic.'

Loveday expelled a sigh of relief. So she wasn't going to be used for frog bait tonight then after all.

'But, there has to be an agreement in place you sees, and that is, no man or woman shall ask for 'elp without the other person's permission, or with the intention to 'arm 'em. Naught good will come from it. Dark magic ain't the way of cunning folk.'

Loveday shivered despite her proximity to the fire. She recalled her pa telling her when she was a cheel that the storm of 1905, which took many of the men in the village, was caused by the spirit of a Spriggan. One of the deckhands had, so say, been meddling with the dark arts.

'And so, me love, it's now up to ye as to whether ye wishes to take up me offer and proceed, and let's be clear, it's not an easy decision to make, I understands that, but it is yours *and* your 'usbands decision.'

Mrs Cromp stopped rocking and got up from the chair, brushing off the speckles of firewood and ash from her pleated skirt. She bent across the flower-laden table and rummaged for a while, eventually picking up a small clump of greenery. Tying it with some red thread, she handed it to Loveday who instinctively lifted it to her nose and sniffed, breathing in the unmistakable aroma of rosemary.

'Right then...all of ye be on yer way. Place the sprig under yer pillow tonight and be sure to remember the first thing from yer dreams on waking. That will help to direct ye to yer decision. Then, when the next full moon comes, providing there's a clear sky, you can come visit me again and 'ear the rest of the tale from

Gribble Gummo. Ye can let me know yer decision then, that's if you've made one. But remember it 'as to be for the right reasons.'

Loveday nodded and without saying anything else, slipped the sprig of rosemary into her skirt pocket. She thought that she might like to ask Mrs Cromp if she could have a candle to help her find her way back, but there was obviously no need.

'Ye be fine 'eading back. The moon is 'igh and will show ye the way.'

Mrs Cromp walked outside with Loveday and the other women and stood watching them as they headed off in the directions they had come from.

She *can* read my bleddy mind, Loveday thought to herself as she hurried along the path. For it did indeed seem that the moon was bigger and brighter than earlier, showing her a well-lit path back to Rowan Cottage.

VIII

Present day

Ben had not got much further than the water's edge before he realised there was a storm brewing. The swell in the estuary was clearly visible and the building waves were beginning to rock the small boats that were tethered in the cove. He could see no sign of Pete's boat and guessed their fishing trip had been called off. Even in the short time he had been stood at the water's edge, visibility was diminishing quickly and the sky had turned a deep shade of industrial grey. He had been looking forward to feeling the wind on his face and some time to himself, albeit with Pete at the helm.

Since moving to Trunrowan his love for the sea and fishing had flourished and if he said so himself, he had become a dab hand at catching the odd sea bass. It certainly beat sitting cooped up in the surgery all day hunched over patients. He would swap the smell of halitosis for seaweed any day of the week.

Ben felt the first drop of rain on his face and reluctantly admitted defeat. He'd never particularly liked storms since his older brother had locked him outside during one as a child, thinking it was funny. He had sat in the rain on the doorstep until their mother had realised he was missing. His mother said it took her almost an hour to stop him shaking. The fear he'd felt from there on in every time a clap of thunder crashed above him was unpleasant. Thankfully he had eventually grown out of the worst of it.

Heading back across the cove, Ben saw a figure at the edge of the wood, waving at him. It was difficult to see who it was in the onslaught of wind and rain, but he recognised the voice calling to him.

'Wasson? Just 'ad to moor up yonder,' Pete said, still waving. 'Blasted storm, ain't got time for it and I ain't risking breaking 'er up on that swell. Now I be stuck on this side of the estuary and the missus will be worrying that I'm still out at sea!'

'Don't you carry a phone then, Pete? You're welcome to use mine or come back to the cottage and use the landline?' Ben rummaged about in his pocket for his mobile phone.

Pete, who was dressed in nothing but a pair of canvas shorts and a now very wet tee-shirt, shook his head.

'Nah, yer all right young 'un, I'll sit it out. It'll pass in no time, ye get yerself back 'ome, the fishing trip will 'ave to wait for another day.'

Thank god for that Ben thought to himself.

'No problem at all, Pete. Are you sure you don't want to join me for a cuppa, or maybe something stronger?' Ben thought that Pete was the type of man who liked a good old drink and a natter.

'Nah, like I said, ye carry on. Say 'ello to yer missus for me won't ye.' Pete had already begun to walk back in the direction from where he came from.

'Yes, of course I will.'

'Right, young 'un, will catch up with ye some other time.' Pete certainly didn't seem bothered by the storm that was for sure.

Ben jogged the rest of the short distance back to Creek Cottage, his feet sinking and slipping on the wet sand and pebbles in his work shoes. He should have changed them for the deck shoes he'd packed in his rucksack. By the time he reached the back door of the cottage, he was soaked right through and, much as he was sure Pete knew his weather, this storm didn't look as though it had any intention of moving on elsewhere.

Pushing the cottage door open he stepped into the warm kitchen, shouting out to Kitty as he did so, and then cursed himself as he remembered she was probably asleep. He'd get out of his wet clothes and put on the dry ones in his bag, make a hot drink, and let her sleep. The day wasn't quite panning out as he'd wished but at least they had not gone out in the boat earlier. He was safe under his own roof and not under the cabin of Pete's boat, wrestling with a force eight or nine gale.

Ben must have nodded off, waking up on the small two-seater sofa that they'd somehow managed to squash into what was their living room. In reality it wasn't really for living in as it was only just big enough for a sofa, television, a small coffee table and half a bookcase. The sofa wasn't the most comfortable but it had been the only one they'd brought down from Bristol that could actually fit into the small space. Getting it through the back door and then the kitchen had taken forever and he vowed to Kitty that it would have to stay where it was until they were dead and buried. He wasn't going through all that palaver again.

He stretched out and rubbed his back. Crikey, how long had he been asleep? He felt as though he'd been out for hours. If the sofa was more comfortable he'd probably still be asleep now. Even the log burner had burnt itself out, as had the storm. Pete was right after all. There were now small patches of blue sky visible through the kitchen window, light slowly emerging and swallowing the darkness inside the cottage. That was another issue with Creek Cottage...in the winter or on dull, rainy days, they had to have all the lights on or else they were literally bumping into one another.

Marmalade appeared from upstairs and sat at the back door meowing loudly to be let out. He must have heard Ben stirring. Pushing the back door open he watched the ginger ball of fluff amble out. The rain drops that'd accumulated on the door frame in the storm came down on him in one huge plop and in protest Marmalade turned and swiped at Ben's legs. He shooed him out into the garden and, as he did so, noticed something dangling from one of his back legs.

'Hey Marm, come here, what have you got caught on your leg then?' Marmalade stopped at the mention of his name and realising there was indeed something awry, twisted the back leg in question around his neck and began licking the mystery object. Ben bent down to get a closer look. Somehow, wrapped around the upper part of his back leg, there was a ragged-looking piece of purple velvet ribbon. Marmalade continued pulling at it. Ben joined in and tugged at it very gently until it unraveled.

'Got it! Go on, off you go then,' Ben said as Marmalade turned and hissed at him. Poor cat, the storm had obviously unsettled him.

On closer inspection, the ribbon showed signs of wear in most places. It certainly had some genuine age to it and wasn't just a piece of ribbon that had got dirty. At one time in its life, it had obviously been a beautiful vibrant piece, but what was of more interest to Ben was the small object that the ribbon appeared to be threaded through. Wetting his thumb he rubbed the small circular object as tiny specks of silver began to show. It would need a proper clean but he was pretty sure it was a coin of some sort that had been drilled to allow the ribbon thread through it. How strange though that it had ended up wrapped around Marmalade's leg when he presumed, given the weather, that he'd been lazing around in the cottage.

Once back inside, he carefully removed the ribbon from the

coin and watched the ribbon practically disintegrate into dust as he did so. He ran the hot tap, found a bottle of washing up liquid under the sink and gently rubbed the object with a piece of cloth.

Slowly but surely years of dirt, dust and grime began to lift off. He remembered as a child his love of cleaning old coins with his grandfather by putting them into brown sauce... He was sure they had some. Placing the coin into a small bowl, he found a small bottle of Daddies Sauce in a cupboard and glugged it over the coin. He would let it seep in and come back to it later. Perhaps Kitty would know where the coin had come from...

Kitty woke with a start. The small vintage bedside clock told her she'd been asleep for over two hours and she was feeling refreshed and ready to take on the world once again.

She wandered over to the bedroom window and saw Marmalade heading off towards the vegetable patch, one of his favourite spots in the garden. As long as he kept away from her wild flower area. She'd planted up various botanicals for harvesting and drying which was part of the module she was currently studying, and it certainly wasn't for cats! Ben might moan a little if Marmalade was caught languishing in the strawberry patch, but she hoped he was heading that way. Giving the window latch a good shove, she pushed the window open to let some fresh air in. She took a deep breath in; the storm had stirred up the smell of seaweed, one of her favourite smells. A walk outside now would do her good, she'd get dressed and get some fresh air.

Pulling on a pair of jeans she'd not worn for a while, Kitty noticed the top button was a little too snug to do up completely. Oh well, she'd just have to cover it over with a long blouse or jumper. She'd make sure she made more of an effort to exercise. Since being in Cornwall she was walking lots more than she ever did in Bristol and was even swimming in the cove, but she was not pounding the running machine or doing spin classes. She glanced in the mirror before heading downstairs. There, that would have to do. At least she didn't look quite as tired as she had done earlier. A dab of lippy and blusher and she'd be back to her old self.

'Hey love; did your fishing trip get cancelled then? That storm was pretty awesome, wasn't it? I was watching it from the bed until Marmalade decided to run around like a wailing banshee.' Kitty stood in the kitchen doorway remembering the shadow she had caught out of the corner of her eye earlier. 'I'm going to get some fresh air now the weather's improving, fancy coming with me?' Walking into the kitchen she shivered. The sooner she was outside the better.

'Yes, sure thing but first… What do you think of this?' Ben handed her a small silvery round object. He was obviously very excited about it, whatever it was. Kitty peered closer, turning it over with her thumb and forefinger.

'Well, it's a coin, an old one; my expertise would say, umm… probably circa 1914.' She laughed, pointing to the date that was just visible.

'Oh well done, Sherlock.' Ben said sarcastically, snatching the coin back from her.

'I thought you might know what it was or where it came from, not the date of it.' Ben's voice softened – as he attempted to tickle her as a way of apology.

'Ah, no tickling please, Ben!' Kitty hated being tickled. 'I have absolutely no idea where it's from. There were a few bronze coins with some other bits and bobs in the bedroom fire grate when we moved in. But I thought I'd thrown them away?' She pulled away from him. She was in no mood for tickling games and to be honest was a little put out at the way he had jumped down her throat.

'Well, Marmalade had it tied around his back leg.'

'What? I certainly never tied it to him, why would I do that?'

'I'm not saying you did, Kit. I'm guessing it got tangled around him somehow, perhaps when he was having his funny turn in the storm. Did he hide under the bed, or somewhere else perhaps?'

'If you count running around the cottage feral, then yes it's possible he did get tangled up in something, but I'm sure I would've noticed.'

'Not necessarily. It was covered in decades of grime and muck, plus it had a piece of purple velvet ribbon threaded through it.' Ben handed the coin back to her.

Looking at it more closely now, she could see a hole through where the lion's crown and King George V's head was.

'How odd, perhaps it's some sort of talisman or good luck charm?' she suggested.

Ben shook his head. 'I think it belonged to a Tommy, of course it could have been a good luck charm too, perhaps his sweetheart was the one who had the hole put through and then hung it on the ribbon?'

'A Tommy... Are we being person-specific here?' She was puzzled, Ben seemed to be so excited about his find but to her he was talking in riddles.

'No, a Tommy as in a soldier. When they signed up in the First World War they were given the king's shilling by the recruiting sergeant – it was a sort of handshake before they had officially signed on the dotted line. An unofficial agreement. I'm guessing most of them spent it in the pub though before they left to fight.'

Kitty remembered that Ben had chosen Dentistry over History and so far there hadn't been much call to be reminded of his superior historical knowledge, apart from the odd pub quiz night.

'Wow! Strange to think the coin is over one hundred years old – how exciting. I wonder if it belonged to someone who lived here in the cottage. Where on earth did it come from though?'

'Why don't you try and find out? It'll give you something to get your teeth stuck into while I'm at work.'

Kitty mumbled under her breath. As if she didn't have enough to do. She was sure Ben thought all she did every day was bake cakes and collect herbs and flowers.

'Look, I've almost finished my module for the summer, so I guess I could spend a little time on research, but I do have to sort out the shed. I need to dry flowers and seed heads and get all sorts of things up and ready for blending elixirs. And Ben, you did say you would help me?' Ben pulled a face.

'Ok, understood. I'm due some time off soon, so I promise I will help you then. Put the coin in your jewellery box so it's somewhere safe for now and out of reach of Marmalade.'

'Yes, I will. Where's the ribbon?'

Ben went out to the kitchen and brought in the remnant of what was left. He handed it to her carefully.

'Now, that has certainly seen better days but I will keep it with the coin. You never know it may be an important piece in our quest to find out who its owner was.' Kitty put it on the wood mantelpiece above the log burner and made a mental note to remind herself to take it upstairs when she next went. Strangely, she felt an odd connection to it.

'You OK?'

Kitty felt shivery again. She didn't know what was going on of late but she seemed to be sensing all sorts of strange things. She'd always been what you could call an empath. Nursing for years had certainly confirmed it. She'd always had an instinctive feel for her patients and when she'd decided to pursue a career in Herbal Medicine, she knew her intuition would somehow aid her on her new path.

'I'm fine, Ben. The kitchen's blooming chilly though. I came downstairs earlier and the window was open even though I'm sure I had shut it. And the Aga's on full blast!'

She rubbed her hands together in front of the wood burner in an attempt to warm them.

It was definitely getting colder, despite the storm having

dispersed. This was nothing too out of the ordinary as the cottage was built of old Cornish stone dating back to the early 1800s, or so they had been told by the estate agent when they'd bought it.

'It must have been the wind. I certainly didn't open it,' Ben offered casually.

He got up and checked the window. It was firmly shut. 'Best find another jumper to put on then.' And he disappeared upstairs.

Kitty decided to stay put, wrapping the woollen throw that was on the sofa over her. It had been the strangest of days what with the previous night's shenanigans. Rather odd too that she was left feeling so apprehensive about being in and around the kitchen. Although if she thought about it on a deeper level, you could say that it was the whole cottage that unnerved her. Hopefully she'd soon be back to normal, but there was a nagging voice in her head telling her something was amiss. Now, to add more intrigue to the whole situation, there was the discovery of the coin and ribbon.

She shuddered. Who could the coin have belonged to...? The person was most certainly dead now but she felt an instinctive urge to find out who it was and whether they were linked to the cottage in some way. Tomorrow was another day and she had always been a great believer in making each day a new start. She decided there and then that tomorrow would be the day she would begin to research the history of Creek Cottage.

IX

1916

They knew there would be bloodshed but no one was prepared for how much. The rain had not let up and no man's land was nothing more than a space between trenches, riddled with barbed wire and littered with bodies, some still alive but with little or no hope of being rescued. Rusty red rivers flowed into man made craters, a mix of blood, vomit and body parts. If he survived, Will knew he would never forget the stench and sights for as long as he lived. The cries from the injured were the worst, wails of fear and pain, and there was naught he could do about it.

Yesterday, as they took the left flank of Delville Wood, he stumbled over a Hun who was barely alive. He'd been caught in the shelling and sat propped up against a beech tree, his head half blown off, blood streaming into his boots, his stomach burst open. The Hun had somehow managed to extend his shaking hand, the gun he held barely visible under mud and blood.

Will didn't have time to stop and put the poor chap out of

his misery, there were snipers everywhere and how did he know it wasn't a lure? He clambered on, head down, over bodies and fallen branches as he heard the close fire of gunshot behind him. He didn't look back; he needed to find the safety of a trench before nightfall.

Later that night as he bunked down in yet another squalid trench, huddled amongst men who had become like brothers, he heard the faint tune of the battalion's anthem, Trelawny, rising up from the band marching through the village below him. Carrying their stretchers they would soon be searching through the mire for signs of life. He thought of home, Trunrowan, of Loveday, the sea and fresh air, but lately he struggled to recall them in any great detail. Gone was the sweet smell of salt, hazy was the image of Trunrowan. Missing was the face of his beloved Loveday, her long auburn wavy hair and green eyes. Everything was a blur.

Colours of grey, black and rusty red permeated his thoughts, like the swirls of a painting that had been accomplished by a dead man.

The shell hit only a few feet from the trench, sending an ear-splitting roar into the air as the earth heaved. For a brief moment he felt at peace, a warm sensation began to descend from the top of his head to the soles of his feet. The last words he heard as he slipped into unconsciousness, were those of the stretcher bearers: '*Come forth! Come forth! Ye cowards all: Here's men as good as ye.*'

Loveday opened the door of the shed and stood back as the flock of hens came running out, clucking. She watched them head over to the vegetable patch and hoped that the wooden boards she had put around it would stave them off. She was fed up of finding her vegetables lifted up by their incessant scratching. If she didn't need them for their eggs and for the table, she would have sold them on by now. She much preferred ducks. Ducks had much more character. They waddled and quacked, and she loved the way they lifted a leg every now and then and stretched, as though practicing some sort of duck ballet. Plus, their eggs made *the* best cakes.

She bent down and scanned the sandy laden floor praying there would be some eggs. Smiling, she spotted two brown speckled eggs in the corner. Good old Bluebell and Dotty, she could always rely on them.

Will had always told her not to name the hens as it made killing them difficult, but she always did, she just never told him. Carefully she put the warm eggs into her apron pocket and then propped the door open with a large pebble. She might get lucky and find a few more when she checked back later.

She headed back up the garden path and as she did so, she caught a glimpse of Daisy riding her bicycle down Chillyhill Lane which ran alongside the front of the cottage. Ah, of course, she'd asked her over for a cuppa and chat about Will's letter; she would hurry inside and get the kettle boiling and see if there were any homemade biscuits left. She may not have much news to tell her about the war effort, but she did have a surprise to show her. Once back inside the cottage she carefully took Will's letter from the dresser and removed the silver coin that was tucked inside the envelope. The king's shilling. She'd felt a pang of emotion when she realised he had sent it to her as a keepsake. She would ask Daisy if their pa could hammer a hole in it for her, so she could wear it around her neck. She picked up the purple velvet ribbon she was using to tie the letters with. It would be perfect for threading the coin through once a hole had been made, and purple just so happened to be her favourite colour.

By the time the kettle had whistled she'd placed a handful of gingerbread biscuits on a plate but Daisy had still not arrived. Loveday wondered if she'd been mistaken earlier, but there was no one else in the village that had such long blonde hair who rode a bicycle. Perhaps she'd been heading to Granby's first. Yes, that would make sense. In the meantime she would read Will's letters again so she was fully armed for any questions that Daisy was sure to have.

It wasn't long after she'd sat down at the table to re-read Will's letters, that the hens started clucking again at the back door. Surely they couldn't be hungry already? Loveday looked at the kitchen clock: 1 o'clock. Gosh! She really should stop procrastinating; there was a whole list of things she should be getting on with. Luckily for the hens she had some scraps saved that would keep them quiet for a while.

She headed to the back door, hands full of wilted cabbage leaves, to find Daisy sat on the garden path, head in hands and the hens pecking at her feet. She was sobbing uncontrollably.

'Oh my, Daisy, are ye OK?'

Loveday had never seen her upset before; she was always such a happy-go-lucky sort.

'Ave ye 'urt yerself...? 'Ere let me 'elp ye up.' Loveday put her arm through Daisy's and gently pulled until she was standing. She shooed the hens away – they were just as curious as to the sobbing as she was. As she did so she noticed a brown envelope on the ground, but before she could pick it up and take a closer look, Daisy scooped it up and looked at Loveday through red teary eyes.

Reluctantly, she handed the envelope over, her hand shaking.

'I'm so very sorry, Loveday. I've been at the bottom of the lane for ages; I just couldn't bring meself to give it to ye.' She rubbed her eyes with the palms of her hand. 'But ye deserves to know and I would rather gives it to ye meself...' She paused before bursting into tears again.

Loveday stood staring at the envelope unable to take everything in. No, this couldn't be happening. She had a distinct feeling her life was about to come crashing down around her, and, for the first time in her twenty-six years, she let out an almighty wail.

Somehow, Daisy had managed to compose herself enough to help Loveday back inside the cottage. She sat her down at the kitchen table and took to making a strong cup of tea. She even managed to find some sugar in the cupboard that Loveday had been no doubt saving for a special occasion. She felt sure this could be counted as an important one, if not exactly special.

The envelope still lay unopened on the kitchen table. Loveday was curling her hair around her fingers like a child.

'There ye goes, get that down ye. It'll make ye feel better.' Daisy put the cup and saucer directly in front of Loveday, wishing she had some whiskey to put in it.

Loveday finally picked up the envelope, turning it over and over in her hands. She looked at Daisy and handed it back to her. 'Ye open it and read it. I truly can't.' She took a gulp of the tea.

'Oh god, I don't think I can. It's bad enough that I've 'ad to deliver it to ye.' Daisy put her head in her hands before taking a deep breath and taking the envelope. 'If yer sure?'

Loveday nodded.

Daisy picked up the butter knife from the table and quickly flicked it through the top of the envelope. She then pulled out the single piece of typed paper, took another deep breath and began laughing.

'E ain't dead!' Daisy was practically hysterical with relief.

'What?'

'It says 'e's missing.' Daisy paused again as she re-read it, just to make sure. 'I mean obviously that's bad enough but… Listen, I'll read it to ye.' She took another deep breath.

'*I regret to inform you, that a report has been received from the War Office, to the effect that Private 52770, William Nance, of the Duke of Cornwall's Light Infantry, was posted as "missing" on 19th July 1916. The report that he is missing does not necessarily mean that he has been killed.*'

Daisy dropped the letter and threw her arms around Loveday, hugging her.

Loveday, still feeling confused and in shock, allowed the tiniest bit of hope to wash over her. Eventually, she managed to free herself from Daisy's tight embrace and clasped her hands together in front of her chest, hardly able to contain her glee.

'I know 'e's still alive, Daisy. I just knows 'e is.'

Without thinking, she grabbed the silver coin on the table and thrust it into Daisy's hand.

'It's a sign – 'e sent me this in 'is last letter. A keepsake for me to wear, I just need ye to ask yer pa to make an 'ole in it so I can wear it like. You know, round me neck. I'm going to use this piece of purple ribbon... Do you think ye could ask 'im for me?' Loveday knew she was sounding desperate but didn't care.

Daisy would have walked all the way to Bodmin to get a hole drilled in the coin, so asking her pa was no bother. She was almost as pleased as Loveday, that there was the slightest possibility that Will was still alive, and the coin was indeed surely a sign. By the end of the day she would make sure the coin was drilled and given back to Loveday, gracing her neck on the piece of purple ribbon.

X

Present day

The beginning of summer was now under way, days and nights were warmer and the sun shone alone in a cloudless blue sky. Creek Cottage was in an enviable position, and although it was protected by woodland either side, it still managed to catch a welcoming on-shore breeze. Ben's surgery days were shorter in the summer season and he found himself with plenty of spare time to go fishing and walking, sometimes with Kitty and other times he was happy to be alone. The only bugbear was that Cornwall in the summer was awash with people. It would seem that no matter where you went there were hordes of them, so more often than not they spent time pottering in the garden or putting the finishing touches to the inside and outside of the cottage.

Kitty had also begun to finally clear out the shed, with a little help from himself as he'd promised, and delighted in finding obscure artefacts in boxes and drawers, undisturbed for decades. Luckily, she'd not had any more bad dreams and life was good.

One glorious sunny afternoon when they were both sitting in the garden after a morning of leisurely swimming in the cove, Ben decided it was the right time to broach the subject of children.

They had not spoken about having a baby for a while now. Back in Bristol, it had been the main topic of conversation. He wasn't sure if this was a good thing or no, because if things were still not taking their natural course, then perhaps it was time to get help from the experts.

He hesitated before picking up his wine glass, taking a large mouthful for Dutch courage. He really didn't want to ruin the lovely day they were having but there just never seemed to be the right time.

He bent down under the table and picked up the wine bottle from the ice bucket, disturbing Marmalade in the process who flicked his tail a few times and then settled back down. It must be hot in summer wearing a fur coat. No wonder he was curled up next to the ice bucket.

'Wine?'

Kitty shook her head, nose deep in a book. How she could read in the glaring sun with no sunglasses on, he had no idea.

'Just a small glass... Go on, I always feel guilty drinking on my own. I fear it's becoming a habit.' He laughed but still continued to pour himself a glass.

'No, I'm fine with my water, thanks. It's too hot.' Kitty put down her book and lifted herself up from the deckchair, stretching her arms as she did so. 'God, my arms are aching today. Ouch! Probably overdid it with that swim earlier.'

'What do you mean, overdid it?! You're as fit as anyone I know... You're not ill, are you? I mean no wine, aching bones. Ha! What's up with you, old bird?' He laughed, peering out from under his sunglasses. She really was glowing these days and looked so different from when they lived in Bristol. Sea air should definitely be available on prescription.

Kitty turned to face him, hands on her hips, the sun silhouetting her body through the pretty white dress she was wearing. She had even put on a little weight, certainly not a bad thing; she was way too skinny before. And then she smiled at him, a huge knowing smile.

'You're not, are you? No, you can't be...' The penny had finally dropped. He jumped up, knocking his wine glass over in the process. Marmalade meowed in protest. 'Oh my god! You are!'

Kitty's smile got broader as she moved her hands from her hips and onto her stomach. 'Yes, Ben. I am,' she said softly. 'I'm carrying our baby.'

And with the confirmation he'd been waiting to hear for such a long time, he scooped her into his arms and swung her around yelling at the top of his voice. 'I can't believe it... Woo hoo! I'm going to be a dad.'

'Ben, put me down. You might drop me.' Kitty screeched.

'Oh, blimey yes, sorry. Are you OK?' He gently put Kitty back down onto the grass, still holding onto her, giddy with emotion.

'I am absolutely fine. I'm pregnant not made of china, although that sudden twirling has made me feel a little nauseous.'

'Here, sit back down.' Ben patted the deckchair.

'Stop fussing! I hope you're not going to be like this for the whole of the pregnancy, Ben Gridley!'

'So, you're already what...three, four months? Why didn't you tell me?' He had so many questions whirling around in his head, he didn't know where to begin. 'I mean how long have you known?' He decided to sit down – it was probably safer. He could feel his legs shaking.

'I did a test about a month ago when I went into Truro to collect the bedside lamps, remember? I've been dying to tell you, but I wanted to be absolutely sure everything was as well as it could be before I did.'

'Have you felt ill, what can I do to help, have you been to the doctor's yet?'

'Well, not really, that's the thing, as I did have a scant period at the beginning, which apparently can happen, so it threw me. I need to go back again next week though and I want you to come with me, so, I had to tell you…obviously!' Kitty said. She was grinning from ear to ear like a large Cheshire cat.

'You are happy, right? I mean, all of this is OK?'

'I'm bloody ecstatic, can't you tell?'

He bent over and kissed the top of her head, ruffling her short hair. 'Finally, we're going to have our own little family. Baby Gridley. Of course, it will be a boy. I've been thinking about calling him Oswald, what do you think?'

'Over my dead body!' Kitty exclaimed laughing. 'I think it's a girl, but we'll have to wait and see. In the meantime, I'm going to ring Mum now I've told you. I can't contain the excitement any longer!'

Kitty eventually reached the eight-month mark, lucky to have had a noneventful pregnancy so far. She'd passed the 'glowing' phase and was now beginning to feel fat and a little anxious about the pending birth. The glorious weather had continued over the summer and her skin had acquired an attractive light tan, while her freckles had almost taken over the whole of her face. She hated them but Ben seemed to love them.

'I have counted every freckle on your face, Mrs Gridley, and there are 210!'

She must have dozed off and woke curled up on the bed with Ben's face close to hers, his hand on her stomach. She stretched like a contented cat and was instantly reminded of the life growing inside her as the baby kicked her.

'Ouch! Someone was obviously comfortable where they were.' Instinctively her hands went to her bump. 'Did you feel that? I'm still not sure if I like the thought of another human inside me, it feels a bit weird to be honest.' She began to sit up in the hope the shift would settle things down again.

'I know it must be odd, but for me it is the greatest feeling ever. Especially as it's obvious *he's* going to be a famous footballer. Up the City!' Ben laughed getting up from the bed. He held out his hand to help pull her to her feet.

'Yes, *she* may well be. I hear there's a really good girl's footie team in St Austell.' She was still pleased they'd not asked the sex of the baby at the twenty week scan. There was no need anyhow, she was certain it was a girl. 'What are your plans for the rest of the day then? Lizzie and Tim's train doesn't get in until 6.30, so I'm going to finish off in the shed. I only have one more box to sort through and then we can clear some space. I can't wait to start using it for drying some botanicals, it won't be much longer before I'll be able to tinker and start making some elixirs.'

Ben pulled a face at her. 'Really, Kit? Are you sure you should still be bending down and lugging boxes around in that dusty old shed? And you need to be careful with some herbs and plant oils when you're pregnant.'

'Yes, Ben, I'm aware of that. It's me doing the degree not you, and believe it or not, I do know what I'm doing. You worry too much. Anyhow, as I was saying, are you OK picking them up from the station? I'll prepare something for supper, but I expect by the time they get here they'll want to put little Ruby down for the night.'

Ben pulled a silly face at her. 'You make her sound like an animal... Put her down, poor thing! Right then young lady, off you go. I'm going into the village to pick up some liquid refreshments for later, do you need anything?'

Kitty would give anything for a cold glass of wine; she missed their cozy nights chatting over a bottle or two. These days her tipple was generally hot chocolate.

'No, I'm good thanks – I did a small food shop yesterday. You might as well get it on your way to the station. If you leave now, you'll have plenty of time. Have fun!' And she padded barefoot down the stairs into the kitchen and headed outside to the shed at the bottom of the garden. She'd put her garden boots on when she got to the shed, that's if she could still get them on. Her feet had begun to swell of late and were most uncomfortable.

The garden shed project had become something of an obsession, although Kitty wouldn't let on to Ben that this was the case or he'd be fussing and fretting she was taking on too much. There was something about seeking solace in the shed that soothed her soul. She felt deeply connected and calm when she was in there, although she wasn't sure why. Baby bump also seemed to love it. Each time she set foot into the space she'd feel a few somersaults as if to say, yeah! I'm back in my favourite place. She thought it must be a coincidence at first but then purposely left the shed and went back five minutes later to find that it happened again. She did this on various occasions and each time she stepped into the shed, she felt the same comforting flips. She didn't question it from there on; it was just one of those things that always happened.

Today she was planning on searching through the final box, getting rid of any rubbish and generally tidying up. The other boxes were literally falling apart after years of being in a closed damp environment and had contained nothing more than old newspapers, dried sprigs of lavender and a few other herbs she didn't know the names of. She was looking forward to searching through her reference book to discover what they were. One box had contained some old bits of pottery – small handmade bowls that she'd washed and were now sitting on the kitchen windowsill. There were also two very old looking mortar and pestles that she thought might come in handy, so she'd kept those as well. The rest of the boxes contained junk. And lots of it.

The newspapers she'd put aside for Ben to look at, seemed to be local with only a few from farther afield. She thought they might be of interest knowing how much he loved his history. If not, then there was sure to be a local historical society nearby that might like them. It seemed wrong to put them in the recycling box when they'd survived all this time. There were even one or two papers with headlines dating from the First World War. She would take them back to the cottage to show Ben and he could muse over them with Tim that evening.

The last box was sturdier than the others, which was just as well as it had visibly suffered the weight of the others on top of it. She tentatively sat on the milking stool that had once been hanging from a hook in the roof, and carefully lifted the lid off the box, brushing away the cobwebs and curled-up woodlice as she did so. A cloud of dust sprang up with the lid and she quickly covered her mouth. Wouldn't do to be contracting some dormant ancient bacteria.

More sprigs of dried herbs covered the top layer in the box, and she moved them onto the floor only to be presented with more newspapers. She guessed the box was going to be no different to the others but just as she was about to put the lid back on, out of the corner of her eye, she saw a faint splash of purple.

Carefully, she removed some of the newspapers and was presented with a piece of faded purple velvet ribbon, approximately six inches or so in length. It was surely the same ribbon that had been caught around Marmalade's leg not so long ago. How odd. There was simply no way he could have got into the shed, let alone the box, so how did the ribbon end up wrapped around him? There must have been a piece lying around in the house somewhere, but she was baffled as to where. She was sure she would have come across it before at some point.

Kitty pondered. Given how old the ribbon was, why had it only come to light now, especially after all the renovations they'd done on the cottage?

She picked it up and gently put it into the pocket of her dress thinking it must have once been a beautiful vibrant piece of velvet back in its day. Maybe there were other treasures yet to be discovered in the box? But after carefully examining all its contents, she only found a bundle of loose envelopes with letters inside.

Ah! They must have been tied with the ribbon at some point. She picked them up and counted six envelopes. The ink address on all of them had either faded or was so badly smudged they were unreadable, but some still had visible post marks on them. A red triangle and a circular mark which she could just about read. One said, *Army Post Office Stamp*, the other, *Passed by...* She couldn't quite make out the rest, it would need a magnifying glass or a strong pair of glasses to read. The letters inside however did look readable. How exciting! Perhaps these were the clues she had been hunting for all this time. Hopefully information as to who had previously lived at Creek Cottage.

Kitty glanced at her watch. It was almost six o'clock. She'd better start tidying up before everyone arrived. Sticking a label marked 'checked' on the outside of the box and ensuring the lid, battered as it was, fitted back on, she slipped the letters inside her pocket and rolled the bundle of newspapers under her arm. As she closed the shed door she realised that for the first time, baby bump had not performed any somersaults since before lunch time. Maybe her theory was wrong after all.

XI

1916

Winter was beginning to take a hold in the village of Trunrowan. The fishing boats rarely left the estuary these days, not only because the weather was so unpredictable, but because there were hardly any men left to sail them. One of the larger boats, the *Billow*, whose skipper, Jez Trevelyan, had been sent off to war with his four boys, was rumoured to be setting sail with the mother at the helm when the weather was fine. Loveday had never heard of such a thing and thought how brave the woman must be. And how desperate. Women on boats had always been bad luck. The Trevelyans weren't from around these parts, apparently, they'd moved up from near Newlyn just before the war started. They must breed them hard down there she thought to herself. She wondered if she could do something like that if she had to, but knew the answer would be no. Although she had been brought up by the sea, her knowledge and strengths were much more akin with those of the land.

Today's routine would be no different to yesterday's, or the day before that. She would wake up and head out into the garden to let the hens out. After a cup of strong nettle tea, she would take the short walk down to the cove and bathe if the tide was in. Come rain or shine, in summer and winter. Then she would make herself some porridge with a small teaspoon of home-made raspberry jam. She would soon have to start rationing herself to half a teaspoon every other day, in the hope that it would last until next summer. She only had two unopened jars left in the pantry.

Then she would do some washing. Although these days there were only her clothes to wash and she wore them for as long as she could to save on soap suds.

Later, she'd walk up Chillyhill Lane to Bramble Farm to help with the milking and if she'd got her days right, there'd be the mucking out of the pigs too. She'd been doing this since Will had left for war and was more than happy to be paid in kind with milk and cheese and the odd hock of ham. She knew she was lucky, much luckier than those in the cities who had no means of feeding themselves other than queuing for hours outside shops. There was even talk of rationing coming in if things carried on for much longer. She shuddered at the thought. Poor buggers, it must be awful.

Since Loveday had received the letter stating that Will was missing, she hadn't been to see old Mrs Cromp in the ancient wood, but she really wanted to know the ending of Gribble Gummo's tale of the standing stones. She sighed. She'd probably never find out now. She was hoping she might have seen Mrs Cromp in the village to explain things to her, but now winter had taken hold such an encounter was highly unlikely. She knew she shouldn't be thinking of a cheel and other such nonsense, especially when her Will wasn't around, but her belly physically ached with longing. She wiped a tear away with the corner of her shawl, ashamed she was crying for a mere want. She gave herself a mental ticking off for being so self-pitying. There were men on the front dying for their country and here she was crying for something she didn't even have.

'Wasson? Loveday, nice day for it!' George Weaver poked his head around the pig pen tipping his cap as he did so, puffing on his pipe.

'Well at least it don't stink as much as in the summer!' She laughed, leaning on the rake, glad to have the chance to catch her breath.

'Our Daisy were looking for ye earlier – think she's got summut ye might like.' George took the rake out of Loveday's hand, shaking his head. 'Use a bleddy shovel, girl. Go on, get yer back into it, won't take ye 'alf as long!'

'Ta, Mr Weaver. I couldn't find one so thought I'd just get on with it like. I ain't got naught to rush 'ome for. And thanks, I'll see if I can find 'er after I've finished up 'ere.' Secretly she quite liked watching the pigs snuffling away while she worked. They were funny animals, and they loved the pen best when it was muddy and messy. The messier the better. She always felt bad when she cleaned them out, as though she was depriving them of something.

'Aye, well, I be off now. Got to mend that there fence up yonder before the winter takes 'old good and proper. There's some ham in the kitchen for ye.' With a pat to Loveday's arm, George Weaver bid farewell.

Loveday wondered what Daisy wanted with her. It must be another letter, probably from her Aunt Dorothy in Truro; she couldn't think what else it could be. If it was to be something she'd like then it wasn't bad news about Will. She'd not had any correspondence from him for months now, nor from the War Office. Still, no news was good news.

Just as Loveday was scattering the final handfuls of fresh straw into the pig pen, Daisy jumped up onto the gate, all long legs and waving arms. She was obviously excited.

'There ye is, been looking all over for ye. Got some news.' She smiled at Loveday, waiting for her to ask what it was.

'Well, I can't mind-read, so ye'd best tell me.'

Daisy turned her nose up in disappointment. 'Well ye be no fun today! Apparently, there's a train load of wounded soldiers coming into Penzance 'morrow and I thought we could go along and show our support. Ye never know...' Daisy paused, then whispered, 'Yer Will might be on it!'

Loveday laughed. 'Unlikely, Daisy. Think I'd 'ave 'ad word by now if 'e been found and was on 'is way 'ome, don't ye?'

'Well, not necessarily. They say that lots of mail ain't been getting through, so, it's possible. I reckon we should still go and support 'em. We could make some flags – Ma's got tons of old pillowcases. We can tie them on some willow kindling. Oh, go on please – naught like ye got anything better to do!'

Loveday could tell from Daisy's enthusiasm that she really wanted to go and remembered she had no one special in her life.

'Oh, go on then, but I ain't standing about on platforms for 'ours waiting for the bleddy train to come in. Ye better find out some more information.' But before Loveday could say any more, Daisy had jumped down from the pen and was running back to the farmhouse waving, her long blonde hair bouncing behind her. Jolly, that was the word that came to mind as Loveday watched her. Jolly Daisy, with the biggest heart she'd ever known.

Despite the jolliness, Loveday had a funny feeling that their trip was going to end in nothing but upset when Daisy eventually realised the true horrors of war. Welcoming heroes was one thing, but physically and mentally scarred ones was the true reality. She'd read about in the newspaper.

It had taken nearly two hours with Loveday sat in the back of Granby's delivery van to reach Penzance. Somehow Daisy had managed to bribe Johnny the delivery boy to take them. She dreaded to think what the bribe had been. Looking at how young he was she hoped it had been with sweets. He drove as though it was the first time he'd ever sat behind a wheel and Loveday's back was aching from squatting amongst the cardboard boxes and vegetable trays, while Daisy rode upfront, laughing and giggling for most of the journey. She was relieved when Johnny pulled into the train station.

'Thanks, Johnny, yer a darling. Promise we won't be long. Looks like perfect timing – I can 'ear the train coming in now. Come on, Loveday, we're gonna 'ave to run!'

Daisy grabbed the flags that she'd made and handed two of them to Loveday. Great, now she was going to have to make her legs move after being curled up underneath her for the past two hours. This was going to hurt, but she had to admit it was turning into quite an adventure.

'Slow down, Daisy. The train ain't going nowhere. It's the end of the line,' Loveday shouted above all the hustle and bustle. Daisy kept on running, oblivious, but soon enough they were both stood on the platform, cheering, waving flags and standing on tiptoe with hordes of others, trying to get a glimpse of the first Tommies stepping off the train.

The steam train had come from Truro and was rammed to the hilt. Soldiers were hanging out of the carriage windows, throwing their caps into the air. There were children hanging onto their mothers, crying in bewilderment, but by the time the carriage doors were opened, they were having great fun picking up the previously thrown caps and parading around the station with them on their heads, wide eyes peeking out under the oversized brims, pretending to be soldiers. Loveday felt another longing ache in the pit of her stomach as she watched them, but quickly dismissed it as Daisy nudged her, reminding her to wave the flags.

From that moment on, everyone was excited. People were rushing forwards, desperate to get closer and see if their loved one was on the train. The nurses in their pristine white uniforms with red crosses emblazoned on their bibs had trouble holding people back, so in the end the station master blew his whistle as hard as he could until people reluctantly gathered once again behind the yellow marker and order was restored.

'Blimey, Daisy, I'm not sure we should be 'ere,' Loveday said, watching all the families and sweethearts surrounding her.

The majority of the soldiers getting off the train were walking wounded. A limp here and there, a shuffle of feet or the dragging of a foot. Some were on crutches with only one leg visible, and some had none, stumps bandaged and wrapped with their trouser legs flapping. People were handing out smokes and pipes and there was an awful lot of hugging and kissing. Standing on the platform with strangers and welcoming their men home with them, Loveday felt as though the war had already been won.

'Oh, Loveday, they poor men and their families. Obviously I'm sad that yer Will ain't 'ere like, but I'm still glad we came and made an effort.' Daisy began wrapping her flags around their wooden handles just as a soldier brushed past her.

'Sorry, love. Ye mind them sticks protruding, don't want to be poking anyone's eyes out now, do we?' He pointed to the flag handles and then to his right eye taped up with a huge bandage wrapped around his head. He was laughing at his own joke. Loveday could see Daisy's face redden, then watched her as she leaned forward, planting a huge kiss onto the unsuspecting soldier's lips.

'Wow! I should go to war more often,' was the surprised response.

Loveday hissed into Daisy's nearest ear. 'We need to go – Johnny will need to get back for his afternoon deliveries.'

And with Daisy properly smitten, they left the station platform and headed back to Johnny who was waiting patiently in Granby's van, eyes as wide as saucers and his face as pale as a corpse. Loveday hadn't thought for one moment that the stream of injured soldiers might have given Johnny a shock. Still, she was hoping the ride back across Bodmin wouldn't be as bumpy. Her backside was bruised enough.

*

The first train had got into Penzance earlier than expected and so the hero's welcome they had all been expecting, wasn't there to greet them. Apart from a few station staff and two women who were sweeping the platform, it was empty, although someone had taken the trouble to string up some colourful bunting in anticipation. Will took a deep breath, and for the first time in a very long while, savored the fresh clean air. He threw his kit bag over his good shoulder and made his way towards the exit sign where he hoped to cadge a lift to Trunrowan. He knew he'd be lucky to get one all the way back home, but it would be better than walking. Since losing his arm he tended to lean slightly, and the weight of his kit bag wasn't helping things.

Less than two hours later, Will was dropped off at the top of the village. The ride on the back of the delivery cart he'd cadged a lift with had been a bumpy one, but he was grateful he hadn't needed to walk all or even part of the journey. The cart wouldn't get down Chillyhill Lane even if it wanted to, so he thanked the driver and bid him farewell.

'Ye alright getting off there?' the driver shouted, as Will threw his kit bag onto the ground and tried to navigate his descent down.

He could feel his face burning up with frustration. 'I be fine!' he shouted back, a little louder than was necessary. So this was what it was going to be like from here on in was it?

'Aye, well if ye be sure then.'

'Yeah, I be sure!' Will mocked back, realising he was probably sounding rude. No one was going to see any further than his absent arm and he'd not even reached home yet.

For a fleeting moment he thought about asking the driver to take him back, where to he didn't know, but the thought of a warm bed and perhaps some ale or cider, managed to persuade him otherwise. If he was lucky, Loveday might not be home which would mean he could take himself off to bed and deal with the aftermath of his unexpected return later. He put his head down and set off down the lane, glimpsing the familiar chimney stack of Rowan Cottage in the near distance. There was no smoke trailing into the sky which could mean only one thing: Loveday wasn't at home.

XII

Present day

Kitty closed the kitchen door and put the bundle of newspapers and the letters on the dresser and set to preparing the chicken casserole to put into the oven. Then, all she would need to do was boil some rice, open a bottle of red for the others and enjoy the rest of the evening. No fuss and no bother. Gone were the glamorous days of preparing fancy meals and making cocktails. Things here in Cornwall were done differently.

'Take us or leave us' had become their new motto, yet they still had plenty of friends wanting to come and stay with them. She didn't mind at the moment, but she certainly couldn't imagine entertaining with a small baby in tow. Lizzie, however, was the exception. She'd been a friend for as long as she could remember. They'd grown up together, travelled the world together and been bridesmaids at one another's weddings. The only thing they hadn't done together was to have children at the same time. Lizzie had fallen pregnant with Ruby straight after she'd married Tim, which was almost four years ago. Ruby was an absolute delight and just like her mum. Blonde bouncy locks of hair with sky blue eyes, and was already showing the quirkiest of personalities. She hoped that her child would be blessed with all of Ruby's attributes – she was an absolute delight. She smiled to herself. There she was doing it again! Referring to baby bump as a girl.

Kitty glanced at the kitchen clock – it was almost seven o'clock. They should be arriving any minute. If she was quick, she'd just about have enough time to give the spare room the once over and make sure Marmalade hadn't snuck in and taken up residence on the bed. She should also put some more wood in the burner; she realised she was feeling cold. That horrible feeling she'd had months ago had suddenly crept over her again, as though someone had walked over her grave. Whatever that actually meant. She'd check the windows; Ben was a bugger for aerating the cottage.

'Hi Love, we're back,' Ben shouted, lugging Lizzie and Tim's bags behind him. 'Kitty, where are you?'

Kitty appeared at the door of the living room. She had changed into a pair of dark blue maternity jeans and a flowery top which emphasised her bump nicely. Ben felt a pang of pride.

'No need to shout, Ben, it's a small cottage you know.' Kitty laughed; she was always telling him they were at the most only ten feet away from one another at any given time. Ruby, who had followed Ben into the cottage, had dived under the kitchen table and was shouting 'Kitty'.

'Aww bless her, she thinks you're calling for your cat, Ben.' Lizzie said, hugging Kitty and then scrambling under the table.

'Come out of there you little munchkin. I expect Auntie Kitty's cat has already fled – you won't find anything under here.'

'Apart from a few crumbs,' Ben added, as he made his way to the stairs to take up the bags to the spare room.

'Hey, let me do that mate, you sort out the drinks – you've

certainly earned yours coming to pick us up. Those country lanes needed your full concentration. Makes navigating the city centre in the mornings a doddle!' Tim piped up.

'Where am I going with them anyhow?' he asked, realising he had no idea.

'The room on your right at the top of the stairs. There are only three rooms up there, you won't get lost.' Kitty chuckled.

'Da-da,' Ruby said, pulling at Tim's hand.

'Come on then, poppet. Let's see where we'll be sleeping tonight, shall we?' and Tim somehow managed to strap the bags on and around him while taking Ruby's chubby hand in his.

'He's so good with her, you're very lucky you know, Lizzie,' Kitty said, pouring red wine into the three glasses on the table.

'I know I am. He's a godsend – his patience is that of a saint. Not like mine. I still need my full eight hours sleep. God help anyone that gets in my way if I haven't.'

The rest of the evening was spent eating, drinking and chatting around the dining-room table. They discussed the newly found newspapers and letters found in the shed and Lizzie agreed to help Kitty with her research of the cottage. Having a friend as a librarian had its bonuses. The casserole was well received and the red wine even more so. Kitty forgot how they all drank like fish when they got together. Ruby was happy lying on the floor in the living room with her colouring book and even though Lizzie warned Kitty that she liked to colour in 'anything', Kitty let her be. She would soon have to get used to having a child around, so now was as good a time as any.

'So, are you ready for the imminent arrival?' Tim asked, topping up the almost-empty wine glasses.

'Is anyone ever ready?' Kitty replied. 'I mean, you're the experts now.' She laughed and nodded towards the living room – realising that Ruby was no longer lying on the floor.

'Hey, where's Ruby gone?'

Lizzie got up a little too fast and knocked Tim's wine glass over in the process.

'Bloody hell, Lizzie! Careful. Shit, so sorry mate.' Tim grabbed a tea cloth from the kitchen drainer as Burgundy seeped over the beautiful embroidered white linen tablecloth.

'Don't worry, my fault for laying the table with white. I'll deal with it – you go and see what Ruby's up to.' Kitty cussed herself. The tablecloth had belonged to her gran and was one of her favourites.

'Ah, there you are, poppet. Where've you been? You know that you shouldn't wander off without telling Mummy and Daddy, don't you?' Kitty heard Lizzie say gently.

Ruby had reappeared at the bottom of the stairs, sobbing, her thumb stuck firmly in her mouth.

'Someone's tired then,' Tim said, scooping Ruby up and giving her tummy a tickle.

'There's a man in my room,' Ruby managed between sniffs, sobs and her thumb.

'Of course there isn't, darling. No one else lives here with Auntie Kitty and Uncle Ben apart from Marmalade their cat,' Lizzie said gently.

'But — there is — a big man in MY room,' Ruby protested. 'And he took Mr Snozzle!'

All four of them looked at one another, puzzled. Mr Snozzle was Ruby's well-loved toy pig that she took everywhere with her.

By the time that they had all made it up the stone stairs and squeezed into the spare bedroom, Kitty was not only panting but beside herself with worry. The bedroom door was wide open, but the window was firmly shut. She checked the iron latch, it was firmly in place. No one would be able to get into the bedroom from outside without breaking the window or at least making a noise jimmying it, and the wind certainly wouldn't be able to blow it open. She checked again just to make sure.

Looking around the room, everything appeared to be in place. The bed was as she had left it earlier, with the late addition of a fluffy pink cushion on the put-me-up bed for Ruby. The soft glow from the bedside lamp was casting shadows on the floorboards, which did give the room an eerie feel, but apart from that, everything appeared normal. Kitty sat on the edge of the bed to catch her breath and spotted Mr Snozzle's tail, poking out from under the small chest of drawers by the window.

'There he is! Ben, grab Mr Snozzle, will you? I can just see his curly tail under the chest of drawers.' Kitty laughed in an attempt to lighten the mood, as a puff of dust followed his retrieval. 'I should probably spend some more time cleaning, I know, but it's difficult to bend down with this bump.' She put her hands on her stomach and smiled.

'Look, I think it's safe to say that no one is here and that Ruby saw a shadow or something. The door must have been ajar. There is no way she could have reached up to open it, so on that note, I think we should all go back downstairs and not make a fuss about it all.' Ben whispered, trying to sound convincing while brushing off the dust from Mr Snozzle.

'Good idea. I think we must all be ready to hit the sack anyway. Agree?' Lizzie said.

'Agreed,' they all said in unison. Kitty checked the window latch again, then drew the floral curtains together as tightly as she could, ensuring there were no gaps. She didn't know why, but she wanted to be sure that no one could see in, even though she knew it was a ridiculous thought. With one last scan around the room, she breathed a sigh of relief and was about to follow the others downstairs when she heard a creak coming from the corner of the room. She froze. There it was again, as though someone was walking across the room.

Oh my god, there was something in the room. What was it? The wind, an echo… She was trying to convince herself it was anything other than the obvious sound of footsteps. She couldn't

84

let Ruby sleep in here now, given what had just happened, she'd have to make up some excuse that the room was too cold, the only problem with that though was that her and Ben would have to sleep in here instead.

Quickly, she left the room, shutting the door hard behind her, trying to compose herself at the top of the stairs. She took a deep breath as her stomach tightened. Someone else wasn't happy either. As she made her way carefully down the stone stairs, she felt the too-familiar cold feeling wash over her again. She'd mention it to her midwife next time she saw her – it must be a hormonal thing. Either that or she was going mad.

XIII

1916

Finding Will asleep in their bed had come as a shock, albeit a pleasant one. She still couldn't comprehend how he had managed to recuperate in the military hospital without her knowing anything about it. He said that he'd written her letters but she'd never received any of them and she knew that if there had been any addressed to her, Daisy would have made sure she'd received them. She let it go though. Will had not liked her prying when she'd started to ask questions, and in truth she was just plain glad to have her Will back in one piece. Well, relatively.

When he'd first come back, everyone in the village had rallied round with offers of help but he'd shrugged them off, keeping himself to himself and going about his business in a quiet and unassuming way. He'd lost his gentleness and drank way too much, often losing his temper at the slightest little thing, but Loveday presumed that when you'd fought for your King and Country, seen the things he'd no doubt seen, you were allowed to, on occasion. What she didn't like however, were his nightmares.

Some nights he would wake in a bath of sweat, trembling and groaning, and the only way to deal with him was to leave him well alone. She'd tried cajoling him, hugging him, kissing him and everything else she could think of, but eventually after being pushed away so many times, she left him alone with his demons. Normally when they happened, he would sit in the bedroom chair by the window wrapped in a blanket, staring out to sea, for what seemed like hours on end, until she could watch him no longer and would eventually fall asleep. If he wasn't there when she woke, he would be sat in the kitchen, his army boots between his knees, polishing and buffing them with his good hand.

One morning, she'd finally snapped. 'Blimey, Will, you'll be able to see yer face in 'em soon!'

'Aye, that's the plan,' he'd replied.

'What's the point though. I mean it ain't like ye is going to be using 'em again, is it?'

As soon as the words had come out of her mouth, she regretted it. Will slammed the tin of polish onto the kitchen table as his boot fell to the floor. As he stood up, the chair tumbled backwards and poor George bolted into the living room to take cover.

'And what would ye know?' Will grabbed Loveday's arm, just a little too tightly.

'Get off, yer 'urting me,' she yelled, trying to wriggle her arm from his grasp.

'Well, shut up then. They might take I back yet, ye know! I've written to 'em to see if there's anything else I can do other than fight!' Will picked up the chair and sat back down, continuing his polishing with even more vigour.

The anger that had been bottled up inside of her since Will's return, suddenly exploded. 'Ye done what?!' she screeched. 'What's wrong with ye? Why would ye want to go back to that 'ell 'ole, eh? Tell me what's so special about all they men that makes ye want to go back… Tell me!' She continued muttering under her breath while she banged the pots and pans around in the sink as loudly as she could.

'Well, they don't bleddy nag me all the time, that's for one! They leaves me be, lets me do things me own way, not the way some nagging woman wants things done! That's why… Oh! And as for trying for a cheel, if ye asks me one more time to make love to ye, I swear I'll take ye up onto Bodmin and string ye up!' And with his final words said, Will marched off down the garden path towards the cove, leaving her sobbing.

That occasion had been one of the worst episodes so far, but there had been plenty of others that had been similar. She'd put up with enough and decided to take things into her own hands once and for all. If he wouldn't seek help, and she'd asked him to on enough occasions, then she would. Tomorrow she would go to see old Mrs Cromp. It was a full moon and god willing she'd be able to give her something to rid Will of his anger and nightmares. He was right though, she had nagged him at every opportunity to make love to her, that was the reality of her desperation for a cheel. She'd been sleeping religiously with the sprig under her pillow each night as Mrs Cromp had instructed, but nothing had materialised.

Their lovemaking since Will had returned had been practically non-existent. They appeared to have lost all connection to one another and when they had made love, if you could even call it that, it was nothing more than an ale or cider fuelled release on Wills part. To add insult to injury, he'd often fall asleep halfway through. She needed to take matters into her own hands and tomorrow, she'd decided, was as good a day as any.

The next morning, Loveday collected the hen eggs and thanked her lucky stars as they almost filled her basket. She'd get some good money for them in the village and perhaps she could put some away without Will knowing. She'd been squirrelling away the odd shilling and pence since before Will had gone off to war. Saving up for a rainy day her ma would call it; she thought it was just being sensible. She wanted their cheel to have the very best of everything, where possible, and the only way that would happen was if they had some money behind them. The only good thing about her not getting pregnant was that she'd managed to save quite a stash.

'Will, I'm taking the eggs into the village, I won't be long. Shall we go down to the cove later and see if we can collect some mussels?' Loveday shouted up the stairs. There was no response. She'd leave him be, it wouldn't hurt him to get some decent sleep while she was out. Loveday shut the cottage door behind her as quietly as she could; the blasted door had started squeaking again. She'd remind Will to oil the hinges when she came back later.

Walking up Chillyhill Lane, she thought how mild it was for the beginning of October. There were plenty of rosehips and elderberries around and the rusty colours of fallen leaves lined her path. She felt blessed to be living in Trunrowan and couldn't imagine what it must've been like for Will in a foreign country. She wished he'd talk to her about it so she could picture where he slept and ate, where he perhaps enjoyed camaraderie and drank with his mates – if only to be able to understand what was going on in his head at times. She didn't need to know what bloodshed he'd seen, that could stay in his nightmares. She just wanted life to be normal again.

The village was unusually quiet for the time of morning and Loveday enjoyed her time walking through, grateful she hadn't been born somewhere other than Trunrowan. Everyone knew one another in and around the village and if they didn't, they knew your ma or pa. There were a few families that had lived in or about the village for hundreds of years. The Cardew family were beef farmers, and there was no meat like theirs this side of Truro. The Weavers had always been dairy farmers, and the Penrose family too, although they were on the other side of the estuary. The Trevelyans were the main local fishing family and had already lost many of their family to the war. Loveday's family surname before she'd married had been Sellers, and they were relatively new to Cornwall in terms of years, or so her ma had told her. They had originated from a small village in Somerset but had travelled, selling their wares, until one day they had settled in Cornwall. Loveday missed her ma hugely, she'd give anything to be able to share her worries. She'd make a cracking cider and apple cake, and a strong pot of tea, and could talk the hind legs off a donkey. She was full of wisdom and wise words and when she'd died some folk whispered she was of Romany descent, but she'd never let on to Loveday that she was; she was pretty sure she'd have told her if it was true. Both her ma and pa died far too young and had left a huge void in Loveday's life.

Even as a cheel, her ma had taught Loveday the names of the local flora. Recently, she had started her own collection of flowers and herbs which she'd tied into bunches to hang up to dry. She didn't know enough to do much with them, but she enjoyed the process. She did know which ones were poisonous though, she'd learned that much and from an early age. Perhaps in the future, once she'd sorted things with Will, Mrs Cromp would be willing to teach her a thing or two. She'd enjoy that.

As she approached Granby's shop, she noticed a group of men, some propped up against the shop front, the others milling around. Normally, at this time of day, the men were working the land or the sea. She immediately spotted George Weaver with his big bushy beard and statement pipe that always seemed to be permanently stuck to his lips. His being there was even stranger as she knew at this time of the morning he should be up at the farm. George appeared to be taking control of the group, or at least trying to, and as she got closer she could see two men rolling about on the floor.

'Right, that be enough, let's be 'aving you.' George was shouting at the two men, while his farm labourers were attempting to prise them apart.

Some of the older women in the village who Loveday knew of but didn't have much to do with were staring at her with smirks on their faces, whispering behind hands to one another.

'Can't ye keep 'im under control!' one of the women muttered as Loveday walked past. Another spat at her, the frothy phlegm landing in front of her feet.

'Ah! Loveday, best ye don't see this, eh? Our Daisy's in the shop, go on in and stay with 'er for a bit, will ye,' George said while ushering her towards the shop door where Daisy immediately appeared and pulled her inside.

By now she realised that one of the two men brawling was her Will. He must've snuck out when she was collecting the hens' eggs, unless he'd been up all night again and had gone out early to walk off his thoughts. She tried to remember if he'd woken in the night from one of his dreams but couldn't recall. For once she'd somehow managed to sleep right through and had felt wonderfully refreshed when she'd woken.

'What's 'appened?' was the only thing she could think of saying to Daisy.

'Apparently, Will arrived at the farm early this morning just as Pa was about to milk the cows, demanding a flagon of cider. Pa said 'e was already lathered and it were only six o'clock,' Daisy replied in the nicest way she possibly could without dramatising it. 'When Pa turned 'im away, 'e started shouting and kicking the door. Then 'e went into the milking yard and was frightening all the heifers. Ma swears blind that the milk's going to curdle due to the shock!' Loveday put her head in her hands. 'Then 'e came down into the village shouting abuse at anyone and everyone, and Pa followed with the farm'ands to try and calm 'im. They be 'ere for a while now and just as ye arrived, the scuffle broke out. I'm sorry to say it, Loveday, but I fear 'e's gone cakey.'

Loveday didn't know what to say. Everything Daisy had spoken about seemed plausible, except she hadn't realised Will wasn't in the cottage when she'd left, and for that she felt awful as well as embarrassed. How could she have not known he wasn't in bed when she'd woken? Perhaps it was her that was going cakey. What was she going to do? Her visit to old Mrs Cromp could not come around soon enough, but for now she was somehow going to have to shamelessly get Will back home.

'I can't sit back and just let things be, Daisy. Will needs me. I don't care what others think about 'im, 'e's been to war and we can only imagine what 'orrors 'ave been seen. 'E needs love and compassion, not bleddy sneers and jibes. I'm taking 'im 'ome right now. Bugger the lot of 'em out there!' And Loveday stood up, put her shoulders back and strode outside with purpose, ignoring the growing group of people that was congregating. She was amazed at where they'd all come from; word had obviously spread quickly. Trunrowan was a small village and it looked as though most of the villagers were now stood outside the village shop.

'Bugger off, the lot of ye, can't ye see 'e's traumatised from the war effort!' she yelled at the jeering faces.

'Lathered you mean!' someone sneered.

George Weaver walked over to Loveday and put his hand gently on her shoulder. His face was flushed and large beads of perspiration congregated in his furrowed brow. He took a big drag on his pipe.

'Come on, Love, I'll help ye get 'im 'ome.'

Somehow, between the pair of them, they managed to stagger down Chillyhill Lane with Will stopping every few feet or so to take a pee or retch up what little was left in his stomach. It wasn't easy propping up a strong man who only had one arm, but they took their time and eventually made it back to Rowan Cottage. Within seconds Will had flopped onto the sofa and was snoring like a pig.

'I'm so sorry, I can't thank ye enough,' Loveday said, physically and emotionally exhausted.

'Aye, well ye needs to sort some 'elp out as soon as possible before someone takes a bleddy gun to 'im. He might be able to get away with that type of behavior on the battlefields but 'ere in Trunrowan, it won't be tolerated, ye knows that. Your ma and pa would turn in their grave if they could see the pair of ye in this state.'

All Loveday could do was shrug. She knew it was true.

'I promise I'll get 'im to see someone as soon as possible. 'E won't be any more trouble, Mr Weaver, I'll make sure of it.' And with a certain assurance in her voice that she didn't feel, she bid him farewell, closed the cottage door and turned the key in the lock; something she rarely ever did. Leaning against the door, she fought back the tears. The evening's harvest moon couldn't come quick enough.

XIV

Present day

The following morning at breakfast, everyone was subdued except Kitty and Ruby.

'Blimey, remind me, exactly how much did we drink?' Lizzie groaned resting her head on the kitchen table.

'Mummy, can we play?' an eager Ruby asked, pulling at Lizzie's dressing gown.

'Oh, good god, I think I'm going to be sick.' Lizzie ran upstairs to the bathroom, her hands covering her mouth.

'Well, obviously it was far too much!' Kitty laughed looking around the table at the sorry faces staring back at her.

'Yeah, yeah, cat that got the bloody cream. If you weren't pregnant you wouldn't have got out of bed by now,' Ben said, pouring himself another cup of coffee from the cafetière.

'Nonsense. I don't know what you're talking about, Mr Gridley. Anyhow, I'm going to take Ruby down to the beach and let you all recover, then later on Lizzie and I are going to Truro

Library so we can make a start on our research and find out exactly who has lived here. I looked through the letters this morning while you were all zonked out, so we have a couple of names to go by, but I didn't have time to go through all the newspapers. Perhaps you guys could have a read before we go? They must've been kept for a reason.' Kitty picked up the bundle of newspapers and placed them in the middle of the kitchen table. Ben and Tim groaned.

'Packing maybe?' Tim offered hopefully.

'Really, Kitty? I can hardly focus on my coffee cup let alone read a newspaper that's almost a hundred years old.' Ben pushed the newspapers back in the direction they had come from.

'Oh my god! What is wrong with you both? Ruby and I will be back in an hour or two and you'd best be looking brighter than you do now. Might be wise, Tim, to check on Lizzie, eh?' Taking Ruby's hand, Kitty left them to it.

Kitty had decided that she'd take Ruby for a nice walk along the cove and perhaps to the edge of the wood if they had time. They could collect shells and seaweed and it would give the rest of them some time to recover from the evening's drinking session. It would also give her some time alone with Ruby and the chance to ask her about what she'd supposedly seen in the bedroom last night.

'Can we swim, Auntie Kitty?' Ruby asked as they made their way to the bottom of the garden.

'Not today, darling. The water's far too cold. Perhaps your feet could see just how cold it is, and then you can decide... What do you think about that?' Kitty knew that the moment Ruby's feet felt the sea water she'd certainly not want to immerse her whole body in it. Ruby squeezed Kitty's hand tight as if they were making a pact and carefully slipped off her sparkly pink shoes, squealing as her feet hit the cold Cornish sea.

'Too cold, Auntie Kitty... Can we find some shells? Mummy likes shells, she has lots in her bedroom. On the floor. I want to find Mummy some shells. Daddy says they pick up must.'

Kitty laughed at her god-daughter's muddled language.

'Do you mean pick up dust, Ruby?'

'Yes. Dust on shells.' And with a quiet giggle, Ruby let go of Kitty's hand and ran off down the beach.

'Hey! Wait for me, Rubes!' Kitty shouted, attempting to run after her while trying to support her stomach as she did so. At times, she completely forgot she was carrying a small child inside of her, but now wasn't one of them.

Kitty and Ruby spent a lovely hour or so wandering along the shoreline collecting shells and seaweed to put into Ruby's Peppa Pig bag. They'd also picked up some plastic straws, a battered yellow flip flop that had seen better days, and a selection of crisp packets. Kitty explained to Ruby why it was important for people to pick up their rubbish and not leave it lying around on the beach, but Ruby wanted to leave everything where it was in case the people came back for them.

'Well, I think we should take it all back home just in case the waves take it all back out to sea,' she'd quickly responded.

Ruby shook her head. 'We can write in the sand and tell them, Auntie Kitty.' This girl was way too smart for her age, which could possibly work in Kitty's favour. Now was as good a time as any.

'Do you think the pieces may belong to the man you saw last night in the bedroom?' Kitty drew breath and waited. She knew she was playing with fire and taking a huge gamble in hoping that Ruby wasn't going to freak out and get upset. Lizzie would be furious if she knew she was asking her questions like this.

Ruby pulled a face. She was obviously deep in thought, but at least she wasn't crying. 'No,' she firmly replied and carried on rearranging the items in her bag.

'Oh, really? Why's that then?' Kitty felt as though she was walking a tightrope.

''Cause he can't hold them.'

'Can't hold them... Why's that then, Ruby?'

'Cause he only has one arm, silly!' Ruby giggled.

'Silly, Auntie Kitty, indeed.' Kitty was even more curious now and not sure whether she should push things further. The last thing she wanted to do was conjure up images of people in the cottage wandering around with limbs missing. It was beginning to sound like a horror film.

'He wanted Mr Snozzle, but I hid him.' Ruby said with a smug look on her face.

'Under the chest of drawers?'

'Yes. Man was sad.'

'And why do you think that was, Ruby?'

'Cause he only has one arm!' Ruby looked at Kitty as though she was stupid, which was quite a feat for a four-year-old. The conversation was obviously going nowhere, and although Ruby was saying it as she saw it, or thought she saw it, whatever it was, Kitty had to stop; she was in danger of making things worse.

'Well, I'm sure he'll feel much better soon and you're not to worry about him, OK?'

'OK, Auntie Kitty. Can we get ice cream now?'

This was the best suggestion she'd heard so far that morning, 'We certainly can, sweetheart. Let's go back to the cottage and see if Mummy and Daddy want one too, shall we?' Kitty glanced at her watch. Surely they'd all be feeling better by now.

'And Uncle Ben!' Ruby reminded her.

'And Uncle Ben!' Kitty laughed.

Slowly they made their way back to the cottage, Ruby stopping every few steps to pick up a shell or piece of seaweed, clutching her Peppa Pig bag tightly.

By the time they'd returned, life appeared to be back to normal. Ben was making breakfast and the wonderful smell of bacon and eggs hit Kitty well before she stepped into the kitchen through the back door. Although technically there was a front door to the cottage, Kitty couldn't actually ever remember using it apart from when they'd first viewed the property. The back door led out onto the garden and then the garden path took them directly to the cove. There was a small slipway which enabled them to catch the ferry across to the other side of the estuary. There was also a shingle path that hugged either side of the cottage and which opened out to a very small garden and a hard standing for the car. They hardly used the car these days and it seemed silly to keep going in and out of the front door when all their activity was at the back of the property.

'Ooh! Smells good. I presume we're all back to normal then?' Kitty looked at Lizzie who was lounging on the living room floor playing with Marmalade, still looking a little pale.

'I am thanks. I've managed some toast and cereal and feel much better now, but the boys are having a fry-up. Their stomachs must be made of cast iron.' Lizzie laughed.

'I just need some food inside me and I'll be fine,' Tim responded, hovering by the Aga.

'Ice cream!' Ruby shouted at the top of her little voice, just in case Kitty had forgotten her promise. Kitty went to the freezer where she kept a small selection of Cornish flavoured ice-creams. Since being pregnant, she'd developed a craving for Roskilly's salt caramel.

'At this time in the morning?' Lizzie pulled herself up onto her knees as Marmalade sauntered off, realising that his tummy tickles were over.

'It's almost midday, you know. And there's never a wrong time to have ice cream, is there? Mint choc chip, strawberry or salt caramel, Ruby?' Kitty thought she might have some as well. She'd bought some lovely caramel wafer cones with chocolate at the bottom which held a really large scoop of ice cream.

Ruby looked at Lizzie for assurance that it was OK before answering.

'Oh! Go on then, you look like you've been very busy on the beach.' Lizzie picked up Ruby's Peppa Pig bag and turned up her

98

nose as she peered inside, amazed at the array of shells, seaweed and rubbish it held.

'Strawberryyyyyy,' Ruby shouted.

'Really, Ruby, could you keep the noise down for Daddy please, he's got a headache.' Tim covered his ears with his hands.

'Look, we really need to get out of here for the rest of the day. Lizzie are you still up for a trip into Truro to visit the library?' Kitty handed Ruby her ice cream and, holding it carefully, she took herself off to sit on the back doorstep, glowering at Tim as she did so.

'Sounds like a great idea,' Ben piped up. 'We can take Ruby crabbing. She'll like that. Oh, and I had a quick look through the bundle of newspapers and found this on the front page of one of them. The rest seemed pretty nondescript, to be honest.' Ben passed Kitty a newspaper, pointing to the picture on the front. 'It looks like a photo of a cottage but it's really difficult to see properly. I've had a quick look with my work loupe glasses but the ink is all pixelated.'

Kitty had just managed to balance a huge scoop of salt caramel onto a cone and, with her spare hand, tucked the newspaper under her arm and headed into the living room. She ushered Marmalade off the sofa and flicked on the sidelamp. The black-and-white photo was, as Ben said, impossible to make out in detail, but you could confidently make out from the outline that it was a cottage. It wasn't clear enough to tell if it was Creek Cottage, but it certainly could be. She noted the date. Tuesday 23 January 1917.

> A dead body was found on Saturday at Rowan Cottage in Trunrowan. Little is known about the circumstances around the cause of death as yet, but it is not thought to be suspicious.

Well, it wasn't Creek cottage then. At least that was clear. In fairness, most of the cottages in and around Trunrowan looked the same and to find a dead body, well nothing really strange about that; people died all the time, even in Cornwall. But there must have been something unusual about the finding for it to be reported on, and on the front page too. She passed the newspaper to Lizzie who had joined her in the living room.

'Don't you think it's strange they have only written a small piece on it, but they took the trouble to take a photo?' Kitty said to Lizzie, who now had Marmalade on her lap, purring.

'Not really. Back then, what, almost a hundred years ago, something like that was a headline in a small village like this. I mean, it would've made a change from writing about the war efforts.'

Kitty nodded. 'Good point, I hadn't thought of that…which is why you're a librarian and I'm not. Come on, we're heading to Truro right now!' Kitty got up and felt a sharp kick in her ribs.

'Ouch, little bugger! You've finally woken up then.' She rubbed her side.

'Ha! The joys, eh? I remember them well. Not long to go now and you'll soon have your body back again.' Lizzie smiled.

'Yep, thank god! Only three weeks left. Saying it out loud makes it seem a little more real.' Kitty picked up a colouring crayon from the sofa and handed it to Lizzie.

'Oh! It's real hun. Just look at that humongous bump!'

XV

1916

Loveday fetched the woollen blanket from the bed and covered Will with it before adding more wood onto the fire. She didn't know how long she'd be gone, two hours maybe, three at the most, but it was doubtful he'd wake up with the amount of drink he'd consumed. He'd been restless most of the day but had finally settled and was snoring loudly. She scribbled a note to say she'd gone up to Bramble Farm to help Mabel and Daisy pack up the cheese, eggs and jam for the Christmas market and propped it up against the milk jug on the kitchen table. He wasn't to know it had already been done. Truth be told, he didn't have a clue what she did most days.

She took a lantern from under the sink, along with a box of matches. Even though the moon would be full that evening, she'd learned her lesson from previous visits. Quietly closing the cottage door behind her, she headed off down the garden path towards the shingle beach. She wouldn't have time to bathe tonight, she was in too much of a hurry; she needed to speak to Mrs Cromp as soon as she could. If she didn't sort something out for Will soon, who knew what the villagers would end up doing. Just the thought made her shudder.

Once outside she realised how cold it was, even the woodland couldn't contain the bitter easterly wind that had picked up, but the sky was clear and there would be a frost in the morning for sure. She pulled Will's heavy Guernsey further down her legs until it almost reached her knees grateful for its warmth. When Will had been at war, she'd managed to knit three of them all with the family pattern on. It had taken her a while to get to grips with the pattern as compared to her pa's, it was rather elaborate with lots of diamonds and cable interwoven, but she'd eventually got the hang of it. It had helped to pass the hours and there was something comforting listening to the clikety-clack of the needles.

Just as Loveday opened the gate, she was greeted by Reverend Jones hurrying along the beach, his cassock flapping in the breeze. He shouted to her above the wind but continued moving in the direction of the coastal path.

'Wasson? Loveday, yer out late. Be careful me dear, there be a storm coming. I'm going to batten down the church hatches... Wish me luck!'

Reverend Jones was new to Trunrowan, yet in the short time he'd done wonders. He'd immediately fitted in with village life and had an ever growing congregation. He was vicar of the small chapel up on the headland, a beautiful 17th-century chapel that was splendid in all of its understatedness. Loveday wasn't a regular churchgoer, but she tried to make an effort on occasion. She and Will had been married in the chapel and had already attended plenty of funerals there in her short life. When she'd been around fifteen years of age, the funeral of the two Trevelyan men lost in the 1905 storms, along with their boat, had made a huge impact on her. She remembered the congregation snaking out through the main door and all the way down the hill that day, that's how many people had come from far and wide to pay their respects. There had been a more private service at sea later and her pa had been privileged to be on board. Her ma had sat with Rose Trevelyan outside Breal Cottage, along with most of the women in Trunrowan.

Loveday had always questioned religion, especially of late. She didn't understand how there could be a god when the country was at war. Seeing her Will come home like he had, well… Why would a god let people suffer so? Still, she liked Reverend Jones and the enthusiasm he'd brought to the village and would always stop to chat if she ever bumped into him. She'd decided that when she or Will passed on, she would quite like them to be buried together in the chapel's graveyard. The graveyard looked out over the headland towards the sea; not that the view would matter much once they were gone. Tonight though, she was pleased he was in a rush; she didn't think his god would be best pleased to know that she was on her way to see cunning folk!

By the time Loveday had reached the woodcutter's cottage deep in the ancient wood, she was beginning to wish she hadn't come. Not only was she petrified at what Mrs Cromp was going to say when she asked for help, she realised that she had no means of paying for anything she might be given. She didn't know how these things worked, whether it was a monetary exchange or perhaps some eggs or butter. For all she knew, Mrs Cromp might well tell her to bugger off! But she kept telling herself that she'd been willing to help her to conceive a cheel…although nothing had come of that as yet. What was really annoying too, was the Droll Teller hadn't been back since her first visit, when he'd only told half his story before heading off to bed the worse for wear. But she had no one else to turn to and she was here now.

She noted the usual smoke curls from the chimney and a faint light through the small rectangular window, so she knocked loudly on the door and waited. Nothing. She knocked again, wishing Mrs Cromp would hurry up and let her in so she could warm up.

'She been ill. Go on in.' The familiar jangling of bells came with the voice behind her, as Gribble Gummo squeezed past her and pulled the door open.

'Oh, sorry, I didn't see ye there.' Loveday stood aside, as behind Gribble Gummo a straggly-looking fox skulked past her.

'Ye got eyes in the back of yer 'ead then?' came the sarcastic reply. Loveday couldn't be bothered to answer, instead she followed them both inside to an empty room and a rather sad-looking fire. Immediately she set to tending it, and in no time at all had the fire roaring again. She rubbed her hands together as she stood in front of it, feeling the heat finally begin to penetrate her cold bones. Where was Mrs Cromp? And Gribble Gummo had now disappeared too, while his fox seemed quite at home curled up on the rocking chair. It lifted its head from under its tail and looked at her as though it knew she was thinking of him. Pesky thing gave her the creeps.

Not quite sure what to do next, she decided to take the fox's lead and reluctantly sat opposite him on one of the cushions on the floor and waited.

After what seemed like an age, Gribble Gummo reappeared from one of the side rooms, a blanket draped over his arm.

'Ere, 'ave this, ye be warm in no time. She can't see ye tonight though, she still ain't right. She's best left where she is, so once yer warmed up, ye'd best get going again.' He wandered over to the fox, patted its head, lit his pipe from an ember in the hearth, and then sat at the kitchen table puffing hard and blowing circles through his mouth intermittently.

'Oh. I really needs to see 'er now. It's very important and I've come a long way 'specially.' She realised she was sounding desperate, but she couldn't leave without trying. The thought of going back home with nothing to help Will wasn't worth contemplating. The fox suddenly lifted its head and looked around the room its nose twitching. He stretched a few times before settling back down, his bushy tail covering his face. Loveday shivered. Sly fox.

'I told ye, she ain't well. Ye'll 'ave to wait,' Gribble said firmly, blowing his smoke rings. He was certainly a very different Droll Teller to the one she'd met a few months ago. He wouldn't capture anyone's imagination at the moment with his sullen disposition.

Loveday thought she'd have one last attempt before admitting defeat and heading back to the cottage. If she gave a little information away, he might find some compassion hiding somewhere.

'Ye see, me 'usband 'ave come back from war and 'e ain't right in the 'ead. I needs to speak with Mrs Cromp to see if she can 'elp him. I wouldn't ask if I didn't 'ave to.' Loveday paused. 'Please?'

Gribble Gummo looked over at her and shrugged. God, he was a miserable so-and-so. Was he really the same Droll Teller? Perhaps they all wore jangly trousers and looked the same.

'She be in there.' He moved his head in the direction from where he'd come earlier. 'But don't be long 'cause she shouldn't be 'aving visitors.' Gribble turned his back on Loveday and put his feet up on the edge of the sink, staring out of the window, still puffing hard on his pipe.

Loveday got up sheepishly. Now she felt bad. She didn't know exactly what she was going to ask for, but she had to give it a go. Slowly, she walked into the small room that Gribble had gestured to, not quite sure what she was going to be presented with and was surprised to see the outline of Mrs Cromp sat on a chair. There was a distinct air there'd been cross words exchanged and she guessed that was why Gribble Gummo was so miserable.

'Umm, sorry to trouble ye Mrs Cromp but I was wondering...' It was very dark in the room and Loveday decided to stand still for fear of bumping into something.

'Aye, I 'eard you. Sorry about Gribble, 'e 'as moods sometimes. Drags me down they do. I ain't ill, love, just me bones giving I gyp. Was hoping no one was going to come tonight, but then realised with the harvest moon, it was unlikely. I guess it must be important… What can I do for ye?' Mrs Cromp turned around on her chair to face Loveday. 'Come and sit on the edge of me bed.'

Loveday carefully made her way across the small room and did as was asked. The bed was squidgy and there was a strong smell of pine coming from it.

'Well, love?' Mrs Cromp said, sniffing and clearing the back of her throat.

'It's my Will. He ain't right in the 'ead since 'e came back from war…and I don't know what to do.' There, she'd said it. Loveday felt a pang of sadness while she tried to hold back tears. Mrs Cromp attempted to stand up but her large frame wobbled and she plonked herself down again.

'Elp me up, love, would ye?' She held out her hand to Loveday, who took it and gently pulled on her arm. Between the two of them, Mrs Cromp managed to stand up and shuffle out of the bedroom into the living area. Hearing movement, Gribble Gummo turned and nodded at them both. The fox flicked its tail, peered out to see what all the fuss was about then settled back down. Loveday thought he looked way too at home on Mrs Cromp's chair.

'Is it the nightmares or the anger…? Which is worse?' Mrs Cromp asked, starting to open cupboards and kitchen drawers. Gribble Gummo eventually moved his feet from the sink and helped to clear the kitchen table, tapping his pipe out on its surface before doing so, his bells jangling as he purposefully moved around. Loveday watched them both in synchronism. It was something they'd obviously done together before.

'Well, the nightmares 'appen most nights, but the anger is getting worse and 'e won't talk to me 'bout naught any more. I've been asking 'im to go and speak to someone, but 'e won't 'ear of it.'

Mrs Cromp stood still for a brief moment as if deep in thought, then went back to the first set of drawers she'd opened, rummaged around, and brought out a bunch of leaves tied together with some vine. She placed them into a large earthenware bowl Gribble Gummo had placed on the kitchen table and gestured to him to fetch the kettle from over the fire. She then collected some muslin and a blue glass vial from a shelf above the sink. Very carefully, she began to pour the boiling water over the leaves and added a handful of small black berries. She then added a handful of red berries until they completely covered the leaves but were still bobbing about on top of the steaming water. Next, she scattered a pinch of what Loveday thought looked like salt, then a few drops of liquid from a large brown bottle. She watched in fascination.

Loveday noticed that although Gribble Gummo was wilingly helping, he was still grumpy. 'Ye sure ye is up to all this?' he grumbled. 'Why not let the girl come back 'morrow and collect it?'

'She's one of us, Gribble, and ye knows it! Now leave 'er be,' Mrs Cromp snapped, continuing to prod and stir the foul-smelling mixture.

Loveday wasn't sure what she'd meant by her comment, but yes, she'd lived in Trunrowan her whole life as had her parents. She was pretty sure however, that Gribble Gummo was not from around these parts.

'Perhaps ye could finish telling the story of the standing stones?' Loveday suggested, trying to make conversation and perhaps cheer Gribble Gummo up a little.

'Well, I could, but I likes an audience and ye ain't exactly that. If yer 'usband ain't right in the 'ead, is a cheel gonna 'elp?' Gribble obviously knew more about her predicament than she realised, but he had a good point.

'Right then, it's almost ready. Give it a bit longer to brew, and ye can take it 'ome with ye, but before ye goes I wants to show ye something.' Mrs Cromp stirred the liquid one last time, then picked up the blanket Gribble Gummo had given to Loveday earlier, wrapped it around her shoulders, and made her way out the back of the kitchen, beckoning for Loveday to follow.

At the back of the cottage was a small twisting path that eventually led to a dilapidated outbuilding, covered in ivy and thick brambles. Even in the dark, Loveday could see it wasn't far from falling down and had been propped up by various pieces of wood and and large stones. On one side, even an old tree stump had been pushed firmly against it, and as Mrs Cromp bent her already hunched back to enter the doorway, Loveday hesitated. What was it about the buildings around here? They all seemed to be built for spriggans.

'Come on child, it be perfectly safe.'

There she was again, thought Loveday, reading her mind. She bent down and shuffled through the doorway, surprised to find that once inside she could stand up easily as there was plenty of height and space.

'Aye, it's deceiving, ain't it? I keeps it looking like this as it means no one will be interested in it, which suits me fine. This is where all me *special* stuff is kept. Not even Gribble knows what I got in 'ere. Well, at least I don't think 'e does.' Mrs Cromp laughed.

Loveday waited for Mrs Cromp to light the candles that were perched precariously on the edge of a wonky-looking shelf. As the darkness dissipated, she was presented with an array of different flowers, leaves and herbs, hanging from the walls and ceiling. The smell was sweet and intoxicating and she was beginning to feel a little giddy. She recognised some of the hanging bunches. Lavender, Nettle Tops and Common Hogweed seed heads, while others she knew by sight but not by name.

'Wow! Is this where ye makes all yer potions and stuff?' Loveday trailed her hand along the wall and put her fingers to her nose and sniffed.

'Careful, girl! Ye don't know what ye is touching. These plants are common enough, but some are deadly. Ye don't need to ingest 'em either, just by touching 'em ye can become seriously ill.' Mrs Cromp raised her voice enough for Loveday to realise how stupid she'd been. She should've known better. Mrs Cromp gestured for Loveday to sit down at the table in the middle of the room.

'Do ye recognise any of these plants and herbs?' Mrs Cromp asked, while she continued searching amongst the bunches that were hanging from the ceiling. 'Ah, there it be, I thought I 'ad some in 'ere.'

'I knows some of 'em, I mean I sees 'em around.' Loveday wasn't sure if she meant by sight or by name.

'No, I mean do ye recognise 'em in 'ere. This place, like ye been 'ere before?'

'Umm…no, I don't think so. Should I?' Loveday said, puzzled.

'Well, when ye was a wee cheel, your ma would sometimes bring ye 'ere.'

'My ma?!' Loveday exclaimed. Why would her ma have brought her to see Mrs Cromp? She remembered walking in the woods with her pa, but she couldn't recollect doing so with her ma.

''Cause she was one of us. She came from a long line of cunning folk up in Somerset, and when the Sellers…that were yer ma's family name before she married as ye knows. When they finally settled 'ere in Trunrowan, we shared our wisdom and knowledge for the higher good.'

Mrs Cromp seemed to have gathered what she needed and was now blowing out the candles she'd only just lit, while Loveday, rooted to the chair in shock, was feeling a little angry. She'd heard rumours before of her ma possibly being of Romany descent, but she'd never told Loveday if it was true. But why would Mrs Cromp make up all these things about her ma? She'd only come here to get a potion to help Will. She didn't want any trouble, or rumours starting. It was downright unkind to start making up stories. She reckoned Gribble Gummo had put her up to it.

'I don't think so. She would 'ave told me if that were true!' Loveday began to protest.

Mrs Cromp stopped what she was doing and gently placed her hands on Loveday's shoulders.

'Perhaps I 'as been a little too forthright, love. Sorry, I ain't been too clever, 'as I? Yer ma passed away, as ye knows, way too soon and didn't 'ave time to tell ye. But, 'er and I, well, we'd spoke about it often enough, and I said if need be, when the time was right, I would tell ye. And the time is right now.' Mrs Cromp removed her hands and patted Loveday's cheeks gently. 'She didn't embrace the gift fully it 'as to be said, and she was only just beginning to understand it 'erself. But, ye needs to know that ye 'as the power to heal too, if ye chooses, and I can 'elp ye with that if ye should wish. Why d'you think I offered to 'elp ye that day in the village shop?'

Loveday sighed. 'Well, that ain't gonna 'appen at this rate is it! Not when 'e ain't right in the 'ead,' she retorted.

'Patience, child, patience. One thing at a time. Let's 'elp 'im get better first, shall we…? I'll give ye a potion that will calm 'im. It's potent enough, can cure many illnesses of the 'ead. But ye must follow my instructions, very, very carefully… Do ye understand?' Mrs Cromp stared directly at Loveday and waited. Loveday nodded.

'Ye is to put one drop in 'is tea every morning, and one drop only. Stir the tea then add some sugar if ye can. I knows there ain't much of it about at the moment, but if ye can't, then some honey will do. It takes away the bitterness. Do this for a month and come back and let me knows if 'e be any better. Is that clear enough?'

Loveday nodded; she was still thinking about her ma as cunning folk.

'Yes, I understands. One drop, every day and no more.'

Mrs Cromp nodded and blew out the final candle.

'That's it, now let's go and finish off the potion for ye.'

XVI

Present day

The journey to Truro had taken about half an hour, mainly along windy country lanes which had proved somewhat of a challenge for Lizzie who was driving.

'Christ! Give me the M32 any day of the week. You must have become an expert at reversing, Kitty. I thought parking in Clifton was bad enough,' Lizzie moaned as she reversed into the tightest of passing places for the umpteenth time since they had set off.

'You get used to it. To be fair, I don't actually use the car much these days. At the moment it's only for hospital checks, normally we get by just using the ferry. We've got everything we need on the other side of the estuary,' Kitty replied smugly.

'Yeah, well let's hope you don't go into labour in the depths of the night. Ben is no Lewis Hamilton… Do you remember that time he almost ended up in the Feeder Canal?'

'Oh, good god! Do we really have to relive that…? Please let's not. In fairness, it wasn't his fault that he had a puncture just as he was going over the Netham lock.' Kitty giggled.

'Maybe, but how we managed to escape with our stomachs in situ I do not know!' Lizzie slowed down as she approached the main Truro roundabout.

'Those were the days, eh? How things have changed. Who would've thought I'd be living in Cornwall and about to pop my first child?'

'Indeed, Kitty, indeed.' Lizzie replied.

Kitty had always loved Cornwall. As a child she had spent many happy holidays on its beaches, and when she was old enough, had taken to surfing like a duck to water, a love that had continued right up to her pregnancy. She also fondly remembered visiting Truro's cathedral when she was in the school choir. It was an imposing building by anyone's standards. She recalled the beauty of the rose windows and the spectacular high altar and would've loved to have visited today and shown Lizzie around, but they only had the afternoon, and time was of the essence.

Lizzie managed to find a spacious parking space, much to her delight, and they headed off along the cobbled Georgian streets, Kitty grateful she'd worn her 'sensible' pregnancy shoes. Eventually, they were presented with the very pretty Victorian library that John Passmore Edwards had funded to build.

'Wow! What a stunning building,' Lizzie exclaimed, admiring its beautiful granite stone.

'It is,' Kitty agreed. 'They've even used Bath stone for its dressings. Look, up there...'

Lizzie and Kitty both leaned their heads back. 'It's impressive, I'll give you that. Let's see if it can impress inside as well, shall we?' Lizzie said, pushing open the main door.

Kitty had always thought there was something magical about libraries and today looked as though it wouldn't disappoint. In the foyer was a huge sign saying:

Kitty looked at her watch just as a very colourful, very tall man, strode past on stilts. He nodded and tipped his oversized purple and orange hat to her.

Lizzie suddenly screeched with excitement. 'Oh my! They have a Droll Teller here, how inspiring!'

'What's a Droll Teller? You'll have to enlighten me... Is it a librarian thing?' Kitty asked curiously.

'It's a Cornish thing. I'm surprised you don't know, what with being a local and all that now!' They both laughed, then remembered they were in a library as they heard someone hiss, '*Shush.*'

'Hey! I've only been down here for eighteen months. I hardly think that makes me a local.'

'A Droll Teller is the Cornish name for a storyteller, like the sign states, they have story time here. What fun! I might nick the Droll Teller name and take it back to Bristol.' Lizzie was showing her library credentials to the receptionist who waved them both through the barrier.

'What, literally? Don't think you'd get his stilts in the car. Right, what now then?'

'Follow me, we need to find the IT suite. We should be able to use a computer and I've got free access, so we won't need to pay for any sites we use.'

In no time at all they had found the IT suite, which thankfully was empty. The Droll Teller must be very popular.

'Tell me, why couldn't we have done this back at the cottage on the laptop?' Kitty asked as Lizzie set about moving chairs and repositioning the computer screen.

'Because, if we find any information here, we can then search their archives, should we need to. They generally hold the original parish records and newsreels, along with all sorts of other information that may prove useful.'

Kitty smiled; she was beginning to feel quite excited.

'There, sit yourself down and let's have a look at the paperwork you've brought.'

Kitty passed Lizzie the handful of letters and the newspaper along with a piece of paper she'd made some notes on that morning. She watched Lizzie methodically spread everything out on the table so they could read it in some sort of date order.

'What do we know so far...? We have an original copy of *The Cornishman* from Tuesday 23 January 1917, stating there was a body found at Rowan Cottage in Trunrowan, but we don't think that's anything to do with your Creek cottage, or do we? We have a handful of letters written from a Will to a Loveday Nance and from their content, it looks as though Will was fighting away at war, possibly in France at some point, and that Loveday was his wife or sweetheart.'

Kitty nodded in agreement. 'Oh! And there's this.' She handed Lizzie the king's shilling with the remnants of the ragged purple ribbon that she'd taken out of her jewellery box before they left. It was the first time she'd looked at it again in any detail since the day Marmalade had unintentionally found it.

'Wowzers!' Lizzie turned it over examining it carefully. 'A love token from the battlefields? Soldiers often sent home coins to loved ones. Although, this is an English shilling. It looks as though someone has drilled a hole in it probably so it could be worn, hence the ribbon. Looks as though its seen better days though...' Lizzie gently pulled at the ribbon.

'Careful! It's survived this long, let's not finish it off quite yet, eh?!' Kitty said laughing.

Lizzie placed it next to the letters on the table.

'OK, so I'm going to put Will and Loveday's names into the search box, here, see? and hope they come up on the 1911 census.' Lizzie tapped the keyboard with confidence and hit the enter button.

'Here we go...' Kitty stared at the screen as names and residences began to fill it. Halfway down the page was the name Loveday Nance. They both shrieked at the same time. 'There!'

Lizzie quickly looked round to make sure no one else had come into the room and was about to chastise them for the noise. Luckily, it was still empty.

'Ah, there's another Loveday below too which has a different birth date... Oh, and another!' Kitty was beginning to feel a little disheartened.

'Loveday is a Cornish name, so I would expect to see it repeated but let's click on the first one and see what it says on the census. It might take us some time. It's going to be a process of elimination. Do you have your notebook and pen, Kitty?'

Kitty took both from her bag and with pen poised waited as Lizzie clicked onto the 1911 England Census icon.

The page appeared and Lizzie zoomed in and read out loud.

Loveday Nance, Age 32. Estimated Birth Year, 1879. Relationship to Head, Wife. Spouse, John Nance. Where born, Mousehole, Cornwall, England.

'Nope, that's not them, although we should be wary as people's real names were often not recorded correctly. Make a note of it, but if I have my geography correct, Mousehole isn't local to Trunrowan and back in those days, they were unlikely to travel far. Let's try the next one.'

Kitty scribbled down some notes and they continued in the same vein until they reached the bottom of the page. Lizzie clicked next and they started over at the top of the new page. This time however they were more successful.

'Yes! This looks more like it. All the details seem to fit... Ah, except the address.' They both peered closer at the screen. Lizzie clicked on the copy of the census which, although difficult to read, proved relatively easy to decipher.

'Loveday Nance, Age 21. Spouse, William Nance. Where born... Trunrowan, Cornwall, England. Bingo!'

Lizzie punched the air, this time more hopeful. 'Ah, but it says the address is Rowan Cottage.'

Kitty looked up from her scribbling. 'Well, that's a coincidence as the photo and write-up in the newspaper mentions a Rowan Cottage.' They both moved to pick up the newspaper at the same time.

'Too much of a coincidence. Do you know, I reckon your Creek Cottage was Rowan Cottage once upon a time.'

Kitty shivered. 'Really? What, you think that a body was found in *our* cottage? Oh shit!'

'Ah! I see where you're coming from.' Lizzie said softly.

'Yes, I am coming from there! A bloody dark place where my cottage appears to be haunted by a dead man – who is roaming about in the upstairs bedrooms. Jesus, Lizzie! What are we going to tell them when we get back? We couldn't make this up if we tried!' Instinctively Kitty held her bump. She needed to calm down, she was beginning to feel a little nauseous.

'Look, come on, let's be rational. We're jumping the gun. Do you *really* believe in all that hocus-pocus stuff?'

Kitty didn't have the heart to tell her how she'd been feeling lately and the odd things that had happened in the cottage. She certainly wasn't going to tell her about the bad dreams she'd had a while back in which she'd seen a body hanging in the kitchen of the cottage. Lizzie really would think she was going bonkers. And, perhaps she was. Surely it must be a hormonal thing? She really should speak to her midwife, just to make sure.

'Well, you know I've always been interested in that sort of thing. I mean, you did actually buy me a book on witchcraft one Christmas, if you remember?' Kitty tried to lighten the mood.

'Gosh, yes, well remembered. I did! Well remembered indeed. Did you actually read it?' Lizzie was now busy jotting things down in Kitty's book.

'I can't remember. It was a long time ago. I definitely still have it though – I saw it in the bookcase only the other day.'

'Perhaps you should have a read of it then.' Lizzie chuckled.

'Ouch!' Kitty suddenly let out a cry and clutched her right side.

'I'm surprised there's any room left inside of you for kicking. When's your next check-up with the midwife?' Lizzie asked.

'Wednesday. I'm hoping she's going to tell me I'm so big I'll be induced early.' Kitty stood up and stretched gently. 'Lizzie, I'm taking myself off to the loos. I'm not feeling great.'

'You do look a little green come to think of it… I'll crack on with this if that's OK. Sure you don't need me to come with you?'

Kitty shook her head. 'No, it's fine. You carry on. See what else you can find out.' She hurried off before she managed to embarrass herself by throwing up everywhere.

XVII

1916

Will stirred and then groaned loudly. Ouch! His head felt as though it had been subjected to a heavy day on the battlefield. His tongue was stuck to the roof of his mouth with a familiar taste of dry fermented apples. Tentatively, he lifted himself up from the couch and slowly moved his head. Darn it. It hurt like hell. He must have had a right skinful – he knew he should have asked Loveday how long the flagons had been in the shed. But then she would've moaned at him. Perhaps this was his comeuppance.

He noticed that he'd been covered with a woollen blanket and guessed Loveday had placed it on him earlier. She must've left him to sleep it off. The trouble was he couldn't recall how he'd got home. The last thing he could clearly remember was being up at Bramble Farm and then walking down into the village, but even that was hazy. After that he couldn't recall a thing. Loveday wasn't going to be happy, especially if he'd made a scene in the village, that was for sure.

He heaved himself up off the couch and slowly made his way into the kitchen, using the furniture to steady himself. A cup of strong tea was what he needed and a few spoonfuls of sugar, if he could find some. He glanced at the kitchen clock: eight o'clock. He had a feeling he'd probably been asleep for most of the day. He'd best add some wood to the fire, or they'd be freezing to death in no time. Still, at least he wasn't wet and cold… Not like in the mire of the trenches, where his muscles twitched and his bones ached. He caught his breath as a loud bang exploded somewhere inside his head. He had to take cover. He was far too exposed where he was. He instinctively felt around his neck, but there was nothing there. A sense of panic began to wash over him. Where was it? He frantically pulled at his jumper. Nothing. He needed his gas mask, without it he faced certain death or at the very least he would be severely compromised. He spun around as another bang erupted, they were close, far too close for his liking. Crouching down he slowly inched forward, feeling the dark space in front of him with his one hand.

'Stay behind me, d'ye hear. I can smell 'em, the filthy buggers,' he hissed, just as his forehead caught the edge of something hard. Ouch! What the bleddy hell was that? He lifted his hand and felt a solid sturdy frame. Holding onto it the best he could, he pulled and then slid underneath it.

'Over 'ere!' He shouted, only to be greeted with a meow from George who was wondering why his master had taken to lying under the kitchen table. And there Will stayed. His body shaking uncontrollably as he eventually curled into a ball, rocking backwards and forwards, humming the tune to the Cornish anthem, Trelawny.

Loveday had run most of the way back to Rowan Cottage and was thankful that with the light from the Harvest Moon and her lantern, she'd soon reached the gate at the bottom of the garden – and in one piece. The cottage was in darkness which she hoped meant Will had not woken up, or if he had, he'd taken himself to bed. She looked up to the chimneys above the cottage. Damn! There was no smoke. She'd have to try and rekindle the fire, otherwise the cottage would be freezing in the morning. Still, thank the Lord for small mercies; at least the storm Reverend Jones had predicted earlier, had not materialised.

As she approached the back door, she thought she could hear a low humming. She stopped as she got closer and tilted her head to try and work out where it was coming from. It definitely wasn't a boat; it was far too late for that. She strained harder, but whatever it was had now stopped and all she could hear was George scratching at the door, meowing. She opened the back door and he ran out. As she closed the door behind her, pulling the heavy curtain across to keep what little warmth there was in, the humming started up again – she immediately recognised Will's distinctive voice. It was coming from where she stood. In the kitchen. Following her senses, she found Will under the kitchen table, curled into a ball, rocking back and forth.

'*We'll cross the Tamar, land to land, Trelawny he's in keep and hold.*'

'Will, what ye doing?' Loveday said, as she slowly bent down so as not to scare him. The lantern she was holding highlighted Will's distorted face and saucer-wide eyes with its flickering light. They looked even more menacing than when he was having one of his nightmares. For the first time, Loveday felt frightened.

'Charge!'

Will suddenly stopped singing and lunged forward, knocking her and the lantern so violently that she hit the back of her head against the flagstones. As she lay there, the room spinning, out of the corner of her eye she could see the candle flame flickering next to a pile of newspapers she'd collected earlier for the garden waste. She tried to shout, but on opening her mouth all that came out was a small squeak. She tried again, this time pushing herself up with both hands and somehow managing to lean across and grab hold of the lantern. She breathed a sigh of relief as the back door opened and she felt a gust of cold air enter the room, extinguishing the flame. Will had fled and she was in no fit state to go after him. She put her hands to the back of her head and grimaced. Considering the thump she'd gone down with, she was amazed to feel only a small bump at the base of her skull. Someone was definitely looking over her this evening, that was for sure.

As soon as Will stepped outside, he felt the cold air hit his face. Trying not to gasp, he held his breath for as long as he could manage. The air smelled fresh with no taint of pear drops that would indicate a poisonous gas. He released his breath, relieved, and breathed normally filling his lungs with the sweet smell of the sea. Blimey he was cold! And then he realised he was stood outside with nothing on his feet. His head had started to bang again which reminded him he'd woken up on the couch...but then nothing. And why was he stood outside in the garden with nothing on his feet? He walked back into the cottage and was greeted by Loveday, sat on the kitchen floor.

'What ye doing down there, love? Get up or ye will be catching yer death.' He shut the door behind him and offered his good hand to pull her up.

'Ye pushed me!' Loveday mumbled at him, her voice shaky, but she took Will's hand and picked up the lantern, the candle miraculously still in place. 'Light this will ye before we 'ave another accident. There be some more candles and matches under the sink. I needs to sit down.'

Will noticed she was rubbing the back of her head as she made her way to the nearest chair. He had no idea what she meant by saying he'd pushed her but he was in no mood for arguing. He lit two candles and placed them on the kitchen table, catching sight of Loveday's note as he did so. 'So, ye been out then?'

Loveday stared at him sternly.

'Ye were on the couch. Sleeping off the drink. I left the note in case ye woke up when I was out. Which ye obviously did!'

Will screwed up his face. He still couldn't remember anything. He'd better apologise. 'Look, love, I'm sorry, alrite. I ain't been getting much sleep lately and ye knows what I'm like when I don't get me kip! I must've woken up with a start, and in the dark knocked ye over or summut when ye was coming in. Come 'ere and give me a cuddle.' Will put his arm out and tried his very best to muster a smile. 'Come on, don't be so teasy.'

Loveday reluctantly got up, noticing her bag and its contents strewn across the floor. Oh god! Please don't let the vial that Mrs Cromp gave her be broken. 'Yer alright, thanks. Ye stinks of the booze and me 'ead's hurting too. I'll make us both a cup of tea.' She bent down and grabbed her bag, immediately looking inside, relieved to find at first glance the vial appeared to still be in one piece.

'Aye, alright then. I'm parched. Me mouth tastes like the bottom of a birdcage. I'll get the fire going again while ye makes it.'

Loveday breathed a sigh of relief and hurridly took the blue glass vial out of her bag. She checked it over carefully. It was still intact and there wasn't going to be a better time than now to try its contents out. Once the water had boiled, she made them both a cup of tea. Carefully, she gave the pipette one squeeze into the palm of her hand, checking the pressure used was correct and that only one drop was released. Easier said than done, but after the third attempt she was confident enough to add it to Will's cup and she watched it splash into the steaming tea, a huge sense of relief washing over her. She didn't think it would matter that it was night-time and not his morning cuppa, what was more important was getting Will back on the road to recovery. She had no idea what she'd walked into earlier, but whatever was going on in Will's head, it needed to stop.

'There ye go.' Loveday handed Will the cup and watched him lift it to his mouth and swallow.

'Blimey! That's rancid.'

Loveday made a mental note. Tomorrow she would remember to add some honey. Just as Mrs Cromp had suggested.

XVIII

Present day

Eventually, after much heaving and bringing up of bile, Kitty
made her way out of the toilet and headed back to the IT suite.
She passed the door that said, '*Story Time*' and looked through
its window. Somehow, the Droll Teller had removed his stilts
and was sat down, having a whale of a time with the attentive
children who were lounging on brightly-coloured cushions set
out in a small circle. She noticed the stilts propped up against
the side of a bookcase, and for a second felt cheated. He really
should have hidden them – they reminded her that he was, after
all, a storyteller. Someone who made up things. She sighed. Still,
at least he was encouraging the children's imagination. She liked
that.

'You feeling better now?' Lizzie asked, briefly looking up
from the computer screen.

'Not really. Do you mind if we head back? I think I may
be sick again at some point. Not that there's anything left in my

stomach to bring up. All I'm doing is heaving up vile-tasting green bile.' She sat down and wearily put on her coat.

'Oooo, sounds nasty. Should you phone the midwife or something, I mean you're almost due... Should you be vomiting at this stage?' Lizzie stopped what she was doing, looking concerned.

'I'll see how I feel when we get back. I'm probably just tired. Too much excitement for me these days!' Kitty tried to shrug off the anxious feeling that was churning inside of her.

'OK, no worries. Let's wrap this up and we'll get going. I can always carry on the research back home now I've got the bones of it.' Lizzie switched off the computer and collated the letters and newspapers, putting them into her satchel along with Kitty's notepad. She then carefully handed over the king's shilling and remnants of ribbon to Kitty.

'Did you find anything else out while I was gone?'

'Yes and no. I was looking for Will and Loveday's marriage entry but couldn't find it. It should have been easy. I mean Trunrowan is pretty small now and I'm sure it was even smaller back then. They may have married out of the area, but I found them both separately on the 1901 census in Trunrowan, so it's unlikely. Records do get lost though. What is interesting... is I did find a death certificate for Will which states that he died on 19th January 1917. I'm afraid it's too much of a coincidence with the report and dates from the paper – it must've been him who was found in your cottage.'

'Oh, great! So the cottage *is* haunted then. Not a word to Ben and Tim about this please. Ben worries enough as it is. I'll keep it to myself for now until we know for certain that the cottage was once known as Rowan Cottage, OK?'

'No problem. You just concentrate on making sure that baby of yours doesn't come along too early. I've only just got my head round the fact that you're pregnant and I'm not sure I'm grown up enough to be a godmother yet.' Lizzie laughed.

'Who said anything about being a godmother?'

'Whoops! Ben mentioned something to Tim the other week,' Lizzie replied tentatively.

Kitty smiled to herself. Men! They were worse than women when it came to gossip.

'Well, no pressure, you still have a few more weeks to think about it'.

'As if I am going to say no... Come on then, let's get you back home before you start being sick again. Don't really fancy stopping on those country lanes for you to expel your stomach lining!'

Luckily for Lizzie, Kitty somehow managed to quell the waves of nausea until they finally pulled into Trunrowan. At that point she had to quickly open the door and hope the wind was blowing in the right direction.

Ben peered out of the kitchen window and watched Kitty and Lizzie walk down the garden path towards the cove. He felt a warm fuzzy feeling as he admired Kitty's bump and the way her walk had now turned into more of a waddle. Perhaps they were going for a stroll along the beach? But then Kitty veered off the garden path heading towards the shed. Ah! She was probably going to show Lizzie where she'd found all the newspapers and letters. Anything to keep Kitty preoccupied into the run-up of the birth was welcome, although he didn't want her becoming obsessed. She did have an awful habit of running away with things. Her last penchant, if he recalled correctly, had been tarot cards. They had come across an old pack in a vintage shop when they'd first moved down and he'd lost count of all the times he'd had to be a guinea pig while she practiced the art of reading them. She'd even taken to sleeping with them under her pillow; apparently it was supposed to connect her to them. But, like most of her obsessions, their interest had whittled out. Last time he'd seen them, they were in the kitchen drawer with a load of wine corks. At least now she was doing her degree, which in his eyes, was something she could potentially make a new career from. He couldn't quite picture her on the seafront reading tarot cards to holiday-makers.

'Is that the girls?' Tim asked, hearing the crunch of gravel outside.

'Oh, Yes. Sorry, I was miles away. They've just gone down to the shed. Kitty is probably showing Lizzy where she found the letters and stuff. What time you heading off, mate?' Ben checked his watch.

'Pretty soon, I reckon. Hopefully Ruby will sleep in the car if we time it right. Don't think I can bear listening to *The Wheels on The Bus*, all the way home! Ah, looks like they're done in the shed.' Tim said, as kitty and Lizzie walked into the kitchen.

'Hiya, where's Ruby?' Lizzie asked, kicking off her shoes and looking around the kitchen.

'She's reading my Dental Anatomy handbook. Well, OK, she's looking at the pictures.'

Lizzie laughed. 'Are the pictures in colour?'

'Oh no! They are now.' Kitty screeched, holding up a handful of colouring pencils that she'd picked up from the floor.

'Tim! I told you to keep an eye on her when she's using her crayons and pencils!' Lizzie was obviously not impressed. 'Anyhow, where is she? Because I can't see her!'

Ruby slowly appeared from under the kitchen table, her hands covering her mouth, stifling a giggle.

'Sorry, Uncle Ben,' she whispered.

Ben smiled. He really was going to be a hopeless father if his child was anything like Ruby. How could he resist such an innocent face?

'Don't worry, Ruby, but you mustn't do it again, OK?' He managed to say without laughing. Ruby nodded her head and then slipped her tiny hand into his.

'And on that note, I think we should hit the road,' Tim suggested.

*

Within half an hour or so, Creek Cottage had returned to normal and order had once more been reinstated, apart from the fact that Kitty had started being sick again and Ben was getting rather concerned.

He'd left her in the bathroom, her head over the sink, with his dressing gown wrapped around her shoulders. He'd never been of any use if someone was being sick. He hated the smell for a start and seeing his wife distressed, concerned him to the point where he would bury his head in the sand rather than address the situation. He busied himself by stripping all the beds, trying to ignore the retching that was coming from the bathroom. As he wrestled with the duvet and cover, he noticed Mr Snozzle on the bedroom window seat.

'Bugger. Kitty! Ruby's left Mr Snozzle behind... Glad I won't be there when she finds out. Do you think we should post it back?' He waited for a reply. 'Kitty!' he called again, making his way to the landing, hovering outside the bathroom door. 'Hey, you OK? Ruby has left Mr Snozzle behind.' He slowly pushed at the door and poked his head around.

Kitty was lying on the floor and groaning. 'Yeah, I heard you. Ben, I think perhaps we should give the midwife a ring. I'm worried I'm doing some damage to the baby with all this retching. Her contact number is on the front of my maternity notes – on the dresser in the kitchen,' Kitty managed to say before groaning again.

'Good idea. You stay there, I'll give her a call.'

'And I need to tell you something too... It looks as though the cottage could have once been called Rowan Cottage and has not always been Creek Cottage, which means that according to the write-up in *The Cornishman*, a body was found in *this* cottage! Our cottage, Ben! So perhaps I haven't been imagining all of the strange things – and neither was Ruby last night. Perhaps the cottage is haunted, and we have disturbed some horrible entity.' She started sobbing. Even though she'd sworn Lizzie to secrecy, she immediately felt relieved telling Ben.

'What…? Are you sure? And what the hell do you mean, *all of the strange things*?' Ben sat down on the toilet seat with a bump.

Kitty cringed. She'd let the cat out of the bag. He'd be furious if he knew even half the truth. Despite feeling really ill she decided to try and distract him. 'Well, Lizzie seems to think so and I'm pretty sure she knows what she's doing when it comes to research.' Somehow she'd managed to stand up and lean over the sink.

'Well if you want my view on it, I think Lizzie is damn well bloody stupid putting ideas like that into your head in your condition! No wonder you feel like shit. Forget it, even if it is true, there's absolutely nothing wrong with the cottage, and there is certainly nothing untoward going on. I haven't felt a thing. In fact, I love the place and am very happy here.'

He seemed to have completely forgotten that she was unwell as he stormed out of the small bathroom, slamming the door behind him.

'Ben, can you phone the midwife, pleeeease!'

It had only taken him a few seconds to find the maternity pack that Kitty had placed in a prominent position on the kitchen dresser. He noted that a small holdall had appeared by the back door. He didn't know why he seemed surprised; Kitty had always been a stickler for planning. He picked up the phone and paced up and down until the ring the other end was answered. After explaining what was happening, the voice on the other end asked to speak to Kitty directly, so off he went upstairs to hand the phone over.

You'd think with all his medical training he'd be a little calmer than he was, but the reality of everything was beginning to close in around him. He hoped the midwife would come out and check Kitty over – he really didn't feel like Kitty was up to another car journey.

Finally, Kitty handed the phone back to him and managed a meek smile. 'Don't look so worried! Midwife says this can sometimes happen, and it's probably stress related. As long as I'm not having any contractions and don't have a temperature, then I should sleep it off. If I'm not feeling any better by tomorrow, then I should ring her again and she will come out and see me. Usual stuff...keep hydrated as much as I can, blah, blah, blah. Any concerns then to phone 999. I need to write up my birth plan anyhow and talk through a few things, so to be honest it would be good to meet her and have a chat regardless.'

'I'm not sure I'm happy with that. I mean becoming dehydrated can be dangerous for a pregnant woman.'

'Stop fussing, Ben. I'm not one of your patients. God, I hope you're not going to be like this when I go into labour.'

'OK, hint taken. Just shout or bang on the bedroom floor if you need anything. I'll find something to wrap Mr Snozzle up with – in the meantime he can keep you company.' He handed over Ruby's toy pig and fetched Kitty a glass of water. For now, he would just have to sit back and try to put his faith in the other professionals. He hated being out of control.

Kitty flopped onto the bed and then remembered she should lie on her left side. Being pregnant was becoming tiresome now. She felt fat, sick, uncomfortable, and tired, plus she was feeling anxious again. She'd made a mental note to mention everything to the midwife, and tomorrow would be as good a time as any. She was probably just tired but...there was something she couldn't quite put her finger on. She plumped up the pillows and made herself as comfortable as she could, putting a pillow in between her legs. There, that was better. She didn't feel quite as nauseous now. Her hand reached for Mr Snozzle; there was nothing quite like cuddling up to a soft toy when you were feeling sorry for yourself. Her hand fumbled. Strange, she'd been sure she'd put him on the bed. Damn, she really couldn't be bothered to get up again now she was comfortable. She moved her legs around, but still couldn't feel him, and reluctantly stretched across the bed to put on the bedside lamp. As soon as she flicked the switch, there was a ping as the bulb blew; instinctively she drew back her hand. Then came a loud groan from downstairs.

'Urghhh, bloody electrics have gone again! Kitty...did you do anything?' Ben shouted up the stairs.

Kitty carefully swung her legs off the bed and sat on its edge. It was pitch black inside the cottage. This wasn't Bristol. There were no street lights in Trunrowan to soften the darkness. She managed to open the drawer of the bedside table and rummaged, hoping to find one of the torches they had placed around the cottage for incidences exactly like this. Typical, it was empty apart from what felt like some tissues, her face moisturiser and a velvet pouch. She pulled out the pouch, remembering they held her tarot cards, then cussed as she dropped them on the floor.

'Bloody hell!'

'Kitty! You OK?' Ben shouted again.

'Not really! I blew the bedside-lamp bulb. Sorry! Can't find a torch either!' Kitty shouted back, bending down to recover the cards, realising it was pointless when she could hardly see them.

'Stay there. I don't want you tripping over in the dark. The trip switch has kicked in. Give me a minute, I'll reset the RCD unit.'

Kitty heard the back door shut and sighed. So now she was a pregnant invalid. Huh! *Stay there.* Since when had she ever done as she was told.

Carefully, she stood up, trying not to slip on the tarot cards. It was only a few feet or so to the window seat that looked out over the garden and beyond to the cove, if she went slowly, she shouldn't have a problem. She looked up to the sky and could sense, even from being inside, that there was a heavy blanket of storm clouds. Looking down onto the garden, she waited while her eyes adjusted to the darkness.

Using the edge of her nightshirt to wipe away the condensation that had formed on the window, she pressed her face as close as possible to the glass without steaming it up. Slowly, she began to make out familiar shapes in the garden. The shed, the bean sticks, the garden waste incinerator bin. She could see the outline of the garden gate now, and the cove further on.

In the distance, she could hear the call of a tawny owl and then…the closer squeak of a floorboard. She froze and turned her head sharply. There it was again, the same noise she'd heard in the spare room last night, as though someone was walking across the room. Panicking, she shouted Ben's name.

'BEN! Hurry up!' There was no reply. She knew he'd gone outside to the shed to where the RCD unit was, but she shouted, nevertheless. There it was again, very faint footsteps at first and then louder ones as they appeared to get closer. Was her mind playing tricks with her?

'BEN!' This time she realised she was yelling, but the footsteps kept coming and now appeared to be from all directions in the bedroom. Maybe there were more than one pair of feet, she couldn't be sure. She turned back to the window and yanked at the handle until it opened outwards and she let out a scream.

'BEN!' She was now gasping as her lungs took in big gulps of stinging cold air. She banged on the glass pane to get his attention and shouted again. Couldn't he hear her? Then she saw him, coming out from the shed and sauntering up the garden path. Why was he walking so slowly? She banged on the glass pane again and this time Ben looked up to where she was kneeling on the window seat, half in and half out of the window, her bump physically stopping her from being able to move forward any more.

'Crikey, Kitty, what the hell are you doing?!' Ben shouted. 'Get back inside before you fall!' Still gasping for breath, she watched Ben bend down and pick something up from the garden path. 'Did you just throw Mr Snozzle out the window?!' he shouted up to her.

Kitty felt sick again and strangely disorientated.

'What? No, of course I didn't! Could you hurry up please, Ben. I really don't feel well.'

She pulled the window shut and secured the latch and sat waiting. She felt too unwell to attempt finding her way back to the bed but at least the floorboards had stopped squeaking. Ironically, the silence was almost unbearable.

Ben had no idea why Kitty was leaning out of the bedroom window in her condition, least of all why she'd dropped Ruby's favourite toy out of it. He'd seen the outline of Mr Snozzle on the garden path and at first glance thought it was Marmalade. He was tired, still a little hungover and the past twenty-four hours had been somewhat of a car crash, and it didn't look as though things were over yet either.

Ben kicked off his boots and shut the cottage door. It was still in darkness. The trip switch appeared to be fine, so he was unsure why all the electricity had gone off. He would have to check in the morning. It was no good rummaging about in the dark this time of night and with Kitty unwell, they'd just have to put up with using candlelight and torches for the evening. He managed to locate some tealights and a couple of torches and took them upstairs, Mr Snozzle securely tucked under his arm.

'At last!' Kitty mumbled to herself as she heard Ben climbing the stairs.

'*Go on do it...*' Kitty turned sharply. Was that Ben speaking?

'*Get some rope and do it,*' came the voice again, this time from what sounded to be a corner of the bedroom.

'BEN!' Kitty screeched. She was really freaking out now. She was sure she'd just heard someone whispering. Forgetting about the darkness and the tarot cards on the floor, she jumped up and rushed out onto the landing, just as Ben reached the top of the stairs. Kitty lunged at him, her bump physically stopping her from being able to throw her arms around him.

'Oh! Thank god you're here. There's someone in our bedroom. I can hear them walking around.' Kitty began sobbing. She knew it sounded ridiculous, but she didn't care. It was all getting far too much for her.

'Hey! Come on now, you've probably had another bad dream. Let's get you settled again, shall we?' Ben tried to lead Kitty back into the bedroom, but she was having none of it. Instead she hovered on the landing.

'I've not even been asleep! And I'm not going back in there, Ben. Especially when we don't have any electricity!'

'Let me go in and check. I can guarantee you that I'll find nothing.'

Kitty stood her ground. She wasn't going back in there until Ben had checked, then she might consider it. The only other alternative was to sleep in the spare room…but then she remembered the incident with Ruby and couldn't decide which would be worse. She was so tired; she really needed to get some sleep.

'Here, hold onto Mr Snozzle.' Ben handed Kitty the fluffy pink pig.

For some reason, Kitty felt a surge of repulsion for the pink pig. Her instinct was telling her not to take it, yet earlier she'd been quite happy to cuddle up to it.

'You keep it, Ben. I obviously can't look after it and we don't want to lose him. Ruby would be devastated.'

Ben shrugged and put the pig on the wooden ottoman that stood on the landing. 'Well, throwing it out of the window isn't going to help the cause, is it?' he joked.

'I did not throw it out of the window, I told you. Yes, I was looking for it because I thought it was on the bed. In fact, I know it was there. I'd brought it with me when I went to lie down. I don't know how it got outside.' Kitty wasn't finding Ben's nonchalance funny one little bit.

'OK, I'm not going to argue with you now. Stay there and I'll check the bedroom, then I think we both need to get some sleep.

Jesus! What a weekend this has been. What with you hearing things *and* Ruby seeing things!' He left Kitty standing outside the bedroom door while he checked there was nothing untoward in the bedroom.

'Clear!' he shouted.

Kitty, feeling overwhelmed and exhausted, had no choice but to go back into the bedroom. She figured that a room where she'd heard something, was marginally better than a room where someone or something had potentially been seen. Amazingly, within five minutes of settling herself back under the duvet, holding Ben's hand tightly, she was sound asleep.

Ben, however, lay there for a good half an hour or more, wondering if his heavily pregnant wife had lost the plot completely...and why the torch had illuminated a circle of tarot cards on the bedroom floor.

XIX

1916

Since the first drop of Mrs Cromp's potion had been put into Will's tea, Loveday had noticed a marked difference in his behaviour. It had happened almost overnight. Gone were the nightmares and wanderings around the cottage in the depth of night, and she welcomed the sound of his snoring, even if it was keeping her awake. It was a whole lot better than the previous worrying and fretting she'd had. Will had even gone up to Bramble Farm to apologise to George Weaver. Despite the very obvious fact that Will physically only had one arm and hand, he was a strong hard-working man and George Weaver knew it. He'd shook Will's good hand and patted him on the shoulder, saying he could do with some regular help over the winter. He'd even pay the going rate. Loveday instantly saw the change in Will's demeanor. Having a purpose each day gave Will the incentive that he needed. Perhaps things were finally looking up?

It couldn't be easy coming back from war the way Will

had. Daisy often remarked on how her pa was grateful he'd been blessed with two girls, the only downside being that he needed to employ manual labour for he didn't have any sons to share the load.

'We'll say no more 'bout it,' had been George Weaver's last words on the brawling incident. There may have been other wagging tongues and fingers behind closed doors, but the gracious act of George Weaver's made the village folk respect his act of kindness, and they kept quiet.

Finally, their lovemaking had resumed, and even though neither of them mentioned a cheel, Loveday was just grateful she'd gotten her old Will back. If nothing came of their lovemaking soon, then she knew she had the option to visit Mrs Cromp again. In fact, she needed to pay her a visit sooner rather than later, just to make sure she didn't run out of potion.

Loveday was contemplating how long it was until the next full moon when Mabel knocked on the back door and let herself in. 'I don't know why ye bothers knocking. I's told ye, just come straight in.'

Mabel smiled. 'Can't 'elp it, it's habit. Blimey, it's bitter out there and looks like we might be in for a battering later. Joe Trevelyan is down in the cove tying up the boats. Sure to be a bad sign.' She kicked off her boots and rubbed the soles of her feet. She needed a new pair of boots, that was for sure. Her feet were either still growing or swelling up. Either way they were uncomfortable.

'Warm 'em in front of the fire. I'll make ye a cuppa. Burdock or nettle?'

'Ooh, nettle please. I could do with a sweet hit. Presume ye got no sugar?'

Loveday shook her head. It wasn't strictly true, but she wanted to keep what she had to sweeten Will's tea.

'So, what have ye been doing to make yer feet sore?' Loveday asked, handing Mabel a cup and saucer.

'Oh! Posh china. It must be Christmas! Ye know, the usual. Ma's had me running errands into the village for people. Me blooming bike's 'ad it and I can't borrow Daisy's as she's still out delivering post. They be too tight, never did fit properly.' She took a sip of the pale green tea and smacked her lips together.

'Yer Will's doing wonders with the 'edge up yonder. Pa's working him 'ard. Truth be told, I think 'e's got a soft spot for 'im. Even took 'im up a pasty for lunch today.'

'Really? Much better than me dry cheese and onion cob I made 'im. I ran out of butter this morning,' Loveday said subtly.

'Ye should 'ave said. I'll give some to Will to bring 'ome when I goes back. Ye knows you only got to ask – just don't go round telling everyone!' Mabel said.

'Do you know, I really think 'e's turned a corner. 'E's so much better. No mood swings, no anger. We've even…well ye know.' Loveday's cheeks pinked up.

'Wink, wink, 'ow's yer father! Well, good for ye, 'bout time we saw a little Nance running around the place. Be good to bring a life into the world with the war and stuff.'

'I can't promise ye that. Well not yet. We wasn't 'aving much luck before, but I guess if it's meant to be, it'll be.'

Loveday for once, was feeling quietly confident.

'So, no more visits to that weird woman in the ancient wood then?' Mabel looked at Loveday with her most serious face. Loveday shrugged.

'Course not. Now, I need to make sure the hens are rounded up before the bad weather yer predicting comes in. Ye be fine to sit there for a while, rest up while ye can.' And seeing Mabel beginning to drop her head and close her eyes, she tiptoed out of the back door and headed into the garden to count in the hens.

Luckily they hadn't ventured too far and were scratching about amongst the sprout stalks. As Loveday approached, they lifted their heads, tilting them to one side, then carried on pecking. Gone were the days when they ran up to her in the hope of scraps from the kitchen. These days most of the scraps, where possible, were saved for broths and such like.

'Come on, time for bed,' Loveday cooed, picking up a nearby bean stick to tap the ground with, while she stretched out her free arm to herd them into the shed.

Normally they were very good at putting themselves to bed at dusk. Hens had no night vision, so weren't stupid enough to stay out, but she was taking no chances today. She counted them in. Eight. Soon to be seven, because sadly the plumpest one would end up gracing the kitchen table on Christmas Day. She pulled the door to and sat inside on a low stool, watching them cluck off to the corner of the shed and rustle around in the straw. Even though there was a small window in the shed, it was surprisingly dark and they soon settled down to roost for the night on the raised wooden planks. She loved watching their individual personalities as they all wrestled for their favourite spot. Funny little things. She did have a favourite though, but of course insisted to Will that she didn't; did no good to get attached. It was the smallest hen, who had a white and black speckled coat and a full red comb who she'd named Fern. Secretly, she was glad she was the smallest, although maybe that was why she was her favourite. It would be a long time, if ever, before they would need to kill her for food.

Sitting in the shed surrounded by all her dried herbs and flowers hanging from the beams, reminded her of Mrs Cromp. What was stopping her going to see her now? If she was lucky, Gribble Gummo might be there too. She really wanted to know what happened at the end of the tale of the standing stones in Madron. She'd only ever visited when there'd been a full moon, but she was pretty sure she wouldn't be turned away. After all, Mrs Cromp had been happy to give her the potion for Will when she'd arrived unannounced before. Right, that was settled then, the sooner she visited, the sooner there was the chance of becoming pregnant. The winter solstice was looming and she knew that the travelling Droll Tellers would soon be visiting the villages in and around Trunrowan, dancing in their guises, bringing frivolity and Christmas cheer to all who lined the lanes to watch. Just as she was contemplating getting up from the stool, her thoughts were abruptly interrupted as Mabel banged on the door.

'I'm off now, what ye doing in there? Ye been gone ages,' she called. The hens began clucking loudly at the disturbance and Loveday reluctantly got up and pushed the stool back under the bench.

'Coming! Sorry, I was daydreaming. How would ye know, ye's been asleep!' she replied, pushing open the shed door. 'Could ye give Will a message for me? I'm off out for a bit. Won't be long.'

'Wer ye going?' Mabel had a horrible feeling she didn't want to know the answer.

'Oh, nowhere special, just fancy a walk to clear me 'ead.' Loveday was being as vague as she could without raising suspicion.

Mabel shook her head in exasperation. 'In this weather?' She pointed to the sky and shrugged her shoulders.

Loveday blushed. 'Look, leave me be will ye. I knows what I'm doing.'

But Mabel had already set off up the back lane and Loveday was left feeling that her best friend wasn't best pleased with her.

Mrs Cromp rubbed her legs. These days nothing seemed to help the aching, apart from resting up on a stool. No amount of rubbing in balms and drinking remedies had helped. She'd tried all sorts of singular and combination teas and had eventually settled with burdock and white willow bark, which gave her some relief. She hated this time of year, it was far too cold and damp in her cottage and she rarely ventured out. She didn't see anyone apart from her cats and the various wildlife that ventured in, either to sit by the fire or sniff about in the hope of finding food. That said, Gribble Gummo was becoming more of a regular visitor these days, which she was secretly pleased about. It was nice to have some human company. She guessed all the years of travelling was taking its toll, for he seemed happy enough to swap a night or two under the stars for a warm bed and roof over his head. Of course, there was the added bonus of food and ale! But she didn't mind. She would always welcome anyone that was in need into her home. Apart from his darn fox. The smelly, flea-ridden creature was good for nothing. Sly was the only word for him; she didn't trust him one bit, but he seemed to keep an eye out for Gribble, a protector of sorts, so she tolerated him.

Just as she was about to rest her feet on a stool, a tapping came from one of the windows. Tap. Tap. Tap. It would be Tapper the crow, he often visited around this time of day. If food was scarce on the ground, Tapper would come a tapping. She heaved herself up from the rocking chair and shuffled into the kitchen. Her legs began protesting, but she wasn't one to give up. If she didn't take some food out for him, he'd be tapping all day and night. Now then, what scraps did she have that would satisfy him. She rummaged through the scrap pot and found a rabbit foot that barely had any meat left on it, but she knew Tapper's sharp beak would make a meal out of it somehow. She'd thought about boiling it up with some of the other bones to make a stock, but there had been a hard frost the last few days and his needs were greater. She had enough meat on her to see her through the winter. She chuckled to herself, not that she would be very tasty though.

As she pushed open the back door, she heard footsteps around the side of the cottage. Soft footsteps like those of a woman, not the heavy feet and jingly bells of Gribble Gummo. She felt a pang of disappointment when she saw Loveday come into view. What did the girl want now? She was in no mood for making up more potions this evening.

Loveday smiled at her in the exact same way as her ma used to do. It was impossible to feel cross. Loveday looked so much like her ma, Rosina, it was uncanny. But as yet, she was showing no signs of using the gift of her ancestors. She wished Rosina had spoken to her about things before her passing. She'd not wanted to weigh Loveday down with the expectation of carrying on the gift of second sight, or possibly frighten her, but it was the way of the cunning folk, no matter whether you were born in Cornwall or Somerset.

'Ello, Mrs Cromp. 'Ow are ye today?' Loveday cheerily greeted her.

'Not so great, me bones be aching and stiff. What do ye want child, 'as the potion been working its magic on yer old man?' She stooped down and put the scraps on the ground for Tapper, who immediately crowed and clasped the rabbit foot in his claws and flew off.

'Yes thanks, 'e be a different man.' Loveday sat down on a large log outside the door, pleased to be able to rest her legs.

'So, why ye be 'ere then? Ye need some more potion?' She was in no mood for small talk.

'Well, yes, I do, but I been thinking and... I was wondering if Gribble Gummo would be visiting ye soon?' Loveday paused as Tapper flew back onto the veranda and cocked his head at her.

'Aye, 'e be passing through soon I'm sure... For the guise dancing like. What do ye need to know for?' She didn't want Loveday thinking they were too familiar with one another.

'Oh! Good. I wanted to ask 'im 'bout the standing stones at Madron.' Loveday paused again, reluctant to continue in too much detail.

'To 'elp get ye with cheel ye mean? I dare say 'e could tell ye a story or two 'bout them stones! If there's anyone who knows the powers they be said to 'old, then it's Gribble.' Tapper had now hopped onto her shoulder and was pecking at her hair. Darn bird, surely he couldn't still be hungry.

'Well, yes. We 'as been, well ye knows, but I think it's time to be 'elping things along.' Loveday blushed.

'Well, I'll mention it to 'im when 'e appears next. Like I said, 'e should be passing through soon for the guise dancing, but I doubt 'e will stay long. They normally goes through all the villages around 'ere, as ye knows. I'll send for ye when I gets word from 'im. No good ye looking for 'im, as 'e'll be in guise, and they all looks the bleddy same to me when they's got them daft masks on.' She shooed Tapper off her shoulder before he pulled any more of her hair out.

'Will ye send for me?' Loveday asked, a little concerned as she didn't want Will finding out, or Mabel for that matter.

'Don't ye worry, me dear. I'll send Tapper to ye with a sprig of mistletoe. That'll be yer sign.' She stood up and tapped the side of her head. If she sat for much longer her legs would seize up. Tapper, hearing his name mentioned, squawked. Loveday flinched.

'E won't hurt you! Daft as a brush 'e is, but a loyal ally to 'ave round these parts. That is as long as ye feeds 'im! 'Ere, let 'im sit on yer shoulder for a bit, 'e can study yer face a little closer. That way 'e won't forget ye.' She called the crow, very gently tapping Loveday's shoulder. Almost immediately the crow spread his wings and made himself at home on Loveday's left shoulder, tilting his head, first to one side and then to the other, studying her face carefully with his beady eyes. Loveday tried not to show how petrified she was, but she couldn't help her body from stiffening.

'That should do. I've 'ad enough entertaining for the evening. I needs me bed.' Mrs Cromp waved her hand at Loveday dismissively and Tapper flew off into the dark of the wood.

'Thank ye,' was all that Loveday could think of saying. She would keep an eye out for Tapper who would hopefully visit her sooner rather than later. By the time she'd stood up herself, Mrs Cromp had disappeared back inside and closed the door. Loveday didn't have the confidence to knock and ask for any more potion, instead she headed back to Rowan Cottage. Hopefully, there wouldn't be too many questions from Will when she got back.

XX

Present day

Ben decided from the moment he woke up: he wasn't going into work. He had woken up early, just as the morning light began slowly filtering into the bedroom, and lay there, staring up at the low, white-washed ceiling. He remembered painting it just before they'd moved in. Being tall and with low ceilings it was always going to be difficult. He'd left it as one of the last jobs, purposely. He now smiled at the cobwebs in the corners and thought how much life had changed since they'd moved to Cornwall. Back in Bristol, there wouldn't have been a cobweb in sight. Kitty used to pride herself on everything being spick and span. But here, well, it really didn't matter, and he loved that they had both become like that. Relaxed. Chilled. And then he remembered last night and felt all maudlin.

He looked over at Kitty who was still sleeping, and carefully moved to the edge of the bed. She looked so peaceful and serene, he didn't want to wake her. She needed to sleep. Last night had been a living nightmare and today he'd make sure she phoned the midwife, whether she wanted to or not.

Once downstairs, he put the kettle on. At least the electricity was back on and there was no need to boil water on the Aga. He set about making himself a strong cafetière of coffee and then picked up the phone to ring the practice.

'Morning, Jenny. I'm sorry it's such short notice, but I'm not going to be in today. Can you cancel all my patients please and rebook? Say I'm ill or something.' He paused and waited for the onslaught of huffing and muttering from his receptionist. He knew it would take ages for her to do, plus she would probably get moaning from some of the patients, but his wife came first.

'No problem, Ben. Are you OK?' Jenny asked, surprisingly kindly. He grinned. Back in Bristol, Ellen his then receptionist, would have torn him to bits.

'I am, thanks. Well, I think I am, but Kitty isn't great, so we're taking no chances and getting the midwife to check her over. Hopefully, it's nothing to be concerned about and I'll be back in again on Thursday. Thanks so much, Jenny, much appreciated.'

'Oh gosh! I hope everything is OK. You take as long as you need. We can manage here. If need be, Nick can see some of your patients, he's got a few spaces in his diary. Give Kitty our best, Ben. You take care,' and without waiting for a reply, the phone line went dead. Ben put the phone back in its charger, with an image of Jenny now cussing at the phone and scrabbling around for patients' notes in a headless frenzy.

Nick was his partner in the practice and was a good sort. Although a fair bit older than him, they had similar views on life. He would happily help out if necessary. He'd send him a text later explaining everything in more detail.

Well, that was much easier than he had expected. Another reminder that life in Cornwall was so much more laid back. Now, to the main task in hand, which he feared would not be so easy. Kitty and the baby.

'Morning, babes.' Ben kissed the top of Kitty's head as he placed a mug of tea on the bedside table. She stirred and protested at being disturbed, opening one eye and then closing it again. Ben balanced the bright yellow maternity notes on top of Kitty's bump and set to picking up the tarot cards on the floor. Kitty lifted her head and groaned loudly.

'So, now you're my obstetrician. Is there any reason why you've brought my notes up with my tea? Did the newspaper not get delivered?' Kitty asked sarcastically.

'Oh, very funny, young lady. They are for you to phone the midwife.' Ben was already handing Kitty the telephone.

'Oh, Ben. I've just woken up! Really, I mean *really*?'

'Yes, really. You were in a right state yesterday. Kitty, I am genuinely worried about you. Humour me, will you? I've taken the day off work so we can sort this together, once and for all.' He wasn't going to let her wrap him around her little finger this time.

'Blimey, you must be worried if you've taken a day off work!' Kitty sat up, plumping up the pillows behind her. 'Leave me in peace for ten minutes and I promise I'll ring her, OK?'

'It's a deal. Now drink your tea and I'll expect to see you downstairs in fifteen minutes, otherwise…I'm coming up with a bucket of cold sea water.'

Kitty sniggered as she reached for her tea. 'Just try it,' she mumbled under her breath, as Ben blew her a kiss and made his way back downstairs. She sat for a few moments gathering her thoughts. How did she actually feel this morning? She still felt tired, which was understandable given how unwell she'd been yesterday. She didn't feel anxious, so that was a good sign, and the room felt normal. Not like it had done last night. Ah, last night. Crikey, what was all that about? She let herself slowly slip back under the covers. Had she heard footsteps? Had she *really* heard someone whispering in her ear? And how on earth had Mr Snozzle ended up outside on the garden path? Had she imagined everything?

In the cold light of day, it did feel as though it was all a figment of her imagination, but even if it was, she knew deep down she needed to speak to someone about it. Too many strange things had happened for them to be a coincidence.

She picked up her maternity notes and punched the contact telephone number for her midwife into the phone's handset and waited. Within two rings the call was answered.

'Midwife speaking, how can I help?'

Kitty paused, tempted to end the call. She was being ridiculous, surely…and then she heard Ben's footsteps on the stairs.

'Oh, yes, umm sorry. My name is Kitty Gridley. My due date is October 31st. I spoke to the duty midwife last night, and I was wondering if it would be possible for me to see someone today? I think I may have some issues.'

There she had said it and just in time for Ben to hear as he walked into the bedroom. He gave her the thumbs up. The midwife asked her a few questions and agreed to pay her a visit later that day. She couldn't be specific but would aim for 3pm. That gave Kitty ample time to decide what she was actually going to say to her. Perhaps now though she could go back to sleep, without listening to the constant nagging from Ben. But first she needed to get up to spend a penny.

'Quick, I need to pee, out of my way!' She laughed pushing past Ben, noticing he was holding Mr Snozzle in his hands.

'Careful, more haste, less speed. You look like a Weeble wobbling.' Ben joked. 'I'm going to package up Mr Snozzle and post him back to Ruby. Lizzie's already sent a text this morning asking for it to be sent special delivery. Ruby's creating.' Ben said, sitting on the window seat and checking the latch on the window. 'I hope you don't mind, but I texted her back and told her you weren't feeling great and that the midwife was visiting later. She said for you to take it easy and that she'd phone later. She's found out some more information about the cottage but would speak to you about it when you were feeling better.'

Kitty just made it to the toilet.

'That's better. My poor bladder. Yep, that's fine, Ben. You crack on. I am going back to bed to see if I can grab a few more hours. The sooner Mr Snozzle is out of here the better.' She shouted from the bathroom.

'Well, I'm going to have to clean him up a bit after his 'fall' from the window, but yes, I'm sure that Ruby will be very grateful to have him back. Oh, by the way, I picked up all your tarot cards earlier that you'd laid out on the floor. Bored, were you?'

'Tarot cards, what are you on about now?' Kitty gave her hands a quick wash. She was desperate to get back into bed; the cottage was bloody freezing.

'They were laid out in a circle on the bedroom floor. I've put them in your bedside drawer. Look, I've got to go. I don't want to miss the next ferry.' Ben kissed her on the lips and opened the bedside drawer for her. 'You go back to sleep. See you later.'

Kitty climbed back into bed and shut the bedside drawer sharply, but not before she saw the card on top of the pack. It was the twelfth card. The Hanged Man. Depicting a man hanging upside down by a rope attached to his right ankle. Its meaning was that of sacrifice, ultimate surrender and being suspended in time. She'd studied the cards well enough to remember. Why they had been on the floor in a circle she had no idea. She had a vague recollection of them falling onto the floor last night...but nothing else, unless of course Ben was fooling around in an attempt to cheer her up.

Within no time, Ben had packaged up Ruby's pink pig and made his way to the slipway at the bottom of the cove. If he made it in time to catch the next ferry, he'd be able to post Mr Snozzle back to Ruby, poke his head round the practice door to make sure everything was running smoothly, and be back in time for the midwife.

'Wasson?' Pete the Fisherman tipped his cap at Ben and took a deep draw on his pipe. Ben watched the small puffs of white smoke filter over Pete's face. No wonder his beard was beginning to turn yellow. He felt as though he should be speaking to him about the risks of oral cancer but thought better of it.

'Morning, Pete. Nice day for it.'

Pete shrugged. 'Yer late this morning. I was beginning to think summut was up... Normally set me watch by ye.' He laughed deeply and then started coughing.

'Day off for me today, going to run a few errands in the village and then spend some time with my ever-expanding wife.' Ben sat down on the wooden seat of the ferry as Pete pushed off from the estuary bank.

'Aye, not seen 'er about much of late. Normally, I sees 'er in the garden or walking along the cove. She be alrite though?'

Ben sensed the genuine concern in his voice and hesitated. Surely it wouldn't hurt to speak to someone about his predicament, it wasn't as though Pete was the village gossip or anything. Talking to a relative stranger had its benefits, a bit like counselling he guessed.

'To be honest, Pete, I'm not sure if everything is alright.' He paused. 'The midwife's coming out to see Kitty this afternoon, so we'll know more then.'

Pete pulled at his beard as though deep in thought. 'What be the trouble then?

Ben realised now he'd opened a potential can of worms. Pete wasn't going to let him get off the ferry without telling him a good story.

'It's complicated, Pete, not enough time on this journey to explain everything.' They were now only a few metres from the slipway on the other side of the estuary, where there were half a dozen holidaymakers already patiently waiting for Pete's next scheduled journey. If he timed it right, he might get away with it...and then realised he had to come back.

'Kitty's been feeling uneasy. Hearing and seeing things, apparently. All total nonsense of course. Overactive imagination, or all those bloody hormones rushing around.' There. He'd said it...and he felt better for it too. Hopefully, it was just enough to keep Pete from asking any more questions.

Ben moved to get up as Pete busied himself with ropes. He appeared not to have heard him or if he had, he'd nothing to say on the matter.

'Right, I'll be seeing you later. Shouldn't be too long.' Ben waited for Pete to remove the barrier so he could get off.

'Aye, well she may well not be imagining things. Strange things 'ave happened at yer place. In the past like,' was Pete's passing shot as Ben stepped off the ferry. Before he could ask what he'd meant, the patiently waiting holidaymakers had turned into impatient ones, pushing past him to get a seat on the small ferry. His answer would have to wait.

XXI

1916

The days and nights were drawing in and within a week or so, the winter solstice would be upon them, thereafter leaving even longer periods of darkness. Trunrowan was also having its fair share of stormy weather of late. Still, things could be a lot worse, at least Loveday had a warm home and food to eat, and she was grateful that Will was no longer fighting for King and Country. Loveday had always enjoyed this time of year, despite the short days and the unpredictable weather. She loved the lead-up to the festive period and the joviality that came with it. Berries on the trees enabling jelly making. The gathering of mistletoe, holly and ivy. Every year she would sit around Mabel and Daisy's kitchen table, all three of them making a willow withy wreath for their homes. It was also tradition in the village, that the wife of the farmhouse, being Mabel and Daisy's ma, Maggie, made one for display in Granby's. One lucky villager would receive the withy, topped with an apple and candle. Their name would be pulled out of an old sweet jar just in time for them to hang the wreath indoors on or around the 21 December to coincide with the winter solstice. It was a tradition Loveday had always known and her ma used to say, '*It welcomed the God of light into the winter eves*'.

They always had great fun around the table, chatting, drinking copious amounts of tea and eating home-made mince pies. This year though they decided that as well as making the wreaths, they would put together a package to send overseas to the soldiers still fighting. Daisy, in particular, was excited beyond belief and had put a notice in Granby's window asking for donations. All was welcome; knitted socks, cigarettes and tobacco or anything else that was felt appropriate. In her role delivering the post to the villagers, she saw this as an extension of her position, and took it very seriously.

'We may well 'ave enough knitted socks to open a shop!' Daisy exclaimed, tipping out the box she'd collected earlier. An array of coloured woollen socks sat amongst pieces of holly and ivy on the kitchen table.

'Careful!' Mabel laughed, removing a sprig of holly that had already attached itself to a brown sock. 'Wow! Who'd 'ave thought that so many people in the village would be so kind? Shall we pair the socks up or mix 'em up a bit. I think it would give 'em a chuckle if they opened up their package to see mismatched socks!'

Loveday raised her eyebrows. 'Maybe... Shall I ask Will for 'is thoughts? Although thinking about it, we'll 'ave to make sure we 'ave a left and a right and they are the same size!'

'Nah! Too much like 'ard work. Let's keep 'em as they are. Ooh look, someone 'as put in some mince pies,' Daisy squealed, overwhelmed with the kindness that had spilled out of the box.

'Agreed. Now, if we gets a move on, we'll be in time to see the start of the guise dancing. Rumour 'as it they'll be with us in the village around six o'clock,' Loveday said, trying to contain her excitement at the prospect Gribble Gummo might be amongst them. Hopefully, she'd soon be getting a visit from Tapper the crow, who as yet, had failed to materialise.

Although it was only a few weeks since she'd visited Mrs Cromp, she was getting more and more impatient, especially as Will had been getting more and more amorous of late, but she was still without cheel and the urge she felt to visit the standing stones that Gribble had talked about, was almost uncontainable. At this rate she'd be setting off to find them herself.

'Why so early, normally they visits us after Christmas?' Mabel asked.

'I'm ain't sure, but that was the message from Rose Trevelyan this morning. She was telling anyone she could find, to make sure we gave 'em a good welcome. I'm surprised ye didn't 'ear about it on yer rounds, Daisy? Are ye going to dress up this year then?' Loveday asked, knowing how much Daisy loved to do so.

Daisy had always dressed up for the guise dancing. She must have given her ma and pa the frights when she was young, getting lost amongst the dancers! Last year she'd worn *the* most amazing dress she'd made herself. It was a gorgeous shade of rose pink, with all sorts of feathers and ribbons sewn onto it, but the best part of the outfit was Daisy's mask. Black and gold with two peacock feathers either side. If she'd not seen her getting dressed, Loveday would never have known it was Daisy.

'Not this year. I don't feel it's right to be dressing up and celebrating but... I'll still join in with the festivities and watch. It would be rude not to welcome 'em into our village, especially at this time of the year. After all, they will 'ave travelled for miles.' Mabel nodded in agreement.

'Let's 'ope it won't be too long before we'll be seeing ye again in your beautiful guises, Daisy, but I agree, it wouldn't seem right packaging up presents for our men on the front, then gadding about,' Loveday said, leaning back on her chair and stretching. 'Let's push through for the next 'our and then we can reward ourselves with a drop of gin.' Loveday tapped her basket with the tip of her boot. 'Made 'specially for ye both as a thank ye for all yer 'elp, advice and, well…' Loveday wasn't great at sentiments and could feel herself beginning to blush.

'Wasson? Did I 'ear someone say gin? Now there's an incentive if ever I 'eard one,' George Weaver said, walking into his kitchen.

'I 'ope you ain't let Will 'ave anything to do with making it, otherwise the lot of ye will 'ave yer socks blown off!' George laughed, pointing to the array of socks on the table.

'Very funny, ye and yer jokes, Dad,' Mabel said wryly.

'Don't worry, Mr Weaver, it's been made with only me fair 'ands. Will don't even know I 'as made it.'

'Just as bleddy well!' George Weaver laughed, pulling up a chair. 'Let's be 'aving ye then… Where's the gin?'

At dead-on six o'clock, above the small village square at the top of Chillyhill Lane, music could be faintly heard. At first, the low beat of faraway drums, but as the dancers got nearer, the drums faded into the background as fiddles and accordions and other musical instruments played their tunes. Villagers had begun to congregate, eager to get a glimpse of the guise dancers as they made their way down the lane into the village. Loveday could not contain her excitement and started tapping her feet from side to side.

'Blimey, Loveday! What's got into ye tonight? Anyone would think ye was excited!' Daisy said, standing on tiptoes, hoping to be one of the first to get a glimpse.

'I am,' she replied, continuing her foot tapping.

'There they be!' Daisy shouted, attempting to make herself heard above the clapping and chattering.

Rose Trevelyan had mustered a very good turnout indeed, and the whole lane was alive with villagers. Children who'd made their own colourful masks waited patiently, holding on to their parents' hands tightly. For some it would be their first time seeing the dancers, and no one wanted their child to go missing.

There was a time, many, many years ago, or so the tale went, that some children would be chosen by the dancers and whisked away with them to be trained in the art of circus tricks, their parents never to see them again. Loveday didn't really think it was true, she was pretty sure that it was probably a made-up tale by someone to make sure that their cheel didn't go wandering. After all, no one had taken Daisy when she was a cheel and she was always following the dancers around. If Loveday was ever lucky enough to have her own cheel, she would certainly continue the tale.

She felt a pang in her stomach, a reminder of her quest. She needed to look out for Gribble Gummo. Surely, she would be able to find him amongst the crowd if she looked for his ginger beard and jangly bells.

'Where's Will?' Mabel asked.

'Oh! 'es being a 'umbug. I left 'im outside The Ferryboat Inn and said I'd join 'im later with the dancers. They be sure to get a good welcome in there and can refuel for the night,' Loveday replied, now clapping her hands in time with the music that was finally getting closer.

'Ooh look!' Daisy yelled above the music. 'Ere they come.' She moved forward as people behind her pushed and shoved to get a peek of the beautifully clad guises as they came down the hill. Lanterns swung and fire throwers skillfully lit up the sky, highlighting the colourful costumes that the dancers wore. Villagers were soon joining the back of the procession, their outfits fit for kings and queens, and Daisy wished there wasn't a war on so she could've joined them with a clear conscience.

Loveday meanwhile, was scanning the dancers as best she could, which wasn't easy when they were swirling around in such flamboyant guises. She tried not to get sidetracked by the beauty of the gowns and masks and concentrated on looking for jangly bells and a ginger beard. People were getting so carried away with the atmosphere, and the ale was flowing, she realised she had little or no chance of spotting Gribble Gummo from where she stood.

If she was to recognise him she needed to be up higher, somewhere ahead of them instead of alongside them. The stone wall outside The Ferryboat Inn would be perfect, if she could get a spot. Without a word to Daisy or Mabel, she picked up her skirt so as not to tread on it and wove herself in and out of the villagers along the lane. People were so engrossed in the parade, it was easy enough to do. She'd left the lantern with Mabel, but luckily she knew every nook and cranny in Trunrowan and eventually she reached the bottom of the hill and climbed up the steps by the side of the pub wall. It was possibly six feet high, maybe a little more, and gave the perfect vantage point from which to watch the dancers coming down the hill and onto the slipway before the final dance. She slowed her breathing to catch her breath, noticing how cold the air had suddenly become. She should've worn another layer, still... Hopefully it would be worth it.

From her vantage point, she was able to fix her eyes steadily on the first dancer that appeared and looked at every one the best she could in the limited light. Gradually, as her eyes became more accustomed to the darkness, she methodically dismissed each dancer that came towards her...until she saw the outline of a man with a beard who wore a large floppy hat, with feather plumes sticking out of it. She couldn't see what they were but if she had to guess, she would've said they were rooster or turkey feathers. She wondered what colour they were and imagined them to be beautiful golds and purples. But what she could see was a pointy face peeping over the man's shoulder. She stared a bit harder, it appeared to be strapped to the man's back in some sort of sack or bag. She dropped her gaze to the man's feet where she could just make out objects that resembled bells, attached to his trousers. As she lifted her gaze, she was now clearly able to make out the face of a fox, its nose sniffing the cold, damp, sea air. It must be Gribble Gummo.

Dizzy with excitement, she wobbled slightly on the wall and stretched out her arm to steady herself. She'd best climb down before she fell. The music which had earlier been pleasantly ringing in her ears now felt as though someone was blasting it directly into them. Her head was pounding from the beat of the drums and she was feeling as though she was on a boat, with the sea crashing against the bow.

Somehow she managed to sit down and thought she could hear Daisy and Mabel calling her name, their voices mingling with the music. Bright flashing lights were boring into her eyes, and she'd gone from feeling hot to cold and back again. She had to get off the wall and try to speak to Gribble Gummo, otherwise she'd never be able to get near him once he was inside the pub. She needed to know when she could visit the standing stones. She needed to know how to get to them.

'Jesus! What the 'ell are ye doin' on that blasted wall, Loveday? Get down, right now, before ye bloody kills yerself,' were the last words she heard from Will, before she blacked out.

XXII

Present day

Luckily, there was no queue in the Post Office and Ben handed over the brown squishy package that contained Mr Snozzle.

'Anything of value in there, Mr Gridley?' the heavily made-up woman, who he recalled was a patient at the practice, said from behind the counter. She smiled at Ben, showing blobs of red lip stain on the front of her teeth.

'Umm...not really, that is unless you're a four-year-old child.' Ben smiled. The woman whose name he couldn't recall, smiled weakly. She'd obviously heard it all before. He took the proof of posting and put it safely in his wallet, then hovered, realising he should have sent it special delivery. Oh, well, it was done now. He was pretty sure it would arrive in Bristol safely. There was nothing else to do other than catch the ferry back home.

'Ye get everything sorted then?' Pete offered his hand to pull Ben on board.

'Yes, all done thanks, Pete.' He appeared to be the only one using the ferry.

Pete headed into the cab. 'Come on in and 'ave a seat. We can 'ave a quick chat before ye gets back.'

Ben dutifully followed him, bending his head and making a mental note to remember not to stand up straight. Good job Pete was on the smaller side.

'So…what sort of things 'as she been seeing and 'earing then?' Pete said tapping his pipe out onto the starboard wooden ledge, one hand on the wheel. He obviously wasn't going to let their earlier conversation go.

'I think you'd describe it as a general sense of uneasiness. I mean she hasn't gone into any great detail with me. She's normally so level-headed, she'd be the last one to believe in ghosts.' At the mention of the word ghosts, Pete turned sharply towards Ben.

'What, ye thinks she's seen a ghost like?'

'Oh, god no! Well, I don't think so. But strange things have been happening. I've just put it down to the pregnancy. She's been very emotional at times. Dreaming and hearing noises, particularly upstairs in the bedrooms. But you know as good as anyone how creaky these old fishermen cottages can be.' Ben couldn't believe he was opening up to a relative stranger. Now he'd started, he didn't seem to be able to stop himself.

Pete nodded. 'Anyone else seen or 'eard anything?' he asked Ben.

Ben wondered whether to tell Pete *everything*…but bringing someone else's child into it, may be taking things a little too far. He didn't want Pete thinking they were complete fruit loops. Especially with his professional standing in the village. But his gut instinct was telling him that Pete knew more than he was letting on, and if he did, he wanted to know about it.

He felt the engine go into reverse. They were almost at the slipway at the bottom of the cove and he could see Creek Cottage from the cracked Perspex cab window. If he was going to mention it, it was now or never.

'Well, yes as it happens. Our friends' child has.' He paused. 'She said she'd seen a man in the spare bedroom and…' Saying it out loud, he realised how ridiculous it sounded.

'Aye, kids can see things that us adults can't. Their minds be open to all sorts. Naught unusual about that,' Pete answered matter of factly. Ben's eyes widened. He'd not had Pete down as the supernatural type.

'And, I's presuming, ye knows about what 'appened at the cottage?' It was a direct question that Ben knew he had to answer.

'You're telling me that Creek Cottage was once Rowan Cottage, aren't you?'

Pete turned his back to Ben as the ferry came to a halt. 'Aye. Not sure who renamed it and when, but yep, Rowan Cottage it was, for many years. The story goes that poor Will Nance who lived there came back from the Great War and weren't right in the 'ead. Rumour 'as it, he 'ung 'imself from the kitchen ceiling one night and 'is poor wife came 'ome and found 'im. Cottage was left empty for decades after that. Understandably of course. Shame 'cause as ye knows…it's a beautiful cottage.'

Ben blinked hard in an attempt to rid himself of the image he'd conjured up. 'Oh,' seemed to be the only appropriate response.

'So, it's entirely possible that, as yer wife says, she 'as been sensing things. Don't being pregnant heighten yer emotions and all that? Makes yer aura more open to these types of things. I believes in all that sort of stuff, ye sees. Not many people knows of course, so I'd umm…appreciate it if ye didn't go around telling folk,' Pete said firmly.

Ben was feeling well out of his depth, it was as though he was hearing someone reading from a book. A fictional one at that, where he'd been cast as one of the main characters and Pete was the narrator.

'So, any bright ideas as to what we should do then?' Ben started rubbing the top of his head. A nervous afliction he'd acquired since infant school.

'Aye. I'd suggest getting Morwenna Cromp in. She'll soon tell ye whether ye got problems with spirits. Ye can find her number in the village journal. She be a diamond that woman. If I'd not married the Mrs, well who knows what may of 'appened.' With a final tap of his pipe, Pete left the cab and set about his usual routine securing the ferry.

Eventually, Ben got up, almost forgetting to stoop as he left the cab. He stepped off the ferry bidding Pete farewell and made his way onto the soft yellow sand of the cove. As he approached Creek Cottage, he studied the whitewashed stone walls and wondered how many other secrets lay within them.

'Hello. You up yet, Kitty?' Ben shouted as he closed the back door of the cottage. 'Umm…' He could smell freshly brewed coffee. 'Kitty?' He stood still and heard the creaking of the stairs.

'I am, indeed. The midwife arrived early and has just given me an examination. She's in the bathroom, won't be long. Hopefully the coffee should be ready by now.' Kitty waddled into the living room and plonked herself down into the armchair, holding her back as she did so.

'Do you want a cup?' he asked, taking three cups and saucers from the cupboard, subconsciously selecting the best china.

'No, best not thanks… It's caffeinated. We forgot to get the decaf stuff, didn't we?' Kitty replied with a hint of sarcasm. Ben had been doing most of the shopping lately.

Ben selected a herbal teabag from Kitty's stash on the windowsill instead and clicked the kettle on.

'Everything OK?' he asked tentatively as he joined Kitty in the living room. Kitty shrugged her shoulders and pulled a face, waving something at him.

'What the hell is this?' she hissed. 'It was on my pillow. Are you trying to be bloody funny? Because I know it was in the bedside drawer earlier.'

Kitty had suddenly changed from exchanging pleasantries to snarling at him like a rabid dog. She appeared to be waving what looked like a tarot card. Without thinking, he snatched it from Kitty's hand and winced as he looked at the picture. The card depicted a man, hanging upside down by a rope, tied around a foot.

'Baby is doing fine, Mr Gridley,' came a softly spoken voice, as the face of an older woman appeared in the living room, placing her small black leather holdall onto the floor. She held out her hand.

'Ben, please call me Ben.' Ben took the offered hand and gestured to a chair. 'Do, have a seat.'

'And please call me Jo.' Jo sat down and brushed down her uniform as she did so.

'As I said, baby is just as we would like it for 37 weeks. Head not as yet engaged, but that often happens with the first. All measurements and heartbeat are textbook, and so…we have no worries about baby at this time.' She paused and took a breath. Ben sensed there was a 'but' coming.

'But…I am a little concerned with what Kitty has told me today.' She glanced over to Kitty to check she was happy for her to continue.

'Oh, yes, please carry on. There are no secrets here. Ben knows exactly how I've been feeling,' Kitty responded, knowing her statement wasn't completely true. She hadn't told either of them *everything*. She was hoping however, that she'd been vague enough to warrant reassurance.

'Sometimes in pregnancy our hormones can get the better of us, and I am sure it's absolutely nothing to worry about, but…'

Ben sighed. There was the 'but' again. Jo continued.

'There is a rare condition that can affect some expectant mothers, and indeed those who have already given birth, but as I say, it is rare. Anxiety during pregnancy, however, is relatively common and as I am no expert in that department, I think it would be wise for all involved, that I refer you on to the Perinatal Mental Health Team in Truro, to assess Kitty.'

Ben noticed that Jo had suddenly become much more professional and matter of fact.

'Ben, I understand that you're a dental surgeon... You may have even heard of Pre and Post-Partum Psychosis?' Jo tilted her head and smiled at Ben as though she was about to ask him if he wanted a cup of tea. Which reminded him...

'Coffee?' Ben asked.

'Oh! Umm, yes, thank you that would be lovely. Milk no sugar please.'

'And yes, I am, but we aren't presented with too many cases in general practice,' Ben replied with a hint of sarcasm that only Kitty was likely to pick up on.

Kitty was glaring at him and still waving the tarot card behind Jo's back.

'No, I am sure.' Jo's response was stifled. 'Nevertheless, for the safety of Mum and baby, I will make a phone call to the team now, if that's OK with you both?'

Kitty nodded, quickly hiding the tarot card behind a cushion as Jo turned to her.

'As I said, it's precautionary and there doesn't appear to be any history of mental health issues or other risk factors, so... please don't worry too much. They're a lovely lot over at the unit and will do their very best to put your mind at rest and work with you, if deemed necessary.' Jo took her mobile phone out of her bag and began to press buttons.

'Please, use the landline if you can't get a signal, or you could go out into the garden. These stone walls block out most things,' Ben suggested as he got up to finally pour the coffee. He needed a hefty shot of caffeine.

'Will I have to have the baby delivered early?' Kitty finally managed to say. Her head was whirling with thoughts and possible outcomes and she was completely baffled by the tarot card, mysteriously appearing on her pillow. Had she said too much? Perhaps she should tell the whole truth, now she realised just how serious all of this could actually be.

She was suddenly overwhelmed with anxiety again, and a strong urge to phone Lizzie. She'd know what to do.

'Let's not get ahead of ourselves shall we now, Kitty,' Jo responded whilst holding her phone up at various angles, walking around the room. 'Try not to fret. Easy for me to say, I know. Let me make this call and we'll soon be able to answer any of your questions more thoroughly.'

Kitty smiled at Jo with as much warmth as she could muster. Bloody fret? That was an understatement. 'Excuse me, will you?' She got up and somehow managed to squeeze between the sofa and chair. She needed to phone Lizzie right now, while she was still able to. At this rate, she could be under lock and key in a secure unit!

Ben went to hand Kitty a mug of green tea, but she pushed past him, heading to the back door theatrically throwing the tarot card into the air. She watched it slowly flutter, then land at Jo's feet. Shit!

'Ooo, what's this?' Jo bent down and picked up the card.

Kitty watched Ben snatch the card from Jo's hands and shove it in his jean pocket.

'Oh, that's umm...nothing. Sorry to snatch,' Ben said apologetically. 'And, where are you going now, Kitty?!' He yelled.

'To talk to someone who'll make sense!' She yelled back. Only twice as loud.

Jo picked up the nearest cup of steaming hot coffee and took a huge gulp.

'Oh dear!' seemed to be all that she could muster.

'Lizzie, can you hear me?' Kitty leaned as close to the small window in the shed as she physically could manage. The line crackled but after a second or two of her changing positions, she heard the warm familiar voice she so needed to hear.

'Hi Kitty, Yes, I can hear you. You OK?'

Kitty sighed. Relieved, she felt instantly calmer. Lizzie would make her see sense.

'Not really.'

'What's up...? It's not the baby is it? Where are you...? You sound all muffled.' Kitty could hear Lizzie's voice carrying a hint of worry.

'No, all is good on that front. I'm in the garden shed...away from the Mafia.' Kitty somehow managed a small laugh.

'You're talking in riddles, Kit...'

'Sorry. Look... I really need to see you, Lizzie, or at least Skype you or something. Ben and my midwife are in the cottage, plotting my confinement to Truro's Mental Health Team as we talk.' A spider scurried across the rotten wooden window frame, dragging its broken web behind it. Kitty knew how it must feel. She mouthed 'sorry' to it; she must have disturbed it trying to get the phone signal.

'You're still not making sense. Slow down. What exactly has happened?'

'I stupidly called out the midwife and told her I was feeling *odd*.' She paused. 'You know, with the weird feelings and last night, well, there was something in my bedroom, Lizzie, I kid you not. And...*it* whispered to me.' She paused again and listened to the silence on the other end of the line.

'Are you still there...? Lizzie?' Kitty waited.

'Sorry, yes, I think there must be a small delay. Are you sure it's not just your overactive imagination again? You know what you're like. Have you told Ben?'

'Most of it, but not about the voice last night, that's the reason I'm now hiding in the garden shed... He kept on and on at me to contact the midwife and convinced me it was the right thing to do. Mind you, I had been vomiting for god knows

165

how long, and I was tired, so I rang her this morning and now she's talking about referring me to the Perinatal Mental Health Team!' Kitty took a deep breath; she was beginning to feel tearful.

'OK, right let's be pragmatic about this. The midwife doesn't know you, so she's only doing her job. Everything will be fine... I promise you. Ben, well Ben is Ben, you know he worries, and he only wants what's best for you and the baby. I'm going to finish up here, collect Ruby from nursery and then, once Tim is home from work, I'll be with you within a few hours. How does that sound? We can sit and talk this through calmly and rationally... OK?'

'Oh! Would you? I feel bad though, you've not long been back in Bristol. Thank you, thank you, thank you! Are you sure you don't mind? What about work and Ruby?' Kitty already felt better at the thought of seeing her best friend and talking to someone who didn't think she was completely crazy.

'You leave all that to me... Anyhow, we have lots to talk about. Did Ben tell you I'd found out some interesting facts about the cottage?'

'Yes, yes, he did... Sounds intriguing.'

'It is and may well answer some of the anomalies we found. Your Creek Cottage was most definitely called Rowan Cottage at one time. I now have proof of that.'

'So, the cottage is haunted. Lizzie, I knew it. It's not me. I'm not going mad or suffering from psychosis or whatever the medical term for it is. You need to get down here as soon as you can and convince Ben that I'm not losing the plot, before he has me committed and they take my baby away from me!' As Kitty said the words out loud, she suddenly froze. That was the reality of all of this. They could take her baby away from her and she hadn't even given birth to it yet.

'Calm down, Kitty. No one is going to take your baby away from you and Ben is certainly not going to let anyone do that!'

Deep down, Kitty knew Lizzie was right. Somehow she had to hold it all together.

'Right, I need to get myself together. What time do you think you will be here?' Kitty looked at her watch, noticing how tight the strap had become in the last few weeks.

'Eight-ish…with a wind behind me and not too much traffic.'

'Eight sounds perfect. Please hurry but stay safe. I need you, Lizzie.' Kitty could hear Ben's voice outside the shed; he was talking to Jo.

'Got to go, they're coming to get me.' Kitty joked, just as Ben opened the shed door.

'Ah, there you are… Good news, the Perinatal team can see you tomorrow afternoon.' He smiled a nervous smile at her as Jo's face also peered around the door.

'See you later then…' Kitty pressed the end call button and quickly put the phone into her pocket. 'Sorry about that, I had to take the call… Reception in the house on my network is practically nonexistent.' She looked directly at Ben, who knew damn well she was lying.

'Oh, no worries. Now, if you are sure you are feeling OK and not nauseous any more, then…I'm happy to leave you in your husband's capable hands. I'll refer you to the appropriate team when I get back to the clinic but…if you have any more concerns, or things get worse, then ring the emergency number on your maternity notes, OK?' Jo looked at Kitty with her stern face again. Kitty smiled weakly.

'Yes, of course, and thank you. Sorry about my outburst earlier. Hormones, eh?!'

'Not a problem, that's what I'm here for. You absolutely did the right thing. Now, if I may suggest that you go back in the warm and get some rest, I'm sure you'll feel much better by tomorrow.' The midwife glanced around the shed.

'This is far too dusty for you and baby to be spending any more time in, now out you come.'

Kitty, for once, did not put up any resistance. She'd got the measure of the midwife and would play it her way. For now. Once she'd spoken to Lizzie later that evening, she'd get things straight in her head. In the meantime, she would be the dutiful patient, wife and prospective mother.

'Well done, Kitty,' Ben whispered, patting her on the back as she made her way back up the garden path to the cottage.

'Patronising git…' she muttered under her breath.

XXIII

1916

'Bed rest and plenty of fluids and she'll be back to normal in no time.' Dr Blake pushed his stethoscope into his worn brown medical bag and fastened it shut. Loveday did her best to prop herself up on the pillows, while Will paced up and down the bedroom like an expectant father.

'Thank ye for coming out so quickly, Doctor,' Mabel said, putting his fee into the large sweaty hand he was holding out. Despite his hoity-toity accent, he stunk of stale alcohol and looked as though he could do with a good bath.

'Let me know if things don't improve.' He made his way out of the cramped room, managing to bump into the door frame as he left.

'Over me dead body,' Will said, sitting down on the edge of the bed and taking Loveday's hand.

'Oh! Stop bleddy fretting will ye all, I be fine!' Loveday cussed.

Loveday looked around the bedroom. She'd never seen so many people squashed into such a small space. She wouldn't mention to the others the words Dr Blake had whispered in her ear as he bent over her, blowing alcohol fumes from his salivating mouth.

'You might be with cheel, too early to tell yet.'

Loveday had been waiting an age to hear those words. But she'd expected the moment to have been in somewhat different circumstances. Oddly though, she felt no excitement. She didn't trust Dr Blake one bit. What did he know, the lathered fool. Surely, she would know if she was with cheel. She'd have words with Mabel for calling him out and lining his pocket with ale money. Most folk in the village stayed well clear of him and especially so after he'd wrongly diagnosed poor old Dolly Penrose's cheel with a measly cold. The next morning the child was found dead in his bed. Dolly, quite rightly, had never got over it. Now the majority of the villagers only called him out if they were desperate.

'Oh, Loveday, I be so sorry. I just panicked,' Mabel said sheepishly, sitting alongside Will on the bed. She'd seen Dr Blake out of the cottage, mainly to make sure he didn't take anything on the way. Will got up and strode over to the bedroom window and opened it to get rid of the lingering smell of alcohol.

'Well, I 'ave to say I'm surprised at ye, but I understands. No 'arm done. Now can I get me bed back to meself please and get some rest?' Loveday slipped down under the heavy eiderdown and turned her back on Mabel, hoping she would get the message.

'Of course, silly me. Look, I'll make sure I calls by 'morrow with some fresh milk and cream. That'll make ye feel better.' Within a minute or so, Loveday could be heard breathing deeply and Will and Mabel headed downstairs. Mabel said her farewells and Will collapsed into the comfy chair in the living room. He was well and truly shattered and could do with a stiff drink if he was honest, but no... Tea would have to do. He owed it to Loveday to be clear-headed and sober in case her condition wosened in the night. She had scared him, seeing her collapse

170

right in front of him. He didn't dare think about what he would do if something really serious happened to her.

Wearily, he got up and headed into the kitchen. He needed to remember to sort the hens out before dusk or he'd be in trouble. He rummaged about in the cupboard above the sink for a mug; he hated the stupid little teacups that Loveday always made the tea in. One gulp and it was gone. As he found a mug, he also came across a small blue glass vial. Carefully as he could, he held it between his fingers, moving it back and forth, as he examined it. He was pretty sure he'd not seen it before. The glass had distinct grooves on it which made it tactile and easy to hold, and it had a brown rubber pipette as its stopper.

Deftly, he twisted it and pulled out the pipette, instinctively sniffing as he did so. He was greeted with a strong smell of burnt almonds, which reminded him of something, but he couldn't quite place where he'd smelt it before. The country lanes perhaps or maybe the fields up yonder? He put the pipette on the sink's drainer and, with one of his fingers, he dabbed the end of the pipette and then on his tongue. Christ! It was worse than rancid. He immediately spat into the sink. What the hell was it? He would ask Loveday in the morning; probably some concoction she'd made up herself. She was always foraging for flowers and herbs. Without thinking any further, he put the vial in the cupboard underneath the sink and finished making his mug of strong black tea. Sitting down in his favourite chair, he pulled a blanket over him. George jumped up onto his lap purring, glad of some warmth. In no time, both were asleep, the mug of tea untouched on the side table.

Loveday stirred and pulled at the eiderdown so it nestled around her neck. Why was it so cold? She tried to settle again, then realised that Will wasn't in the bed. No wonder she felt so cold. He must have fallen asleep downstairs, although she was surprised she couldn't hear him snoring. But she could hear something.

A light tapping every now and then that seemed to be coming from the window. There it was again. Tap-tap. Tap-tap-tap.

She slowly sat up, surprised she felt okay; a little woozy perhaps but otherwise there appeared to be no after-effects of the night's events. She held her breath and listened. There it was again, this time a little louder. She swung her legs out of the bed, placing them on the cold floorboards and instantly felt a cold draught of air. The window must be open. No wonder it was so cold.

As she walked over to close it, she saw something move outside – the silent flap of bird wings. An owl perhaps, there were certainly plenty of them around. But she'd heard no warning call. As she reached for the window's handle, she saw an outline of something on the window ledge. Carefully, she picked up the object, delighted to find it was a sprig of mistletoe, its waxy white berries glistening in the light of the almost-full moon. Gribble Gummo had arrived. It must have been Tapper at the window; how silly of her not to realise. Mrs Cromp had promised her that he'd visit. Good old Tapper. Tomorrow, she would visit Mrs Cromp and Gribble Gummo in the hope she could persuade him to take her, or at least show her the way, to the standing stones at Madron.

Beginning to feel lightheaded again, she placed the piece of mistletoe over the end of the cast iron bed post, and gingerly got back into bed, forcing herself to close her eyes. Despite her excitement, she fell into a deep sleep, where crows wore guise masks and danced along the sandy cove to the music of fiddles. Nearby, was an expanse of land, where ancient stones stood, adorned with sprigs of mistletoe, and their plump berries took the form of newborn babies. Hundreds of them wailing, naked and cold.

'Morning!' Will said cheerfully, handing Loveday a mug of steaming hot tea. "Ow ye feeling now then? Ye gave us all a scare that's for sure… Dunno what ye was thinking of last night – you could 'ave been badly hurt.'

Loveday sat up and rubbed her eyes, taking the mug of tea. She hardly noticed the fact these days that he only had one arm and hand; he was so adept at everything.

'What the 'ell be this?' Will exclaimed, picking up the piece of mistletoe from the end of the bed frame.

Loveday pulled a face. Damn, she'd forgotten she'd hung it there. 'Umm, not sure. Gift from Mabel, perhaps. Maybe she left it there by mistake last night?' That was the best she could offer. Will seemed to accept the explanation well enough.

She tentatively took a sip of the steaming hot tea. Tea! Almost immediately, she felt panic well up inside of her. She hadn't been making Will's tea. He hadn't been having his drops! Oh! Dear god. She put her cup down and started to move in an attempt to get out of bed.

'And where do ye think ye is going maid! Bed rest for ye. Doctor's orders.' Will gently guided her back onto the bed.

'But I feels fine now. I ain't staying in bed all day. I got too much to do before Christmas.'

'Yes, ye are. Mabel said she'd look in on ye later as I needs to go up yonder and 'elp George with the winter feed. 'Opefully I won't be too long. Now ye stay there and drink yer tea.' Will held the mistletoe over Loveday's head and bent forward to kiss her. 'And give I a kiss before I goes.'

Loveday reluctantly offered her cheek and sighed. 'Well, at least let me make ye a cuppa eh?' she offered.

Will shook his head. 'Already done. I'm enjoying me tea in a mug!'

Before Loveday could protest any further, Will could be heard banging around downstairs and then finally came the familiar sound of the cottage door shutting and the crunch of shingle as he headed off down the path.

Loveday jumped out of bed and peered out of the bedroom window, watching Will disappear from sight. He'd be gone for most of the day, even though he said he wouldn't be too long. He always was. George Weaver was a dab hand at finding him things to do, which meant she had plenty of time to visit Mrs Cromp and Gribble Gummo. If she left now, no one would be any the wiser. Then she remembered that Will said Mabel was going to look in on her... Damn it! She'd scribble her a note to say she'd gone into the village to get some medicinals. Hopefully, no one would be any the wiser, and anyhow, she felt absolutely fine this morning. In fact, she almost had a spring in her step.

Despite it being well into December, so far the weather had been mild enough, although Loveday knew that the storms would be upon them again soon. Trunrowan nestled on the estuary and was surrounded by headland on one side and ancient woodland on the other. In the main it was a safe harbour from the wild weather extremes that Cornwall often encountered. But not completely. Every year there would be at least one huge storm that would roll in and batter the small fishing village. They had become accustomed to it over the years, and precautions were always at the ready. Sandbags, shutters for windows, and a general community feel, made sure all the villagers felt safe. The village had really pulled together since war had been declared, although so far the village had not felt the effects that the big cities were beginning to. Loveday reminded herself every day how lucky she was to have Will back home, even if he wasn't quite in one piece. She grabbed her woollen coat and pulled her knitted hat hard over her ears. There, that should keep the wind out; she really didn't want to be catching a chill before Christmas.

Within minutes of leaving the warmth of the cottage, she was walking along the cove towards the wood, her arms wrapped across her chest, head down into the driving wind. Once she was in the shelter of the wood and out of sight of others, she could relax. The last thing she needed right now was for someone to spot her and ask her where she was heading.

After a brisk walk, treading a now familiar path, Loveday knocked gently on the half open door of Mrs Cromp's cottage.

She could hear the rhythmic sound of a flute, coming from inside. She knocked again, louder this time, and called out, 'Mrs Cromp, it's Loveday...'

Mrs Cromp hobbled to the door and smiled. At least she looked a little happier to see her this time.

'Ah, so Tapper found ye alrite then. Good. Come in me dear and warm yerself. That easterly wind is a bugger. Gribble is waiting for ye by the fire. I've told 'im why ye wants to see 'im and as it 'appens, 'e's off Madron way later today and says ye is more than welcome to go with 'im. I've packed ye a basket with some food and drink. Ye shouldn't be gone for more than a day.' Mrs Cromp paused, realising she was babbling. 'That's if ye is still serious about visiting the standing stones?'

'Of course. Yes, I must go. That's why I've come,' Loveday replied, jigging up and down to keep warm.

'Well, come on in then, girl, come on in.' Mrs Cromp ushered Loveday in and without turning to greet her, Gribble Gummo, who was sitting cross-legged on the floor very close to the roaring fire, lifted his hand to acknowledge Loveday's presence.

'Go, take a seat. I'll fetch ye a warm drink.' And Mrs Cromp disappeared into the adjoining kitchen.

'Ello,' Loveday said, sitting down next to Gribble, putting her hands out in front of the fire to warm them.

'So, ye wants to visit the standing stones then?' Gribble said, putting his wooden flute on the floor.

'Yes, if that's alrite with ye, and ye don't mind taking me there? If it's not out of yer way of course.' Loveday shifted slightly; she could feel the fire burning her cheeks.

'Aye, I be off up that way later, so ye is welcome to tag along. But...' He hesitated, turning towards the fire, his back now facing Loveday. 'Ye, will 'ave to make yer way back on yer own. It ain't too far, ye could walk it or cadge a ride from one of the traps coming into Penzance. Up to ye. But we needs to go before the full moon wanes.'

Mrs Cromp reappeared and handed Gribble Gummo a pewter mug, then passed Loveday a cup of sweet-smelling yellow liquid. She lifted the cup and sniffed.

'Get it down ye, girl. It'll warm yer cockles,' Mrs Cromp said, standing so close to her she had no choice but to drink the foul-tasting liquid.

'Don't taste as good as it smells,' she said, handing back the cup.

'Naught that does ye any good, ever does,' Gribble Gummo piped up. 'So, no time like the present. We'll 'ead off now, while the weather be on our side.' Gribble stood up and pulled at his beard. Loveday hoped he wasn't trying to remember the way.

'Ye grab the basket, girl, and we be off.' Gribble sauntered out to the veranda, his bells jingling as he moved.

Loveday was a little taken back at the suddenness of the situation, but reluctantly picked up the small wicker basket.

'I needs to let me family know first. They thinks I've gone to the village for some medicine, as I ain't be feeling too great.' Loveday could feel panic rising in her throat.

'Is ye coming or not girl? I ain't got time for wasters,' Gribble called.

'Ye'll be back in no time, now be off with ye. Stop fretting, they won't even know ye 'as gone,' Mrs Cromp added, jollying her along.

Loveday picked up the basket and wondered how she would manage to carry it all the way; it felt like there was a lead weight in it. She was pretty sure Will would realise she'd gone, and he'd have the whole village out looking for her, especially after last night's drama. Oh, good god! What was she doing? But it was too late now, this might be her only chance for a long while, and she had to take it. She'd just have to worry about the consequences after.

'Yer ma would be proud of ye,' were the last words offered by Mrs Cromp, as she waved from the veranda.

'See ye in the spring maid,' was Gribble's parting comment before she closed the wooden door. No kisses or tokens of affection... Perhaps they really were just good friends.

So, Gribble wasn't heading back this way then? Poor Mrs Cromp. Spring seemed such a long way off. One good thing though was there was no sign of his mangy fox. Perhaps things were looking up after all.

XXIV

Present day

At dead on eight o'clock, there was a knock at the back door and Kitty heard the warming voice of her best friend.

'Hellooooo, anyone at home…?'

'Lizzie, come on in, we're in the living room,' Ben called back. Neither he nor Kitty moved, they were far too snug on the sofa, which was remarkable given Kitty's huge bump.

'Hey, how are my favourite two people… Sorry, three people?' Lizzie laughed, bending over the back of the sofa and kissing the tops of their heads. She sat down in one of the armchairs and kicked off her shoes. 'Well, that was the journey from hell. Two crashes on the A30 near Bodmin and for a moment, I thought it was going to be Jamaica Inn for the night.'

'Oh, Lizzie, thank you sooo much for coming back down, you really have no idea how wonderful it is to see your face again and hear the voice of normality and reason,' Kitty enthused, removing her legs from Ben's lap and sitting up slowly.

Ben pulled a face at her. 'Charming, but she's right. It's good of you to come all this way. Hope Tim and Ruby didn't mind too much?' Ben got up and made his way into the kitchen. 'Tea or coffee?'

Lizzie shook her head and looked at her watch. 'Don't suppose you have any wine, do you? It's been one hell of a day!'

As if reading her mind, Ben had already opened the fridge door and took out a bottle of Prosecco. 'Well, as it happens…' Lizzie smiled and gave him the thumbs up, watching him balance two glasses, the Prosecco and a small dish of nuts on a tray. 'Sorry, love, but your time will come,' Ben said, smiling at Kitty's forlorn face.

'I'm surprised either of you want to drink again after the other night…and so you keep saying. Believe me, am I going to make up for it when it does,' Kitty replied.

'So…you've been causing havoc in Trunrowan then?' Lizzie took a big gulp from the glass and slumped back into the chair.

'Oh! Yes. Apparently, I *may* have something called Pre-Partum Psychosis. Very rare it is too.'

Lizzie practically choked on a nut.

'Everyone's fussing over nothing. It's not me they need to be concerned about, it's the cottage!' Kitty huffed. 'I'm telling you – this bloody cottage is haunted. And Lizzie has come all the way down here to confirm it, haven't you, Lizzie?'

All eyes were now on Lizzie who'd already drained her glass. She shifted uncomfortably. 'Well, odd as this may sound, yes, I guess if you believe in those things, it could well be. Haunted that is. It appears that someone did in fact die here. To be precise, they…well, they hanged themself.'

Ben breathed in sharply and buried his nose in his glass. If Kitty found out what he already knew from his conversation with Pete, things could get messy.

Eventually Kitty found the words she'd wanted to say to Ben for a long while. 'So, I'm not actually going mad after all then…' It was a statement rather than a question.

'Oh, this is all ridiculous!' Ben said dismissively.

'You would say that though, Ben, being a scientific man. But do you *really* think I'm going mad?' Kitty was glaring at him, searching his face for an answer. Her eyes met his and he lowered them in defeat.

'I guess not,' he said, and then added, 'but the baby will be with us any minute and I'm not sure we should be entertaining the possibility of a malevolent spirit. Pete suggested to me that we contact a local medium who lives in the village...' As the words slipped out, he felt his face redden. 'Shit!' he said out loud, realising the implications of his words.

'What the hell?' Kitty replied.

Lizzie shifted uncomfortably.

'What has Pete got to do with this?' Kitty spat.

'May I ask umm...who's Pete?' Lizzie added in an attempt to diffuse the situation.

'Oh! no one important, just the local ferryman!' Kitty huffed. Ben reached for the Prosecco bottle and shook it. It was empty. 'Look, it's not how it sounds.'

'And how exactly does it sound, Ben? Have you been telling everyone in the village, that I've been seeing and hearing ghosts, for crying out loud. Jesus! You really take things to another level, don't you? It'll be all around Trunrowan by now and if the midwife, god forbid, should get wind of this then my fate is sealed. I'll be locked up in no time!' Kitty felt breathless and took a few deep breaths to try and steady herself.

'Oh, stop being so dramatic,' Ben replied, a little too dismissively. 'It was a passing comment he said earlier today on the ferry, that's all. And, to be fair, he didn't seem too surprised. In fact he told me that a Will Nance had once lived here and that the cottage used to be called Rowan Cottage, not Creek Cottage as it is now.'

Lizzie nodded her head in agreement. 'Correct.'

'Apparently, he came back from the Great War and wasn't quite right in the head... His words, not mine.' Ben paused, wondering whether to carry on. 'Lizzie is right... Rumour has it, he hanged himself.' Ben watched Kitty's hands cover her face.

'Oh my god! What? *Here*, in our home?' Kitty had now got up and was pacing around the small room. 'So, it is haunted then. I'm not going mad. Hallelujah! At least we can all sleep well now... Not!'

'Kitty, sit down, please. You're not doing the baby any favours by getting uptight,' Lizzie said, trying to placate Kitty.

'Oh! And then there's the small incident we forgot to mention, of me finding one of my tarot cards on my pillow. The hanged man as it happens!'

Ben scratched his head, she had a point. 'Well, there was a distinct circle of them on the floor, like I told you, but I picked them all up. And I put *all* of them in the bedside drawer.'

Lizzie was struggling to keep up with what was going on.

'Whatever! I'm not going to that Perinatal unit or whatever it is they call it. There's nothing wrong with me.'

Ben groaned. Kitty could be stubborn at the best of times but now, well, there was no way he was going to be able to get her to the hospital for her appointment tomorrow.

'What else did Pete say, Ben?' Lizzie offered.

'That was about it really, he just suggested that we contact this woman in the village. He said her name was Morwenna Cromp and she would be in the village journal?'

'OK, so let's give her a call and see what she has to say then?' Lizzie looked at them both reluctantly nodding, and started sifting through the pile of papers and magazines on the small wooden table.

'What, we are doing it right now?' Kitty asked Lizzie, looking at her watch.

'No time like the present. Ben, how about you stick the kettle on and make us all a cuppa. I think we'll leave the drinking for another night, when all this has been sorted.'

Ben knew when he wasn't wanted and decamped into the kitchen.

'What a mess!' Kitty said, exasperated.

Lizzie began flicking through the village journal, her practicality a welcome change from Ben's overbearing fussing of late. Of course, she understood that he was worried about her and the baby, but he'd seemed quite happy to go along with the midwife's suggestion and have her assessed by the mental health team. She knew better than most that most of the time the medical profession stuck together. He wasn't listening to her and if she really thought about it, he'd hurt her feelings deeply by not believing her.

'Ah, here you go. *Morwenna Cromp. Psychic Medium. Over 50 years of experience. Contact: 01736 879 67901.*'

Lizzie handed the small paper journal to Kitty.

'Do you think it's too late to ring her now?'

Lizzie shook her head. 'OK, pass me the phone will you. Let's do this before Ben comes back in and talks me out of it.'

Within minutes, the phone call had been made, just as Ben came back into the room, this time carrying cups and saucers on the tray and an unopened packet of chocolate Hobnobs.

'She's coming out tomorrow morning,' Kitty said to a puzzled-looking Ben.

'Who is?'

'Morwenna Cromp. Psychic Medium *Extraordinaire*,' Kitty said, nervously laughing.

Ben placed the tray on the table. 'And what about your appointment with the Perinatal team? Jeez... I literally can't believe this is happening.'

Kitty sighed. 'I need my bed. You two carry on with the tea,' and she picked up the journal to take upstairs with her. 'The spare room is made up, Lizzie. Thanks for coming down, I really appreciate it. I'll see you both in the morning.' She blew them both a kiss.

Tomorrow was going to be interesting, that was for sure, and she needed to get some rest. It had been one hell of a day.

XXV

1916

Strangely, for a Droll Teller, Gribble Gummo had little to say. They'd been walking for at least an hour through the ancient wood and were about to turn away from the coast and Trunrowan. Loveday had never ventured farther than Mrs Cromp's cottage and it was a surprisingly pleasant walk, taking them along a babbling brook that gurgled away for a good mile or so. Gribble stopped and cupped his hands, sniffed the water and gulped a few mouthfuls. Loveday followed his lead; the water was icy cold and tasted as fresh as any she'd ever tasted. Then they walked across a rickety-looking wooden bridge where they found themselves in a huge open field that went on for as far as the eye could see. There were a few sheep grazing who lifted their heads as they passed, but so far, they'd encountered nothing other than the occasional bird and rabbit.

Eventually, after a good hour of walking around the edge of fields, they were back in the wood again. Loveday had lost her bearings miles back and realised she hadn't seen the coastline for a while, but by the position of the low sun, she knew they must be heading towards Penzance.

She was thankful she'd put on an extra pair of socks that morning and her good walking boots, not the ones with the hole in the sole she normally wore if it wasn't raining. Luckily, today it wasn't, the sky was a crisp pale winter blue and void of any clouds. Cold weather would definitely soon be on its way.

Eventually, they stopped alongside a copse and, sitting upon raised clumps of grass, Gribble gestured to Loveday to open the basket. He had made no offer to carry it for her and she was glad of the rest. She pulled back the elasticated white cloth and peered inside.

Mrs Cromp had packed them a feast! Apples, cheese, a tall jar of chutney. Nuts and some berries as well as some very well-cooked chicken thighs, and a large Hevva cake. Loveday smiled to herself seeing the familiar criss-cross pattern across the top of the cake.

'Pass it yer,' Gribble said, reaching for the basket handle. It was the first thing he'd said since they'd set off.

She watched him turn his nose up when he realised there was no ale in the basket, but began to rip the meat off a thigh bone regardless. Well, this is fun, Loveday thought to herself. She wondered if she should start up conversation but thought better of it. She was pretty sure Gribble wouldn't want to be disturbed when he was eating. Instead, she bit down into an apple and broke off a small piece of cheese, keeping a close eye on what Gribble was taking out of the basket. She didn't want him eating all of the contents. As he took his third chicken thigh, Loveday decided to take the basket back under her control, if only to ensure they still had some food for later. She didn't know how long they were going to be walking for, plus she had the return journey to make too. Then there was the question of water; they'd have to find another water source, but she felt confident that Gribble, being a travelling man, knew where the next watering hole would be.

'Let's go. Not much further. We should be there 'fore nightfall,' Gribble said, throwing the thigh bones onto the ground. And they were off again, Loveday lengthening her stride this time to keep up with him. She let her thoughts slip back to home for a brief moment, and quickly dismissed them again when she envisaged Will, Mabel and Daisy scouring the village for her. They'd soon realise when they found her note and visited Mr Penrose in his chemist shop, that she'd not been there like her note had said she would be. Then, well...she had no idea what would happen.

After another few hours of solid walking, Loveday was losing hope of ever reaching the standing stones, until Gribble finally stopped and rested his hands on his hips.

'There they be, just over yonder, not long now and then we can rest up before it gets dark. Sky is clear. We should 'ave a good full Cold Moon later.' He took a deep breath as though filling his lungs with more fuel, and they were off again.

Loveday could barely see the standing stones. There were a few hills in the distance and possibly, if she really squinted, an outline of what could be stones. She had no other option than to take his word for it, realising she could well be a lamb to the slaughter. No one would know where she'd gone, well, apart from Mrs Cromp, but she was pretty sure there weren't many in the village who even knew the whereabouts of her cottage. Come on, Loveday, you can do this, she said sternly to herself. Just think of the reward if it works. She'd never wanted anything so badly in her whole life. Her, Will and a cheel. A real family.

Digging even deeper and with a renewed energy, she eventually caught up with Gribble.

'Bout time – thought ye was never gonna give I a bit of company.' He laughed, winking at Loveday cheekily.

Finally, she caught a glimpse of the Gribble Gummo that she'd first met. The jolly Droll Teller, who told wondrous, colourful stories.

'So, tell me 'bout the standing stones again, Gribble, and what I 'ave to do when we gets there?' she asked.

'All in good time, all in good time. Ye be guided by the light of the moon and the energy of the stones. They will tell ye. With a little 'elp from the story of the land. An ancient land, with ancient stones. All in good time, all in good time.'

Darkness had almost fallen when they eventually reached the standing stones. There were four stones in total, although one had fallen and appeared to have merged with the ground at some point. The other three stones stood in a line, the middle stone with an almost perfect hole through it. Surrounding it was a small trough that had filled with rainwater, but it was definitely not for drinking, which was disappointing as Loveday was parched.

As if reading her mind, Gribble took the basket from her and removed the tall glass jar that had previously held the chutney. 'Right, I be off over yonder to fetch some water, but before I goes, let me tell ye 'ow the stones work their magic. Come sit 'ere while I lights a fire.' Gribble patted the ground. He'd been gathering bits of kindle since they'd left Trunrowan and filling his cloth bag with them. He now tipped them out onto the ground and out of his jangly pockets he took two small stones and what looked like tufts of horsehair; it was difficult to be precise in the creeping darkness, but within minutes, a small fire was burning. Loveday sat next to Gribble, her knees tucked up in front of her as she tried to stop herself shivering. Facing the stones, Loveday realised she could just about see the moon through the middle-holed stone if she bent down far enough. There was certainly something tranquil and special about the place, she could feel it in the earth below her, whispering to her, reassuring her. It was the strangest feeling she'd ever experienced, but she still didn't know what she was supposed to do.

'Can you feel it?' Gribble asked. Loveday nodded.

'Take yer time, then when ye feels ready, take yer boots and socks off and 'ead for the middle stone. Then, ye is to ask the guardian of the stones for whatever it is ye needs… When ye is ready, ye must go backwards through the middle-holed stone seven times, and seven times only.'

Loveday nodded again to show she understood, this time with more confidence.

'People comes from far and wide to these stones. I knows folk who 'ave 'ad many ailments cured and I 'as often thought of asking the stones to rid I of me back pain.'

Loveday wondered why he hadn't then… Perhaps his pain wasn't bad enough or else he didn't believe in the stones' magical powers, but then why bring her here?

'Right then, I be off to fetch some water, ye do what ye got to do.' Gribble picked up the glass jar and disappeared into the creeping darkness.

Loveday sat for a while, her eyes closed, and clasped her hands tightly together in her lap feeling the coldness of the moor underneath her. It was eerily quiet, only the sound of a gentle wind could be heard rustling grass and nearby gorse. There were no sounds like those heard in Trunrowan. No waves lapping against the shore. No owls hooting in the woodland.

It was time.

Removing her boots and thick woollen socks, she stood barefoot and instantly felt the energy of the earth beneath her. She wasn't sure who the 'guardian' was that Gribble mentioned, but she tried to listen to her inner voice and slowly approached the stones.

'Please, grace me with the joy of a cheel,' she whispered under her breath. She paused and was sure she could hear the echo of her words bouncing off the granite stones and into the darkness. Slowly, she placed a small piece of apple at the base of the nearest stone as an offering, and then approached the middle-holed stone, gently running her fingertips across it. It felt cold, ancient, evoking a powerful feeling within her. Somehow, she knew she was safe here. She looked at the hole... If she bent down, she'd be able to pass through it easy enough, although going backwards would be a challenge. But nothing could stop her now. Putting her hands together and blowing a kiss to the full Cold Moon, she bent down and stepped backwards through the holed stone.

One. Two. Three. Four. Until she'd repeated the ritual seven times as Gribble had instructed. Stretching her back, she placed her hands on the middle stone and said a prayer of thanks, returning to her spot beside the fire, eager to put her socks and boots back on.

Within minutes, Gribble had returned, almost too timely. She wondered if he had been watching her in the shadows?

'There ye be, drink this and then let's get some shut-eye. I be leaving early 'morrow so ye be on yer own but ye will find yer way back with no problems. The 'edgerows and paths will show ye the way,' Gribble said, handing her the glass jar that was now full of what she hoped was water.

'We needs to snuggle up to keep warm, so ye can 'ave this for the night. Don't worry, I ain't got naught nasty, so ye be fine.'

Loveday gratefully took Gribble's jacket and wrapped it around her. It smelled of smoke and sweat but it wasn't the time to be fussy. She drank some of the water, which thankfully tasted as fresh as the water from the brook earlier. Then like an old married couple, they laid down on the ground in front of the fire, their backs to one another. It wasn't long before Gribble was snoring and Loveday closed her eyes, hoping that sleep would soon come. Exhausted and drained, she drifted off into the deepest of sleeps, dreaming that the whole village had turned out looking for her, while Will wandered like a lost soul, back and forth...across the wind-swept headland.

XXVI

Present day

The next morning, Lizzie was up with the birdsong, tidying the cottage and making it as presentable as she thought it should be for a psychic medium. She wasn't sure whether Kitty was supposed to be going to Truro to see the mental health assessment team, but she figured that having a tidy cottage to wake up to would make everything seem brighter, regardless.

She had woken way too early; but after all the excitement of yesterday, her head was working overtime and she'd given in and got up. She'd make some fresh coffee and lay the table for breakfast and hope that Morwenna Cromp didn't arrive too early. Marmalade had stuck his nose in through the cat flap, then back out again when he realised the breakfast cooking wasn't for him. Normally, she would've gone after him, or at least opened up a can of his favourite food – she was a sucker for cats – but this morning she didn't have time for distractions; he would have to find himself a mouse or two.

By 8:15, she was settled on the sofa with a steaming mug of coffee. All she had to do when Kitty and Ben woke up was to fry the eggs; everything else had been cooked and was keeping warm in the Aga. She contemplated the surreal situation she'd found herself in. Her best friend had been provisionally diagnosed with Pre-Partum Psychosis, and could at any minute, apparently, be whisked off to hospital. Then there was the psychic medium, Morwenna Cromp, who was about to potentially connect with the spirit of Will Nance, who had apparently hanged himself in the cottage. Life in Cornwall was certainly not the quiet option that Kitty and Ben had hoped for.

'Hey, morning, Lizzie.' Kitty stood in the doorway rubbing her eyes.

'Good morning. Did you sleep well?' Lizzie asked, getting up to make Kitty a drink.

'You could say that. Best night's sleep I've had in months. I didn't even need to get up for a pee. I can't tell you the relief, knowing both you and Ben don't think I'm going mad.' Kitty flopped onto the sofa.

'Tea or coffee...? Aww, bless you. I'm sorry I didn't tell you earlier what I had found out, but to be honest I was worried it might spook you and send you into an early labour! Is Ben still asleep?' Lizzie looked at her watch.

'I think I'll treat myself to a coffee this morning. Thanks Lizzie. Yep, dead as a dodo. He deserves a little lie-in, let's face it when the baby is here, he'll be wondering what sleep is!' They both sniggered.

'So, I've been busy cooking breakfast, but wasn't sure what time Morwenna Cromp said she was coming?'

'I thought I could smell bacon.' Kitty pushed herself up, resting her hands in the curve of her back. 'Christ, my back's hurting this morning. I must have slept awkwardly.'

'Time please, madam!'

'Oh yeah, right. Midwife said she'd call me this morning. Bloody waste of time. I have a good mind to call them and—'

They were interrupted by the landline ringing. Kitty picked it up quickly, in the hope that it hadn't already disturbed Ben.

'Yes, it is.' There was a lengthy silence as Lizzie watched Kitty's face eventually erupt into a huge smile, giving her the thumbs up.

'Oh, OK. Yes, I understand. Next Tuesday at 12. And of course I will – not a problem. Thanks for ringing.' Kitty replaced the phone and did a little dance. 'Oh, *YES!* Result.'

'What's happened? And sit down before you fall down will you. Jesus, if Ben wasn't awake, he certainly will be now.'

'Midwife says that she's now had the chance to speak to my consultant, and he is happy to wait and see how things progress, as long as I explain to Ben that he needs to keep a close eye on me. I have my check-up next week anyhow but to contact them before, if need be.' Kitty could not have felt more relieved.

'Great news. I guess with Ben being in the medical profession they are happy to leave you in his capable hands and wait to see how things pan out.' Lizzie handed Kitty her coffee.

'Whatever the reason I don't really care, at least we can relax a little knowing that the psychic isn't going to bump into the psychiatrist, ha, ha.'

'What's that?' Ben walked into the room looking just as sleepy as Kitty had earlier.

'Sorry, babes, did the phone wake you?' Kitty stood on tiptoe and kissed Ben on the cheek.

'No, I think it was your shrieking. What the hell is going on down here…? I need a coffee.'

'Coffee's been made,' Lizzie shouted as Ben shuffled into the kitchen. 'Blimey, is he always so grumpy in the mornings?' Lizzie asked Kitty.

'Pretty much, yeah. Look, can I leave you to tend to breakfast while I go and take a shower. We've got about an hour or so before the psychic arrives, and I need to look half presentable and not so much of an unruly crazy pregnant woman who's been seeing and hearing things.' Kitty made for the stairs.

'Sure thing, you go do your stuff. Scrambled or fried?

Kitty shook her head. 'No eggs for me, thanks.'

At the top of the stairs, Kitty stopped and grimaced as her back twinged again. The baby must be lying on a nerve, or maybe she shouldn't have been so enthusiastic on the stairs. Much as she was greatful for the life that was growing inside of her, and after waiting for so long, she thought she would be prepared for the nuances of pregnancy a little better. She certainly wasn't one of those women who had a glow about them and felt all mother earth. Nope, instead she'd somehow managed to attract a ghost!

Breakfast was a rushed affair. Ben shoveled his bacon, eggs and beans down as though he'd not eaten for days, while Kitty was already suffering from heartburn and she'd only managed a few mouthfuls of bacon. But she was grateful that Lizzie had offered to cook. Lizzie had always been great at knocking up a cooked breakfast. Living in France in her early 20s, had equipped her with all sorts of skills, and not just culinary ones. She was fluent in French. A dab-hand at making cheese. And, she had learned the art of making artisan milled soap in the way only the French do.

'I'm a bit nervous about the psychic to be honest. Do you think we're doing the right thing inviting a stranger into our home?' Kitty asked.

'We'll soon find out,' Ben said, looking out of the kitchen window, noticing the growing storm clouds scudding across the skyline. 'Because if I'm not mistaken…Morwenna Cromp, Psychic *Extraordinaire*, is currently walking up our garden path, with Marmalade close at her heels!'

'Blimey, she's bright and early,' Kitty exclaimed, glancing at the kitchen clock. It was a little after nine.

'Bright. Yes.' Ben said.

'No time like the present,' Lizzie added, quickly clearing the kitchen table of plates and bowls. 'I have to confess, I'm well excited. I've never met a psychic before.'

'I don't think any of us have Lizzie,' Kitty said, just as there was a loud knock at the back door. It was a knock that meant business. They all looked at one another, hoping one of them would open the door. The knock came again, and Ben eventually stepped forward and opened the door.

Morwenna Cromp had obviously, at one time, been a very good-looking woman. Her complexion was like alabaster, with red rouge brushed across her cheekbones. Her eyes were a deep green and her eyelashes were to die for – long, black and full, framing her green cat eyes perfectly. The clever flick of black eyeliner on her upper eyelid, added to the effect. She had a smidgeon of dark red lipstick on her lips and a touch of gloss. Just enough to complete a very pretty picture. She certainly knew how to make the best of herself, that was for sure. But her pièce de résistance was her hair. Curly auburn locks piled high on her head, secured in place with a beautiful silk embroidered headband. The handsewn sequins and beads, cleverly caught the light, sparkling every time she moved her head. She fitted the perception of a psychic medium perfectly, even though none of them were quite sure what that was supposed to be.

'Good morning. I'm Morwenna Cromp. Very pleased to meet ye.' She offered her hand and Ben felt a firm and confident handshake.

'Ben Gridley. Pleased to meet you too. This is my wife Kitty, and our friend Lizzie.' Morwenna smiled and shook hands with them both, stepping into the kitchen before Ben had the chance to invite her.

'Ah! I see you have already become acquainted with our cat!' He laughed, watching Marmalade rub himself up and down Morwenna Cromp's legs.

Morwenna Cromp bent down and tickled the back of the cat's neck.

'Lovely to meet you,' Kitty added, completely enthralled by the woman who stood in front of her, who had just a hint of a Cornish accent.

'Thank you so much for coming over at such short notice. Where would you like to go first?' Ben asked, unsure what the correct protocol was for psychic mediums.

'Oh, let's sit and talk first shall we?' Morwenna replied casually, settling herself at the kitchen table. 'Let me get my bearings first.' And she began rummaging in her bag, bringing out all sorts of unfamiliar items and placing them on the table.

'Let me turn on some lights for you. The cottage gets so dark when the weather's not great. One of the many joys of living in an old fisherman's cottage.' Ben flicked some switches.

Morwenna looked up and instantly smiled at Kitty, who was unashamedly staring at her. 'So...ye are the chosen one. When is the baby due?'

Kitty laughed nervously. Morwenna Cromp, in the main, seemed relatively normal and rather pleasant, certainly not what she'd expected. 'Three weeks to go, so not long now.'

'And did the disturbances begin with your pregnancy, or are they more recent?' Morwenna asked.

'Not straight away no, but they've certainly been getting more frequent of late. My midwife thinks I'm going mad. Something called Pre-partum Psychosis.'

'And do ye think ye are?'

Kitty shook her head fervently. 'Absolutely not! Apparently, someone hanged himself in this cottage and I'm pretty sure it's his spirit I've sensed, hence my phone call to you.'

Morwenna nodded as if she understood.

'Well, let's see, shall we. I need some quiet, just for a few minutes while I collect my thoughts but first I need ye all to understand that anything we may see, hear or feel, is not something to be mocked at or taken in jest. We could be dealing with a malevolent spirit, so it's important that ye listen to what I say...*and* do exactly what I tell ye. The crystals I have brought with me will do their best to protect us.' She waved her hand over the colourful array of crystals she'd emptied from her bag. 'This is not something to be taken lightly and...' She looked Kitty up and down with a hint of concern in her eyes. 'I cannot guarantee the safety of ye all...or that of your unborn baby should the spirit, if there is one, decide it wants to play games.'

'Wo! Hang on a minute, what's that supposed to mean?' Ben puffed out his chest, running his fingers though his hair.

'What I mean is, I have no control over the spirit, if indeed there is one here. I can only do my best to protect ye all, but I come with no guarantees or promises. Such is the uncertainty of the spirit world. Take it as a disclaimer if ye like.'

'OK, let's stop this right here shall we... Kitty, I can't have you subjected to this. My god, if the midwife found out what we were doing, we'd *all* be shipped off to the loony bin. I have a respectable job in the village you know... I could get struck off for meddling in the dark arts!' Ben sat down with a heavy thud and put his head in his hands.

Morwenna Cromp kept her composure. She'd obviously heard it all before. Instinctively, she gently put her hand on Ben's arm.

'Don't fret – it's highly unlikely the spirit is here to cause torment. They rarely are. Usually, they are troubled and for some reason or another, have not passed over in the way they should have. This is why ye have called me, to help facilitate the crossing...ensure that they are finally at rest.'

There was an audible sigh of relief from everyone around the table.

'Ben, it's absolutely fine, let's not get carried away with all the drama, eh?' Kitty said, very calmly. She was surprised at Ben's reaction; he was normally so pragmatic. Perhaps the spirit was playing games with him too.

Lizzie nodded in agreement. 'I'm with Kitty on this. Morwenna's here now, and at least it will put our minds at rest knowing what's going on, if indeed there is anything.' She winked at Kitty.

'Huh, drama! Says the one who has been hearing and seeing things.' Ben huffed.

Morwenna Cromp, oblivious to the domestic bickering, was now laying out the crystals in some sort of pattern on the table. 'No one is to touch the crystals unless I say so, or I give ye one to hold…understood?'

Everyone nodded. Ben realised he was outnumbered and resigned himself to handing over his relatively rational and sane life, to that of an unknown psychic medium that happened to be sitting in his kitchen. Marmalade jumped up onto his lap to see what all the fuss was about and meowed as if in sympathy.

'Right then, if we could all hold hands and relax, I will say a few words. Ye can close your eyes now if ye want, but under no circumstances let go and break the circle without my say so.'

Everyone nodded again.

'Kitty, you might find this a little more difficult because you have a rather large bump in front of you, but we won't be like this for very long.' Morwenna handed Kitty a large black crystal, and a smaller one each for Ben and Lizzie.

'The crystals are black tourmaline. They are a powerful stone used for protection and will keep ye grounded on this earth plane. Put them about your person, either in a pocket or down your bra if you're wearing one. They are your trusted friend.'

Kitty immediately put hers in her dress pocket, patting it as she did so, hoping it would do its work. She watched Morwenna Cromp as she said a few words, calling in her spirit guide, her head held high and eyes closed. She looked every bit in command of whatever it was she was doing and Kitty slowly relaxed, trying to trust her intuition that everything would be OK.

Kitty gave Ben's hand a little squeeze and reassuringly felt him squeeze back. As they sat in silence waiting, a blast of cold air came out of nowhere and whistled past them. Kitty tightened her grip. It felt like the icy wind that blew up on the headland in the depths of winter. Morwenna gave her hand a firm squeeze, as though to say, I know, it's fine, I felt it too.

'Welcome,' Morwenna said, breaking the silence.

Kitty tentatively opened her eyes, almost expecting someone to be in the room with them. But there was no one visible.

'We are here to help ye. We mean ye no harm.'

Suddenly, Marmalade let out a loud hiss and jumped off Ben's lap, bolting for the door. The last thing Kitty saw was him trying to squeeze through the cat flap, his fur stuck up like a puffer fish, almost doubling his size.

'Do not break the circle.' Morwenna reminded them. 'Your cat will be fine. They often sense spirit energy.'

Kitty thought back to the various occasions when Marmalade's behavior had been strange. It was obvious now that he'd been sensing similar things to herself.

Kitty shivered. She was freezing and whatever was causing it was not going anywhere anytime soon. She wished she could put her hand in her pocket and touch the crystal Morwenna had given her for reassurance, but she daren't break the circle.

'We're here to help ye. Was this once your home? If so, it's time to move on to your new one, my friend. Ye will find your loved ones waiting for ye. They're not here any more.' Morwenna took a deep breath in through her nose and slowly exhaled through her mouth.

Kitty could feel the warmth of her breath settle on her hand. She was still watching Morwenna, everyone else appeared to have their eyes firmly shut. But there was no way she was going to miss some meddlesome entity come into the cottage and try to take them over. No, she needed to be in control and if necessary, she would break the circle and be out of the cottage's back door before you could say *expecto patronum*.

She could now also hear a faint noise coming from above the kitchen and recognised it as the familiar sound of floorboards creaking. It was the same noise she'd heard the other night when she'd heard the voice whispering to her.

She froze… There it was again.

'Take a last walk, my friend,' Morwenna said calmly. 'Say your goodbyes if ye need to, but it's time for ye to leave.'

Kitty felt Morwenna pull her hand away and watched her put her hands together in the prayer like position. The circle was broken. Immediately, she reached for the crystal in her pocket.

'Now, what?' Ben asked, standing up and stretching. 'Is that it?'

Morwenna was rummaging about in her bag again. This time she pulled out what looked like a small bundle of herbs and a clear glass vial. 'No. Sadly not. There is indeed a spirit here and it is the spirit of a man. A soldier. He is sad. So very sad.' Morwenna rubbed her left arm vigorously. 'He is confused and angry and keeps showing me his arm, but I can only see the one. I don't know if that means anything to ye?'

They all shook their heads.

'Is he Will Nance?' Lizzie asked, taking her jacket off the back of the chair. She was freezing.

'He hasn't told me his name yet, but yes, I believe him to be Will Nance. I know of the family name. He lived here, in Trunrowan, with his wife, Loveday.'

'And he hanged himself, right?' Lizzie was beginning to get frustrated.

'Yes, I'm afraid he did. But I can't be a hundred percent sure it is him yet. Not until he tells me.'

'What the bloody hell is he waiting for, an invitation? Jesus, this is ridiculous, what the hell are we doing?' Lizzie was feeling scared, and it was beginning to show.

'Hey, come on, let's all calm down. We invited Morwenna here and she is doing her best to find out what is going on, so let's just give her some slack, shall we?' Ben said authoritatively. Realising they weren't raising the devil after all, he was feeling a little more in control.

Kitty had left the table and was still listening to the floorboards creaking, trying to work out where the sound was coming from. It sounded as though whatever it was, or whoever it was, was moving around upstairs. Ben caught her arm just before she got to the bottom of the stairs.

'Hey, don't go wandering off on your own. Do you need the toilet or something? I'll come with you.' Ben put his arm around Kitty's shoulders protectively.

'Wait a moment, my dear, will ye.' Morwenna had lit the bundle of herbs she'd taken out of her bag earlier and was wafting sweet smelling smoke around the kitchen with a large white feather.

'Blimey! Now it smells like a weed factory in here.' Lizzie huffed, finally declaring defeat and taking herself off to the living room. At least it was a warmer there.

'Do ye have anything that was in the cottage when ye moved in by chance?' Morwenna asked, still wafting.

'The cottage was pretty run down when we bought it, just a shell really,' Ben replied, holding Kitty a little tighter.

Kitty nestled into Ben. She was tired, cold and really needed a pee. When was all this nonsense going to stop?

'Hey! What about the coin, Kitty?' Lizzie shouted from the living room.

Kitty lifted her head from Ben's shoulder. 'What about it?'

'Oh, yeah, we found an old king's shilling,' Ben continued. 'Well, Marmalade our cat found it actually; it was tied around his back leg… It's a long story. We're certain though that it's somehow connected to the cottage. It dates from the First World War and has a hole drilled though it, so it could be worn on a chain or a piece of ribbon. Which we think at some point, it probably was.'

'That would be perfect. If it isn't anything to do with the cottage or the spirit, then it won't work, so no harm done. Could ye fetch it for me dear?' Morwenna directed the question at Kitty, who reluctantly let go of Ben.

'Let me go upstairs first.' Morwenna said, still wafting her bundle of herbs around.

'What on earth is that stuff?' Ben turned up his nose.

'I think it's sage, although I might be wrong. I can smell cedar too,' Kitty whispered, following Morwenna.

'Really...? And why is she burning it? Don't you use sage when cooking?' Ben whispered back.

'Ha! Yes, you do, but sage, and in particular California sage, has been used in ancient ceremonies for years. It's said to get rid of negative and unwanted energy.' Kitty and Ben were now at the top of the stairs.

'All that studying herbs has come in handy after all then.' Ben chuckled. Kitty nudged him in the ribs. 'Ouch!'

'Sshhhh.' Morwenna Cromp stood on the landing and turned sharply, glaring at them as though she was chastising two naughty school children.

'Let me get the coin. It's in my jewellery box.' Kitty disappeared into the main bedroom and returned to the landing holding the coin.

'Here you go, maybe you can tell us a bit more about it?' Kitty handed over the silver coin.

'He wants us to go into this room here.' Morwenna pointed to the spare bedroom, taking the coin from Kitty as she did so.

It was the only other bedroom in the cottage, the one where Ruby had said she'd seen the figure of a man and Kitty had heard someone or something walking across the floorboards. The arm! Kitty suddenly remembered the conversation she and Ruby had on the beach. She'd not told anyone about it and couldn't really bring it up now, otherwise there would be 101 questions, especially from Lizzie. It certainly would tie in with Morwenna only being able to see one arm in the image she'd been shown.

Morwenna briefly looked at the silver coin then pushed open the stable style door of the spare bedroom and flicked the light switch, as an audible *ping* sounded as the light bulb blew.

'What the hell! What's happened?' came a yell from downstairs.

'Bloody electrics. Don't worry, I'll head out to the garden shed and sort it. The RCD unit is out there. It will have tripped that's all. I'll have us glowing like Blackpool Illuminations in no time.' Ben headed downstairs before Kitty could protest.

The weather had worsened and with storm clouds gathering outside and the heavy curtains closed in the bedroom, it was dark without any lights on. All she could make out was the soft glow from Morwenna's bundle of herbs, but strangely, she didn't feel frightened or anxious any more.

'Here, my dear, hold my hand.' Morwenna reached out and Kitty took her hand.

'Let's see if he wants to play now it's just the two of us. I think he may have done this on purpose.'

'*Play*?' Kitty managed to splutter. She was desperate to go to the toilet. The baby had started jigging up and down on her bladder, and she didn't want to end up peeing herself.

'Figure of speech, my dear. It means he's being mischievous. Not necessarily malevolent, just meddling. Can you feel his presence in here?' Morwenna didn't wait for an answer, instead she held out her hand, the coin resting on her palm. 'Is this your coin, young sir? Did it once belong to ye?'

Kitty waited, although she wasn't sure what for. She felt as though they should be saying, one knock for yes, or two for no. But there was nothing, and where the hell was Ben? Why had the lights not come back on yet?

'No, I can't sense anything, but I'm beginning to feel a little odd. My head's spinning, although it might be because I *really* do need to pee.'

Kitty felt as though she had downed a bottle of Prosecco, a little too quickly, and the bubbles were having a right old argument in her head.

'Sit down. We don't want any accidents.'

Kitty, for once, did as she was told, and reluctantly sat on the edge of the bed. The darkness wasn't helping; it was very disorientating. She really wished Ben would hurry up and turn the electric back on.

Morwenna began walking around the room, humming. It sounded like an old sea shanty mixed in with Siouxsie and the Banshees. Strange how things from your past came to you in the oddest of moments.

'It's time to move over now, my friend. Is there something ye wants to show us before ye do?'

Kitty was beginning to feel sick. She really needed to go to the bathroom.

'Show us, my friend – we are here to help ye.'

What the bloody hell was Morwenna suggesting? Kitty wasn't ready for the games that Will Nance, or whoever the spirit was, wanted to play.

Kitty sniggered. Chess anyone? She was getting hysterical and her mind was conjuring up all sorts of strange things. Then silence. Morwenna had finally stopped humming and chanting. Even the creaking floorboards appeared to be resting.

'Are you OK, Kitty?' Morwenna's voice sounded as though she'd somehow made it to the other side of the room.

'Sorry, but I need to pee.' It was now or never. Kitty pushed herself up off the bed, her legs feeling like dead weights. She recollected the same feeling when she'd first practiced some skiing exercises, before she and Ben had set off on their first holiday together. She racked her brain for the name of the resort.

It was in France, she remembered that. Les Deux something? For god's sake what did it matter, why was she thinking about skiing holidays?

Kitty fumbled for the bathroom's door latch. There, she'd made it, and as she stepped forward, the lights finally came on. She heard a loud cheer from Lizzie downstairs, and then a shriek from the spare bedroom at the same time.

The last thing she recalled as she lay on the floor in the bathroom, was a warm feeling between her legs and an overwhelming sense of relief. Then someone must have blown the lights again, as everything was plunged into darkness.

XXVII

1916

Loveday woke shivering, wondering why she was so cold, and then remembered where she was. The December sun was slowly beginning to rise but it would give off no heat at this time of year. Still, at least it wasn't raining. She sat up and stretched. Every bone and muscle was stiff and aching, and the thin velvet jacket Gribble had loaned her for the night, had gone, as had Gribble.

She was out on the moors alone.

Quickly, she stood up and almost fell into the embers of the fire that a few hours previously had been a welcoming roar. She scuffed her feet around the edges to smother the embers and picked up the basket. She peered inside. Surprisingly, Gribble had generously left her some cheese and an apple.

How long had she been lying asleep alone in the middle of the moor? The thought made her stomach turn, and now she had to find her way back home to Trunrowan and face the music.

What would she say to Will? He was going to be so angry she daren't even contemplate what mood he would be in.

His mood… By now he'd have gone almost two days without any potion in his tea. She prayed it wouldn't make that much difference. The best thing she could do right now was to find her way back and quickly.

Scanning the horizon and trying to get her bearings, Loveday recognised a small mound in the distance and instinctively set off towards it. Perhaps she should listen to her instincts more, but right now she had a bad feeling in the pit of her stomach, which told her all was not well at home. She was sure she was going to be in for a right telling off.

Will had put in a good day's graft at Bramble Farm. George Weaver was a good sort. Ever since the 'incident' in the village, when Will had made a right fool of himself, George had seemed to take pity on him and taken him under his wing. He didn't have a lot to say conversational wise, but he made sure any work that was available on the farm was put Will's way, and for that he was more than grateful. He certainly didn't make a song and dance about the fact that he only had one good arm. He'd adapted well physically, ensuring that he gave everything a go, and there were few things he couldn't manage. The thing he did still struggle with were the thoughts in his head. Although he'd felt a lot better of late, less anxious and irritable, on occasions he felt as though he was living on a knife-edge.

The slightest noise would send him into a panic. The drink didn't help; he'd worked that one out for himself. He was getting better at staying clear of the rough cider and today he'd put in a good day's graft. He'd stop off in The Ferryboat Inn for a swift half on his way home. Loveday had seemed much better that morning after the previous night's escapades, so he was sure she wouldn't mind.

By the time he walked into the pub, he'd practically convinced himself he'd even earned more than a half.

Mabel walked up the garden path, shooing the hens away as they gathered around her legs, pecking at her skirt. 'Ye hungry?' she said, looking around and noticing there were very few scraps on the ground. In fact, there was very little sign of anything. Normally, at this time of the year, there would be a welcoming curl of smoke from the chimney, a sure sign that a warm fire was burning inside. But the chimney showed no sign of life. Mabel hoped that Loveday had not taken a turn for the worse. She cussed herself. She really should have come round earlier and not got so involved with helping Daisy put the paper-chain decorations up. Then she remembered seeing Will in the dairy yard. Surely he wouldn't be out working if Loveday was still unwell?

'Loveday, ye in?' Mabel pushed open the back door and stepped into the kitchen. 'Ellooo...'

Mabel made her way to the bottom of the cottage's stone stairs and called a little louder this time. Nothing. No sound whatsoever. She noted the fire in the living room had almost gone out, so added some kindle, stoking it for a few minutes. Where on earth was she? Given the state of the fire, she must've been out all day, which was unusual. She had better check upstairs to make sure she'd not passed out or something worse had happened, but she sensed she wouldn't find her there. If her instincts were right, she'd have to go and find Will immediately. For all she knew she may have been taken ill elsewhere. Hopefully he would still be up at the farm.

'Daisy, 'ave ye seen Loveday, or for that matter, 'ave ye seen Will?' Mabel threw her basket over the back of a chair and unraveled the long scarf from her neck. Daisy was up to her eyes peeling tiddies and by the look of things, thoroughly enjoying herself.

Mabel had never understood women who actually enjoyed spending hours in the kitchen, cooking and baking – she'd much rather be outside working up an appetite. That wasn't to say that Daisy didn't spend a lot of time outside, after all she delivered the post for the village every day, but she was certainly much more at home in the kitchen than Mabel ever would be.

Her ma had once said, 'God 'elp yer future 'usband, everyone 'ere knows ye can't even peel a tiddy!' And it was true.

'No. I thought ye'd gone down to see 'er? She must be feeling better then, if she's not there.' Daisy put down the last tiddy and wiped her hands on her apron.

'Do ye think them tiddies will be enough? Pa has invited the farm'ands in for dinner.'

Mabel glanced at the pile on the draining board and nodded. Enough to feed a small army she thought to herself.

'She's not there and the fire was almost out, so am guessing she be gone for a while. 'As Will left the farm yet?'

'Yes, 'e left just before three o'clock.' Daisy replied.

'It's blooming cold out there. That wind is blowing off the top of the 'eadland like it means business. Think we might be in for a bad snap of weather this Christmas.' Mabel flopped into their ma's armchair and kicked off her boots.

'Wouldn't it be wonderful if it snowed? I can't remember the last time I saw any.'

Mabel laughed. 'Ye don't want much then. It never snows in Trunrowan, ye knows that. Ye needs to go into Truro to see snow.'

'Where do ye think she is then?' Daisy said, still at the kitchen sink now shredding cabbage.

'I 'ave no idea, but I need to find Will and tell 'im just in case we needs to send out a search party. If it gets any colder, she be in trouble.'

'Then what are we waiting for?' Daisy exclaimed. 'Dinner will 'ave to keep. I'll ride into the village and ask around. Ye let pa know what's 'appening and ask 'im whether Will mentioned if 'e was going straight back 'ome.' Daisy snatched the mug back from Mabel's hands, which had only just warmed up. Within minutes the tiddies and cabbage had been put into a pan of cold water and Mabel was once again wrapping the scarf around her neck.

*

'I'm telling ye, the last I saw of 'im was about an 'our ago. 'E'd finished up 'ere for the day and I said I'd see 'im back 'ere in the morning. 'E 'eaded off down the lane, so I presume 'e was going 'ome.' George Weaver was trying his best to push the last stubborn cow through the gate.

'Come on then, don't just stand there watching.'

Finally, with Daisy's help, the cow sauntered off, lifting her tail and letting them both know exactly what she thought of them.

'She's a bugger that 'un. Always the last one in and out.'

Daisy nudged her pa and laughed. 'Ye loves 'er really. Stubborn, just like ye.'

'Aye, well, sometimes there's one who just needles ye. Like kids they are. Always one who's bleddy trouble.'

This time it was Daisy's turn to have her ribs nudged and she squealed like one of the pigs in the yard; she'd always been ticklish. Bidding her pa farewell, she jumped on Betsy her trusty bike and made her way into the village. She knew Will wasn't at home and so her best guess was he'd taken himself off to the pub. Within minutes she was resting Betsy against the wall of The Ferryboat Inn, just as Mabel came running around the corner, panting.

''E's in the pub!' she exclaimed, holding her sides while bending over, trying to catch her breath.

'I guessed that,' Daisy said, looking concerned.

'Mary Wiggins said she'd seen 'im walking down about an 'our or so ago. Whistling 'e was, seemed cheery, so I'm 'oping Loveday's in there with 'im.'

'Or 'e don't know that she's not at 'ome and ain't got a clue what's going on,' Daisy added, pushing open the heavy door of the pub. She looked around for Will but couldn't see him.

Mabel followed Daisy in and they made straight for the snug bar.

'Wasson, Daisy? What ye doing in 'ere?' Will said, putting his hand of playing cards down onto the table and picking up his glass. 'Cheers.'

Daisy didn't like what she was seeing. Will was lathered. Not to the extent of falling over, although it was difficult to say for sure while he was sat down, but he was well on his way. He was going to be little to no use with helping them find Loveday.

''Ave ye seen Loveday?'

'Eh? She's at 'ome, ain't she?' Will turned his back and picked up his playing cards.

'No, she's not.' Mabel said, squeezing herself between two bar stools until she was standing in front of Will with her hands on her hips. She took a deep breath in and Daisy watched her sister grow at least two inches.

'Ye needs to go there now. She ain't there and we don't know where she be.'

There, she'd said it.

Daisy studied Will's face. At first, he appeared to be deep in thought, then slowly his face turned red as though he was holding his breath. Finally, he stood up and banged his fist on the table. Mabel stood her ground.

'And what gives ye the right to come in 'ere and meddle, eh? While I'm 'aving a quiet pint and a game of cards with me mate?' Will's face was turning from red to a deep shade of purple. He resumed banging his fist on the table. His pint glass and the playing cards were soon on the floor.

'Eh there, Will, calm it down, mate. They's only concerned. Perhaps summut's up?' Bobbie Trevelyan, who was sat opposite Will, said with a hint of annoyance.

'And ye can keep yer bleddy nose out of this in all,' Will retaliated, pushing the small card table over.

Daisy had already started to inch backwards out of the snug, gesturing to Mabel, who annoyingly seemed intent on standing her ground. As stubborn as that bleddy cow earlier, she thought. This wasn't going quite the way she had hoped. The whole scene reminded her of the incident outside Granby's shop when Will had been lathered and brawling. She wished her pa was here now. Perhaps if she hurried, she could go and get him…

'Sit yerself down and listen to me. Ye don't scare me, Will Nance. Loveday is missing. Yes, that's right. She ain't at 'ome and no one knows where she is. Now, I don't care whether I've disturbed yer little game of cards and drinking session. I just wants me friend back 'ome safe. She ain't been well, ye knows that. So, if ye is really a man and cares about 'er…ye'd best clear up 'ere and start looking for 'er.'

For a few seconds there was silence. Daisy could have heard a pin drop she was sure. Then came a small guttural howling. At first, she couldn't quite make out where it was coming from, although she knew it was in the room. Gradually it became louder, like the painful cry of an animal in distress, and she eventually realised it was coming from Will who was now rolled up in a ball on the floor, rocking back and forth.

'Oh god, Mabel, what 'ave we done?' Daisy shouted across the noise.

'We ain't done naught. If 'e can't be 'elping us, then I knows pa and the farm'ands will.'

Mabel was still looking ten feet tall. Daisy had never seen her so commanding.

'Bobbie, are ye alrite looking after Will while we tries an find Loveday?' Mabel asked Bobbie Trevelyan, although it was more of an order than an ask.

Bobbie nodded, the look of fear on his face was making Daisy nervous. She hesitated at the door, watching Will still rocking back and forth. It felt wrong to leave him, but time was not on their side. They had to find Loveday before nightfall. Will's issues would have to wait.

*

Will hadn't been in The Ferryboat Inn for a long while, but it was still the same. Smelt of baccy and spilt ale and the same old faces propped up the bar and graced the seats. Jago the landlord seemed surprised but pleased to see him and before he'd even got to the bar there was a pint waiting for him. It felt good to be back. He would have the one pint, two at a push and be home in time for dinner. No harm done; except he hadn't counted on Bobbie Trevelyan being in there. He and Bobbie had worked on the luggers and the drifter boats together, years back. Bobbie's family came from a long line of fishermen. They worked hard and played hard, and both of them were fond of a drink or two. At sea it was just you, your crew mates and the fish, and the fish weren't much company. After the storm of 1905, Bobbie threw in his nets and took up with the boatyard further down the coast. The Trevelyans had lost so many men in the storm, much as he wanted to go back out to sea, he couldn't put his family through the worry again. It had seemed the right thing to do at the time, but Will knew he wasn't happy. He'd started drinking heavily and spent more and more of his time back in Trunrowan in The Ferryboat Inn, so his family never saw him anyhow. Will had gone off to war and they'd drifted apart. Bobbie hadn't passed his medical on account of being deaf in one ear. At least his family had that saving grace.

The only thing Will did miss about the army, was the camaraderie, so it was good to see Bobbie's cheerful round face and bushy black beard once again. Before he knew it, they had set up home in the snug and despite him only having one hand, they were playing cards just like the good old days. One pint became two, then three, and at that point Will genuinely did think of going home. For a very brief moment. Then another pint appeared in front of him and all rationale went out the window. He convinced himself he'd be fine; nothing a good brisk walk in the fresh air wouldn't cure on his way back home.

By the time Mabel and Daisy turned up, he wasn't really sure what was going on. The hearts and diamonds on the cards were merging into one big red blob, which reminded him of bloodshed every time he dealt a hand. And all the shouting was making his head spin, what with talk about Loveday having gone missing, it was making him feel queer, as though his head and body didn't belong to one another. He'd felt like this before, on the battlefield. He'd been watching himself from above no man's land, detached, hovering, lying in the mire of mud, blood pumping from his arm. Only his arm wasn't part of him. His arm was five foot away from his body and try as he might…there was no way he could reach it.

Then he blacked out. When he eventually came too, his head and face were stinging from the bucket of ice-cold water Bobbie had thrown over him.

'Jesus, Will! Ye gave me a fright then, man! Must 'ave 'ad a dodgy pint or summut.'

Will was doing his best to cough up the water he'd inhaled, while poor Bobbie was looking down on him with concern.

'Best get ye 'ome before ye does any more damage.' Bobbie said, putting his arm under Will's good one. He heaved, trying to steady him. His legs were wobbling like jelly.

'Where's Loveday?'

'Don't ye worry about 'er – the maids 'ave gone out looking for 'er with George Weaver and some of the farm'ands.'

Will groaned. That was the last thing he needed, to be in George Weaver's bad books again.

'They'll 'ave found 'er already. Mark my words. Now come on, let's be 'aving you.'

It must have taken them a good half hour to walk a route that normally would take five minutes. Will's legs were still shaking uncontrollably. Each time he placed a foot on the ground, his leg jerked back up. In between trying to master walking, like a nine-month-old cheel, he had to keep stopping to be sick. Perhaps there had been something wrong with the ale like Bobbie suggested. By the time they were walking up the path to Rowan

Cottage, Will was just about able to walk unaided, even though Bobbie insisted on seeing him to the door. The lights were on and he could see a figure at the kitchen window. Loveday must be back. He breathed a sigh of relief.

'Blimey, ye took yer time. I'm frantic 'ere waiting for news. Loveday's still not back. Pa and the boys 'ave gone up over the 'eadland to make sure there ain't been a cliff slide or naught.' Daisy handed Will a blanket and thanked Bobbie.

So, Loveday wasn't home. The figure had been Daisy.

'She left a note saying she'd gone to get some medicinals, but we 'as checked with Mr Penrose at the chemist earlier... Apparently she never showed up.' Daisy shoved a mug of steaming tea in his hand, which tasted as though she'd put in half a bag of sugar. He hoped that she hadn't used the stash that Loveday had been saving for Christmas, or there would be trouble.

'Do ye have any idea where she could be, Will? Ye were the last person to see 'er after all. Think 'ard. What was the last thing she said to ye?'

Will pulled up a chair to the table and wrapped the blanket around his shoulders. His head was still feeling fuzzy but at least his legs had settled down. He tried to recall earlier that morning in the bedroom. Loveday had seemed much better. She was chatty and had told him not to fuss. She'd been insistent on making him a cup of tea, but apart from that there was nothing out of the ordinary.

'It was a normal morning; I did give 'er a kiss under the mistletoe I found at the end of the bed. Apparently Mabel had left it there. But naught else. She said she were feeling better.'

Daisy pulled a face.

'I don't know naught about the mistletoe, ye'd have to ask Mabel about that. We're just going to 'ave to sit tight.'

There was no way he was going to sit in the kitchen drinking tea when other men were out looking for his Loveday, plus he had a nagging feeling that he'd done something wrong. Maybe she'd been looking for him and saw him in the pub with Bobbie and had gone off in a huff. Perhaps, and he couldn't bring himself to think that she would, perhaps she'd left him, had enough of him and his moods. What he did know though was it was no good waiting for her to come home. If indeed she was going to. He had to do something.

Lighting a lantern he headed for the back door.

'And where do ye think ye be going then?' Daisy asked calmly, hovering.

'Get out me way, Daisy. I needs to find 'er.' He really didn't want to have to push past her, but if she was going to stand in his way, then he'd have no other option. No one was going to stop him looking. He had to know for himself if she'd decided to leave him, and if she had, well, he would deal with the consequences then.

Daisy stepped aside, realising it was pointless trying to get in his way.

'Be careful, Will. This ain't the time for 'eroics. Like I said, pa and the farm'ands 'ave gone up yonder, why don't ye try the cove and the edge of the wood?'

Will sidled past and nodded. 'Thanks, Daisy. Pray we find 'er, eh?'

Within minutes he was walking along the cove towards the wood, placating himself with the fact that Loveday had seemed okay with him that morning, and if she'd indeed seen him in The Ferryboat Inn earlier…surely it wasn't enough to make her leave him?

By the time dusk had hit Trunrowan, most of the village was out looking for Loveday. The woods had been searched the best they could, the shoreline walked by many. The fields up yonder had been gone through with a fine-tooth comb, even one of the fishing boats that was preparing to go out later with the crab pots offered to scour the cove. The tide was on its way in, so if Loveday had somehow got into trouble and drowned, it was likely she would be washed ashore. Will had joined up with George Weaver and the farmhands and although nothing was said, he knew he wasn't in anyone's good books. Some of the women of the village had congregated by the slipway and were handing out mugs of tea to keep the men going. Mabel made sure that Daisy was kept informed of what was happening by showing her face at Rowan Cottage every now and then, but everyone agreed, including Daisy, that it was best she stayed there just in case Loveday should return home.

'I think we is going to 'ave to call it a night,' George Weaver said, wearily sitting down on the wall near the slipway. He took off his cap, running his forearm across his brow.

'It's way too dark now to do anything meaningful. That Cold Moon ain't coming out from behind them storm clouds for love nor money. If we all goes back 'ome and gets a good night's sleep, we can be up at the crack of dawn and start over again.'

Mabel handed her pa a mug of tea and watched him take a small silver hipflask from his coat pocket and empty it into the mug. She'd never seen him with a hipflask before. Maybe he'd been at ma's Christmas brandy?

'Ye all 'ead off – I'm going to keep searching,' Will said.

'Don't be daft, man… With only one lantern? Go and get some shut-eye. I'm sure she'll be back 'ome by the morning,' one of the farmhands said curtly.

'E's right, Will. I'd put me life on it that she'll 'ave got all consumed by some new berry or plant up on the 'eadland and forgot the time. Get yerself 'ome. I'm sure our Daisy will make ye summut to eat,' Mabel said, feeling pretty hungry herself after all the commotion of the past few hours.

Reluctantly, Will nodded and accepted defeat. He hoped that Mabel was right. She knew Loveday well enough, probably even better than he did. He figured that if she knew Loveday was going to leave him she wouldn't be coordinating the search. He'd get himself off home, eat something and put his head down. It was still hurting like hell from the ale he'd downed earlier.

Loveday had somehow managed to find her way home, which in itself was nothing short of a miracle. She was normally hopeless with directions but she could now see Trunrowan in the distance. It had been a pleasant walk and was a beautiful morning, the sun was low but bright, searching out all the cobwebs in the hedges that had been spun overnight, highlighting dewdrops which glistened as though left behind by the spiders to entice flies into their lairs. Nature was a wonderful thing.

God, she was hungry. All she'd had to eat over the past day was what Mrs Cromp had packed for her and Gribble, and that hadn't lasted long. The piece of cheese and apple she'd eaten earlier hadn't touched the sides. She'd picked a handful of wood sorrel which had quenched her thirst with its sharp and sour lemony tang but had set her stomach gurgling wanting more. The sooner she got back home the better. She was cold, thirsty and hungry and she desperately needed the warmth of her bed.

But first, she would have to face the music.

It must've been around ten o'clock by the time she walked out of the wood and into the cove. She could hear the hens clucking as she got nearer to the cottage, no doubt they were hungry too. She didn't envisage Will would have thought of feeding them, regardless of the noise they were making. As she walked up the garden path, she literally had to fight them off, realising they'd probably not been put to bed in the shed last night. Poor mites, it was a miracle they'd not been taken by a fox. She wondered whether Gribble Gummo's fox had to fend for himself. She doubted it. She was pretty sure she now knew *exactly* where the word *sly fox* came from. Thank god he'd not gone to the standing stones with them. She shuddered at the thought.

'Oh, Loveday! There ye be. We's been so worried! Where

the 'ell 'ave you been?' Daisy said, suddenly appearing at the back door. She flung her arms open, ready to embrace her.

'We've 'ad the whole village out looking for ye. They's started out again this morning already. My, you're cold. Where 'ave ye been?' she asked again.

'Come in and warm yerself up in front of the fire. I's been 'ere all night keeping it going. Thank the lord ye is back safe and sound. Ye 'ad us all worried to death.'

Loveday knelt down in front of the fire, rubbing her hands together. 'Where's Will?'

'E's up to bed. I thought 'e might 'ave got up early to go out with the others but...' She hesitated.

'Look, I might as well tell ye, ye's sure to 'ear it from someone. 'E had a skinful in the pub last night and then 'ad one of 'is funny turns. Pretty bad it was. 'E's probably sleeping it off. Best leave 'im be if I was ye.'

Loveday groaned. So, the few days without the potion *had* made a difference. She needed to make sure he started taking it again as soon as possible. There was no goodwill left in the village when it came to Will and his drinking, let alone his funny turns on top. She'd warm up first and then take him up a cuppa.

'If ye don't mind, I think I'd best go and let the others know ye 'as returned?' Daisy said gently. 'Pa will need to get back to the farm. I bet he's left Mabel and ma to see to the cows this morning. Ma won't be best pleased.'

'I'm so sorry, Daisy, that I've put everyone through all of this. I really didn't realise what the time was and ended up sleeping in the wood. Thought it was safer than trying to find my way back in the dark. Will ye pass on me thanks to yer ma and pa? It was totally selfish and stupid of me. I realises that now,' Loveday said sheepishly.

'It don't bother me, I'm just glad ye is back safe. But ye might need to do a bit of explaining to Will. Frantic 'e was last night. Convinced you'd left 'im.'

'Don't worry, I'll put things right. Ye get back to the farm. I'll catch up with ye later.' Loveday kissed Daisy on the cheek before seeing her out and smiled, watching her walk down the garden path, trying to dodge the hens – which reminded her, she needed to find them some scraps before they started pecking one another to death. Daisy turned and waved, and Loveday shut the back door firmly, pulling the curtain across.

Thank god she was home safe. There was no way she would be able to tell anyone what had happened last night. Not even Mabel. She'd have to keep the secret to herself. Instinctively, she placed both her hands on her stomach, and rested them for a few seconds. She had never wanted anything more than for the ritual she'd performed at the standing stones to come right. She'd have to wait and see whether her next bleed came. Thinking of it, she was pretty sure she was due one around now. She was normally as regular as clockwork, but with everything going on of late she'd lost track of time. She remembered what Dr Blake had said the other evening, about her maybe being with a cheel, but it was more likely to be her time of the month. She often felt out of sorts before her bleed. Anyhow, enough nonsense, she needed to make Will's tea. While she waited for the water to boil, she took out a mug and felt at the back of the cupboard for the blue glass vial. Strange, she couldn't feel anything. She stood on tiptoe but still couldn't see, so dragged one of the kitchen chairs across and stood on it. Nothing. All she could see was dust. A wave of panic washed over her as she steadied herself, holding onto the top of the chair. She'd best get down before she fell, she didn't want a repeat of the other night. Where the hell was it? Without it Will was sure to get worse and she couldn't think about the consequences of that happening right now. There was no way she would get away with returning to Mrs Cromp's and asking for more. She'd only just arrived back home. It had to be here somewhere.

Frantically, Loveday opened all the cupboards, thinking she must have put it back in a different one without realising. Perhaps

Will had moved it? Or even Daisy when she was waiting for her to return and no doubt making copious amounts of tea. But surely, if one of them had found it they would have questioned what it was and left it out for her? Where the bleddy hell was it?

Just as Loveday was beginning to physically shake at the thought of never finding the potion, a flash of blue caught her eye from the cupboard under the sink. Moving cloths and a can of Brasso, there stood the blue glass vial. Carefully, she picked it up and felt the liquid swish about inside. Thank the Lord, it wasn't empty.

Removing the pipette stopper, she sniffed it just to make sure… The bitter smell of burnt almonds filled her nostrils and, with a sigh of relief, she set to making Will's tea. Collecting her secret stash of sugar from the pantry, she added two large teaspoons and stirred.

Drawing up some liquid from the bottle with the pipette, she remembered Mrs Cromp's instructions; one drop every day and one drop only. Will had been without any for potentially three days if she took into consideration her being ill…so she would add those too. Carefully, she released four drops of the brown liquid into the mug and stirred for a good minute. Dipping her little finger into the hot liquid, she dabbed it on her tongue. Perfect, she couldn't taste a thing apart from the sugar. Preparing for a proper telling off about her absconding, she climbed the stone stairs of the cottage and tiptoed into their bedroom.

Will was still sleeping, his nostrils flaring each time he breathed out. It was a shame to wake him. He looked so peaceful lying there, his face devoid of any stress or worry. Loveday was tempted to get into bed with him, if only to warm herself up. Instead she sat on the edge of the cast iron bed which let out a little creak, and gently shook Will's shoulder.

'Morning.'

Will stirred and slowly opened his eyes, rubbed them, then

sat bolt up, almost knocking the mug of tea over that Loveday was holding in her hands.

'Jesus maid! Ye frightened me to death.'

Loveday smiled weakly.

'Where the bleddy 'ell 'ave ye been? The whole darn village 'as been out looking for ye.' Will wasn't happy.

'Tea?' Loveday pushed the mug towards him, impatient for him to drink it. Thankfully he took it. 'I know, I'm so sorry. I lost track of time and it was getting dark and I didn't want to walk back through the woods. I thought it was sensible to stay put. But I'm 'ere now.' She batted her eyelashes at him and saw his face soften.

'Me 'ead's 'urting, so yer lucky I can't be bothered to argue with ye. Truth be told, I thought ye might 'ave left me.' Will's voice became softer and he patted the bed, indicating for Loveday to join him.

'What, leave ye, William Nance? Ye be joking!' Loveday laughed and began undressing.

'Let me finish me tea up and then I can warm ye up. Proper job.'

Will took a few large gulps and the mug was soon empty. Loveday finally relaxed and climbed under the sheets. Having spent a night out on the moor in the cold on hard damp ground, she told herself she would be forever grateful she had a soft warm bed to sleep in. At least she would never have to lie next to Gribble Gummo again.

She felt Will's large rough hand touch her breasts and giggled. Maybe today wasn't going to be so bad after all.

XXVIII

Present day

Lizzie waved at Ben as he hurried off down the garden path carrying Kitty's maternity bag. The ambulance had taken a mere fifteen minutes to arrive after she'd made the 999 call. Apparently, the crew were eating sandwiches in a lay-by on the coastal road, just outside of Trunrowan when the call came through. From the minute they arrived they calmly took control. Kitty's finger was jabbed which showed her blood sugar was low, as was her blood pressure, no doubt from all the recent vomiting. The older paramedic of the two decided that Kitty's waters had broken and she'd not peed herself like she kept apologising for. The stomach cramps were confirmed as definite contractions and not stress-related. Ben was fussing like an old woman and Lizzie really didn't understand how he'd ever become a dentist.

Finally closing the door of the cottage, Lizzie collapsed on the sofa. Morwenna, who had carried on chanting and wafting upstairs while Kitty was being seen to by the paramedics, had now made herself comfortable in one of the armchairs and it was obvious she wanted to talk.

'Do you have time for a cuppa, Morwenna? Or maybe something stronger? I can see what's in the fridge...' Lizzie got up and opened the fridge door, thinking she could die for something alcoholic right now. Morning drinking wasn't normally her thing, but she reckoned she'd earned at least a small glass.

'Tea is fine, thank ye, but ye go ahead. Not every day ye happen to witness what ye have,' Morwenna replied all Zen-like.

'Well, if you don't mind, I'm going to have a glass of wine. I'm really not sure what you were doing upstairs, but I'm guessing the electrics going off wasn't part of a theatrical stunt?'

'Absolutely not!' Morwenna sounded horrified at the suggestion. 'Things like that often happen when there are restless spirits around. They tinker, ye know, meddle with things.'

Lizzie handed Morwenna her tea and took a large gulp of wine.

'It's obvious that the spirit of William, or Will as he was known, had suddenly become restless. I think the reason may have been triggered by Kitty's pregnancy, and I will explain why in a moment, but first I ought to fill ye in on some background.'

Morwenna shuffled, lifting her feet and curling them underneath her bottom. Lizzie noticed her feet were bare and wondered at what point she had taken her shoes off. She must be freezing.

'I come from a long family line of folk who have lived in and around Trunrowan for almost two hundred years. Let's say, shall we, that we have a gift. Some have the gift of sight; some have other types of gifts. Mine happens to be that of mediumship, where I can feel, see, hear or talk to spirits on the other side. Or in Will's case, those who have not passed over properly and have been left in limbo. For whatever reason.'

Lizzie listened attentively. Finally, she was going to get some answers about Creek Cottage, or Rowan Cottage, whatever it was called, and find out once and for all what had happened all those years ago.

'My great grandmother was called Myrtle Cromp. She knew Will's wife, Loveday, who as it happens, also came from a family of cunning folk.'

Lizzie nodded, even if she didn't fully understand, 'We came across the names, Will and Loveday Nance when we were researching the history of the cottage in Truro library.'

Morwenna reached forwards and seemingly absently picked up Lizzie's glass of wine and took a large mouthful.

'Apparently, and this is only what has been passed down from one person to another you understand, so we cannot be one hundred percent sure how accurate it is…but Loveday sought the help of my great gran Myrtle, to help her conceive.'

Lizzie thought what a captivating storyteller Morwenna was, with her soft Cornish voice.

'Now, as I've already mentioned, it could all be hearsay, tales that have been made up or contorted throughout the years, but what we do know to be fact, is that Will went off to war.'

'World War One.' Lizzie said matter of factly.

'Yes, or the Great War as it was sometimes called.' Morwenna said, continuing to drink Lizzie's wine. 'I'm sure there is plenty of information held within the military records about his war history. I would imagine that the king's shilling Kitty found was indeed Will's. A keepsake as such. Although most men spent it in the pub before they went off to war. So…the story goes, he came back from war with what we now know to be PTSD, or as it was known in those days, shell shock and Loveday also sought help from my great gran Myrtle to help with Will's black moods.'

Morwenna nodded towards the glass she'd drained.

'I think I might like a small glass now, if that's alright with ye?'

'Of course.' Lizzie got up and smiled to herself. Didn't she realise she'd just drank hers? The poor woman must have needed it. She still couldn't quite believe everything that unfolded. Taking the bottle of Sauvignon Blanc out of the fridge and collecting a fresh glass from the kitchen dresser, she handed Morwenna the bottle and sat back down eager to listen to the rest of the tale.

'And that was why he hanged himself?' Lizzie offered.

'Most likely yes. What is very sad, and unbeknown to him at the time, was that Loveday was actually carrying their child. When she arrived back here at Rowan Cottage to tell Will the long awaited news, she found him hanging from a meat hook in the kitchen ceiling.' Morwenna gestured with her head in the direction of the kitchen.

Lizzie shivered at the thought of a body once hanging there. 'Oh my god! So Kitty had been picking up on his presence because she's pregnant?'

'Highly likely he was trying to protect her in some way, make amends so to speak, and confusing her with Loveday because she is living, in what he believes, sorry, *believed*, to still be his cottage. There can often be problems with passing over when death has been sudden and traumatic.' Morwenna yawned, and Lizzie thought how much older she suddenly appeared.

'Rowan Cottage, that was?' Lizzie was finally beginning to piece everything together.

'Yes, the name was only changed to Creek Cottage recently as a marketing ploy by the estate agents – the cottage had lain empty for so long.'

'So, is Will's spirit still here?' Lizzie asked tentatively.

'No, he has passed over now, with my help, and the cottage has been cleansed of any residual negative energy. Hopefully, he will now find peace on the other side and finally be reunited with Loveday.'

'And what about the child of his that he never knew? He won't come back again when Kitty returns home with her baby, will he?' Lizzie couldn't bear the thought of having to go through all of this again.

'No, my dear. I have made sure that he understands. He would not have passed over if he didn't. What do ye think I was doing for so long up there while ye were all seeing to Kitty?' Morwenna chuckled.

'So, what happened to their child?'

'The baby girl was born healthy and named Lamorna. She lived to the ripe old age of ninety. After she died, the cottage was put up for sale. She lived here alone, as a spinster for most of her life. Never married, never had any children and stated that the proceeds from the sale of Rowan Cottage went to the Lost Gardens of Heligan. She was a famous botanist ye know.'

Lizzie could tell that Morwenna was thoroughly enjoying relaying everything to her, almost as much as the wine.

'That is so strange. Kitty is doing a degree in herbal medicine. There are so many threads and connections, it's quite remarkable. I can't wait to tell her.'

'Life is indeed strange at times, but I think my job here is done.' Morwenna uncurled her feet and stretched her legs.

'Thank you so much, Morwenna. You have literally been a god send... Ah! You need paying, don't you? Let me get my purse. Hopefully I will have some cash in it!'

'Just this once, I'll waiver my fee. Instead ye can pass me some silver. It's been a pleasure, in a strange sort of way. Ye be sure to let me know how Kitty and the baby are doing, won't ye? I'm guessing it's a girl...but don't quote me on that.'

Lizzie pulled a face. Silver? Surely, she couldn't be serious. Wasn't that what gypsies asked for when they read palms?

'Anything will do, ten pence, fifty pence.' Morwenna was holding out her hand. Lizzie managed to find a fifty pence piece in her side pocket – it was the one with a picture of Kew Gardens on. She'd been meaning to add it to her collection but decided that Morwenna had more than earned it.

'Ye won't forget to let me know, will ye?'

'No, of course not. As soon as I hear any news, I will ring

you.' Lizzie instinctively moved forward, feeling an urge to give Morwenna a hug. Morwenna blushed and hugged Lizzie back. Somewhere between the awkwardness was a strange sense of connection. It had been the most surreal day.

No sooner had Morwenna left, Lizzie's mobile rang.

'Hello?'

The line was crackly, and Lizzie could barely hear anything other than a muffled voice. Bloody cottage and its two feet thick walls. She went outside and the line cleared.

'Hello, is that you, Ben?'

'Lizzie, can you hear me? It's Ben. We have a baby girl! I can't believe it. Kitty was amazing, only had gas and air, it was all so quick, we barely got here in time, oh, and the paramedics were amazing and she has jet black hair, don't know where she's got that from, and Kitty was amazing, or have I already said that?'

'Ben, slow down. Wowzers! Congratulations. I'm so happy for you both. Does she have a name yet? How heavy is she?' Lizzie was almost as excited as Ben.

'Eight pounds and four ounces, and she is sooo long. Lizzie... can you hear me? You're breaking up again...'

'Just about, Ben. Does she have a name?'

'Yes... We are going to call her Loveday. Kitty thought it rather fitting and well, after all...it's a Cornish name.'

Lizzie smiled. She would've expected nothing less from Kitty. Then the line finally went dead. Morwenna would certainly be happy to hear she was right about the sex of the baby, and the name couldn't be more perfect.

XXIX

1916

Christmas was always a wonderful affair in Trunrowan, despite the fact the war was still hanging over them. The USA had declared war on Austria and Hungary, and people were saying that the Russians and Germans were about to suspend all hostilities on the eastern front but, to most, it was a long way away from the relatively sleepy coastal village.

Christmas Eve was always spent at Bramble Farm as was tradition, only this year Will had taken to his bed, proffering that he was unwell, and Loveday secretly thought it was the best place for him. There would be plenty of ale and cider on hand at the farm and he was best kept away from it. George Weaver had thankfully not mentioned the incident when Loveday had gone missing, and was still giving Will regular work, but things weren't the same any more. Instead of coming back from the farm in good spirits, tired from a good day's hard graft, Will was sullen and uncommunicative, each day descending further into a cloud of darkness. But at least he wasn't raging or having his funny turns, thanks to the daily potion. Loveday had managed to slip away and visit Mrs Cromp's to ask for some more, but only after she'd presented her with a small hock of ham in way of a Christmas gift. She'd told Mrs Cromp that their cat George had knocked the vial over; luckily there were no further questions.

When Christmas Day finally arrived, it was just the two of them, although Will was no company whatsoever. In the end, Loveday gave up trying to jolly him along and let him sup himself to sleep, at least then she didn't have to tiptoe around him. These days even the slightest noise made him jittery. She'd accidentally tripped over his boots he'd left by the back door one evening, knocking over a chair as she did so. You would've thought that the cottage had been bombed by Will's reaction. It took her at least half an hour to stop him from shaking. She was beside herself with worry and had almost called out Dr Blake, perish the thought. It was a shame that there was no one else in the village that had been to war that he could talk to, but all the men that had gone, and there weren't actually that many from the village, were still out there fighting. God bless them. She daren't think of the state they would come back in, if they were lucky enough to come back at all.

Loveday was now having to add the potion to his ale over the festive period as he wasn't drinking any tea but, on the plus side, at least she didn't have to use her sugar stash up. And, on top of all the worry, she wasn't feeling all that great herself. She'd had to slaughter a hen for Christmas dinner, which had set her off crying, and then when she cooked it and laid the table with all the trimmings, she couldn't face eating any of it because she felt sick. They were turning into a right old pair. She'd be glad when the year was over in the hope that 1917 would be a better one.

1917

January was almost over. Strangely, it was Loveday's favourite month. She loved the stillness of everything. The anticipation of knowing greater things were to come. Yes, it was cold and frosty, yes, it could be wet and stormy, but there was something wonderful about snuggling up in front of a warm crackling fire and not having to tend to the garden, or the vegetable patch. Life could stand still, for a brief moment, before slowly gathering momentum and pushing up new shoots as a new cycle began. The war had changed things though. Even in Trunrowan. It had changed them both and the thought of being holed up in the cottage with Will's unpredictable moods during a spell of bad weather, was too much to contemplate.

Mabel had popped down one day after New Year with a hock of ham, but apart from that, she'd seen no one and kept herself to herself. Even Daisy wasn't around so much these days, now all the Christmas mail had been delivered.

It had been at least one full moon since her last bleed, maybe even two, but apart from the intermittent nausea, which she'd put down to worry, there were no other obvious physical signs of her being with a cheel. She'd not put on any weight, she wasn't tired, and her breasts weren't sore – all signs she'd remembered her ma having when she'd fallen pregnant with little Freddie. Her ma had been at a time that she called her 'change' and had surprisingly fallen pregnant. Sadly, little Freddie didn't survive his first year. Ma had never got over his passing. Loveday could feel her eyes welling up, remembering the day he died from the fever, in Ma's arms, limp as a wet rag he was. So, knowing how her Ma had suffered when she was pregnant with Freddie, surely, she couldn't be? If, by the next full moon, she'd still not had a bleed, she would go and see Mrs Cromp to see what she had to say on the matter. She couldn't bear the thought of going to see Dr Blake and his dirty, podgy hands touching her again.

'What ye doing today then?' Will asked, expertly tying the shoelaces on his boots with his one hand.

'Not sure yet. I might 'elp Rose Trevelyan with some

mending, apparently two of the boats came in yesterday with 'uge 'oles in their nets. Not sure what caused them, but they were down at the 'arbour saying it was a mine. Do ye think that's possible? I mean we's been lucky so far not to 'ave been affected by the war, ain't we?'

As soon as Loveday had said it, she realised how stupid a comment it was. They'd been affected by the war more than anyone around these parts, not forgetting the fact that Will was minus an arm. She could have kicked herself for not thinking before she spoke, but Will seemed unconcerned by her comment.

'Ye ain't going far, is ye?' Will said, all of a sudden seeming perturbed.

'No, I ain't. Like I said, ye can find me down at Breel Cottage if ye needs me. Stop fretting.' Loveday planted a kiss on Will's cheek and ruffled his hair. 'What are ye doing today? Up at the farm?'

'Aye, one of the bulls has escaped over yonder, so we'll be tasking that today. It won't 'ave gone too far if it's got any bleddy sense. Too cold. We'll take some fodder with us and 'e'll be back in no time.'

Will stood up and stamped his feet.

'Read this yesterday, one of the farm'ands picked it up in Truro.' Will thrust the rolled-up newspaper he'd had in his jacket pocket at Loveday. ''Ere.' He pointed to the front of the paper.

Loveday scanned the headline and then read it out loud. '14th January, German destroyer bombards Yarmouth… Oh! My god, Will, so they is coming then? Where is Yarmouth?'

'Up north. Thankfully, a very long way from Trunrowan, it was some days ago but…we still needs to be on our guard. Them 'oles in the netting *could* well 'ave been made by mines,' Will said seriously.

'I'll be sure to mention what ye 'as said to Rose, make sure she warns the men,' Loveday said, opening the back door and following Will outside. There was a heavy mist rolling in from the sea and the cove at the bottom of the garden could hardly be seen.

'Ye take care today. I 'as a bad feeling summut's brewing.' Will said, returning the kiss, lingering a little as their lips touched.

'Go on, ger off will ye.' She laughed. 'It's too bleddy cold to be standing out 'ere getting amorous.'

'Ye knows I loves ye don't ye? Ye wouldn't leave I would ye?'

'Course I do, and no I wouldn't. How many more times do I 'ave to tell ye, silly bugger. What's got into ye today? Go on, off and find yer bull.' Loveday shooed Will off in the direction of Bramble Farm, then made her way into the village and out the other side towards Breel Cottage where the Trevelyans lived. She'd already decided that after spending some time with Rose Trevelyan, tending to the nets, she would pay Mrs Cromp a visit. She would use Will as an excuse. Then she would drop a hint about possibly being with cheel. Maybe, with Mrs Cromp's sixth sense, she would know without the need to examine her. She hoped so. It would certainly help Will take his mind off things and his recent paranoia about her leaving him. It might even put a smile on his face. Despite what Will had mentioned earlier, about today being a bad day, she was feeling quietly positive. Maybe, finally, everything was coming together. The start of a new chapter in their lives.

Will had been handed the heavy length of rope by George Weaver's leading hand and was told to head out to the far field where the bull had last been seen. How he was supposed to catch it on his own, he didn't know, especially with only one arm. But out of stubbornness, he slung the coiled rope over his shoulder stump and trudged over the hard, frosty ground towards the far fields. It felt for some reason as though this was some sort of punishment. A test of some description perhaps? As if he hadn't been punished enough. Yes, life was tough farming. He knew that better than most, but *they* really didn't know how tough life could *really* be. On the battlefield, fighting for King and Country, killing innocent young men, for what? Yes, freedom, but from where he was standing right now, it was a difficult concept to swallow. Trunrowan was as far removed from the effects of war as could be. No one had a bleddy clue what was happening out there. Not that he wished what he'd seen and done on anyone, it was just… he couldn't let go. It was always there, in his head. Waiting to rear its ugliness every now and then, and normally when he was least expecting it. He could deal with the physicality of losing a limb, but his mind? It felt as though it had been lost on no man's land, along with his arm and hand. Now, he was left with a new battle. Not on the fields of the Western Front, but on a patch of land in Cornwall. His battle was invisible. Unheard. And there was no one who could help him fight it. Even when he was sleeping, they came for him. Nightmares of the worst kind, the ones that continued to haunt you even in daylight.

Will had taken refuge under a hawthorn hedge at some point during the morning, although he couldn't remember why or when. He'd paced up and down the field, then had gone over into the next, and the next again, and then back again, still with no sighting of the bull. But at least he felt safe under the hedge because out in the fields he was exposed. There were probably snipers hiding and watching him; it was best if he took cover.

He must have nodded off, even passed out? for when he came to, he was cold and stiff, the heavy rope having chafed the side of his neck. Rubbing it, he felt a sticky substance and on putting his fingers to his mouth, he recognised the unmistakable metallic taste of blood. It was a stark reminder he was alive; blood was still pumping through his veins. Fuelling his heart, his lungs, his brain. For once, in a very long while, everything seemed clear. He knew what he needed to do. Finally, there would be no more worrying and heartache. Soon, he would be at peace.

*

Loveday put the final thread through the net and smiled. A job well done. For once she felt as though she had actually achieved something worthwhile, and Rose Trevelyan was more than grateful.

'Ye, young un, can come again. What a difference another pair of 'ands makes. Can't thank ye enough. Ye'll stay for a drop of something, will ye?' Rose began rolling up the net, her arms as strong as any of the men who skippered the boats. Loveday felt she should be helping her, but Rose wouldn't hear of it.

'Ye 'as done enough as it is. Go inside and our Joe, if he's around, will put a tot of summut in yer tea. Warm yer cockles.' Loveday hesitated and wondered if now was a good time to mention the Yarmouth bombardment and the possibility of mines.

'What's on yer mind? Go on, spit it out.' Rose Trevelyan was no fool.

'Oh, I'm just daydreaming. If ye don't mind, I've got things to be getting on with back 'ome, but thanks for the offer.' Loveday hoped she wouldn't be offended.

'Certainly not like yer old man, are ye?' Mabel replied.

Loveday presumed she was referring to the drink. There was no point acknowledging the comment, it would only start off a conversation that she didn't want to have.

''Ow is he? Joe said there was a bit of a ruckus in The Ferryboat Inn before Christmas?'

Loveday faltered; Rose wasn't going to let her go without getting some sort of an answer.

'And summut was said about ye 'ad gone missing? But I said to our Joe, they must 'ave got that bit wrong. I mean there ain't anywhere to go missing to round these parts...is there?' Rose Trevelyan was staring straight into Loveday's eyes. It was then she realised the real reason she'd been asked to Breel Cottage in the first place, and it had nothing to do with mending the nets.

'I ain't got naught to say to ye on the matter, but I'll tell ye this much...apparently, a German Destroyer bombarded

Yarmouth the other day. Yeah, I knows it's a country mile away, but ye wants to ask yerself this – 'ow did those nets get damaged? I'd put me last penny on the likelihood it were done by mines. So, ye'd best tell your Joe, and anyone else going out, to be extra careful.'

Loveday was cringing. She felt awful saying what she had. It wasn't in her nature to be so vindictive, but she'd had enough of everyone being so harsh on Will. She knew that the Trevelyans had suffered more than their fair share of bad luck over the years, and Rose had lost many sons in the great storm, but none of them had gone to war. None of them could even imagine what her Will had been through, and they didn't have the right to judge neither.

She watched Rose huff, then, with her head down, she walked away from Loveday, half the woman she'd appeared to be only moments earlier. There was nothing more to be said. They had both said their piece and from now on, Loveday hoped there would be an unsaid mutual respect between. They knew one another had endured and lost. There was no need for any further words.

The mist that had previously lingered in the cove had now turned into a dense fog. Loveday firmly shut the wooden gate outside of Breel Cottage and set off in the direction of the ancient wood. She had no worries that anyone would see where she was heading. Hopefully, that would also mean that Trunrowan would be obscured from the enemy. The thought of the sleepy coastal village being bombarded by the Germans had scared her senseless, but she daren't let on to Will, he didn't need the extra stress. Still, hopefully by the end of the day, she would have some good news for him.

Loveday walked at a brisk pace, now knowing her way to Mrs Cromp's cottage like the back of her hand. She recalled her very first visit and how timid she'd been, it all seemed like an age ago now. In no time, she had reached the cottage and was knocking on the familiar rickety door. Almost immediately, the door opened.

'Ah! Loveday, come on in. I thought ye might be Gribble. Not seen 'im since 'e took ye up to Madron before Christmas. I know 'e said 'e wouldn't be this way for a while, but…' Mrs Cromp waved in Loveday, obviously disappointed she wasn't Gribble.

'Ye feeling sick yet?'

Loveday shut the door behind her, startled at Mrs Cromps comment.

'A little…'

'Well, I can give ye summut for it if it's too bad, although it shouldn't last much longer. Ye be over the worst of it now.'

'So, I am with cheel then?' Loveday said, feeling a sense of excitement stirring in her belly.

'Of course ye is. Didn't doubt it did ye? Come and sit by the fire and warm up. No good getting too cold in yer condition. Although, I ain't convinced that ye wasn't with cheel before ye went to the standing stones, although Gribble wouldn't 'ear of it if I suggested so.' Mrs Cromp laughed, followed by a long protracted sigh.

'Oh, I do miss Gribble ye know. This place ain't the same without him 'ere, it 'as to be said. Eating and drinking me out of me larder. The depths of winter be the worse. I 'ardly gets any visitors. But I sensed ye was coming so, I made a crumble and we can 'ave a nice cuppa and a natter… That's if ye 'as the time?'

Mrs Cromp looked at Loveday, her eyes filled with sadness.

'Of course I can stay, for a little while. I got in trouble ye see for staying out all night when I went to Madron.' Loveday was feeling sorry for her. It must be lonely living in the depths of the wood, with only birds and small mammals for friends, no matter how used to it you were.

Mrs Cromp nodded, as if she understood.

'I did come 'ere to see if ye could tell if I was with cheel. I thought ye might know by feeling me stomach or summut?'

Loveday sat in the rocking chair and took the mug of tea that was handed to her, careful not to spill its contents.

'I can indeed, but I don't really need to. Still, come 'ere and let me place me 'ands on you.' Mrs Cromp blew on her hands, rubbing them together vigorously.

Loveday squirmed a little as she felt a strange prickly heat from Mrs Cromp's hands, as she placed them on her stomach. She waited patiently, until finally Mrs Cromp removed them and disappeared from the room without saying a word. By the time Loveday was about to get up and go looking for her, she reappeared holding a cotton reel.

'Give us yer wedding ring.' Mrs Cromp was holding out her hand.

Loveday hesitated. She'd never taken her wedding ring off before, not since it had been placed on her finger by Will on their wedding day.

'Come now, it's only for a minute or two. I wants to show ye summut.'

Loveday swiveled the ring on her fingers for a few seconds, then decided that no harm would come from taking it off for a short while. She handed over the thin gold band and watched Mrs Cromp thread a piece of cotton through it, then tie a knot.

'There. Now sit back and relax, let's see what sex this cheel is, shall we?'

Mrs Cromp dangled the ring over Loveday's stomach, and they waited. She watched the light from the fire catch the gold ring as it began to slowly move in a clockwise direction. Amazed, she checked to see if Mrs Cromp's hand was moving, but it was as still as could be.

Mrs Cromp smiled and patted Loveday's stomach gently, handing back the wedding ring. 'It be a girl. As I expected. Strong and 'ealthy, and when the hay is 'arvested, she'll be born.'

Loveday could feel tears welling up but was grinning from ear to ear. Finally, after years and years of waiting, she was going to have a cheel. She and Will were going to be a proper family. She couldn't contain her delight any longer. She needed to leave right now and tell Will. She couldn't wait to see his face when she told him.

'More nettle tea?' Mrs Cromp offered. 'And I'll bring ye summut to eat too. Got to keep yer strength up now ye will be eating for two.' She passed Loveday a bowl of delicious-looking blackberry and apple crumble.

'Thank ye.' She would have to contain herself a little longer, it would be far too rude to leave now.

'And 'ow's that 'usband of yers doing...? 'As the potion 'elped?'

'Yes, it did, but then I missed a few days and when I got back from the standing stones, 'e was in an awful state. Worse than before.' Loveday paused so she could take a few mouthfuls of the delicious crumble. She didn't realise how hungry she was.

'Aye, that can 'appen, but ye only needs to start it up again.' Mrs Cromp raised her eyebrows. 'As long as ye sticks to the instructions I gave ye. One drop per day and one drop only and 'e will be right as rain.'

Loveday didn't have the courage to tell her that she'd doubled the dose. She'd already managed to get away with telling Mrs Cromp that George, their cat, had knocked some over when she'd asked for the second lot not that long ago, how was she going to ask for more now? She'd put two and two together, that was for sure.

Loveday shifted uncomfortably, just as a robin flew in through a small window that had been left slightly ajar. It perched on the top of the fire mantle and cocked its head looking at her, then puffed out his red breast and flew over to the kitchen table. Loveday shivered as though someone had walked over her grave.

'Ye must never give more than I 'as told ye to. Too much can make things worse and ye don't want that 'appening...that's for sure.' Mrs Cromp was looking concerned.

'Yes, I understands. Look, I best be off now…if that's OK? I'd like to tell Will the good news. 'E will be pleased as punch.' Loveday tried to lighten the mood in the room, which had all of a sudden become rather oppressive.

'And ye is sure 'e's alrite?'

'Yes, yes, just a bit tired ye knows. Time of year probably.' She started to make her way towards the door, hoping she wouldn't be challenged any further.

Mrs Cromp rested her hand on Loveday's arm.

'Ye be sure to come back and see me if things ain't right, ye understand? And if all is well, make sure I sees you when ye starts getting bigger. Yer ma would turn in her grave if she thought I wasn't keeping an eye on ye.'

Loveday suddenly felt an overwhelming urge to hug Mrs Cromp. She missed her ma badly as it was, but having a cheel of her own, well she was sure she was going to miss her even more now. Without thinking, she threw her arms around Mrs Cromp and hugged her tightly.

'I promise I will. Thank ye. For everything.'

As Loveday turned, she thought she saw Mrs Cromp wipe the edge of her cheek with a hanky.

'Myrtle. Call me Myrtle.'

Will wasn't sure how he'd got back to the cottage. Presumably he'd walked, but he couldn't remember doing so. He wondered if he was blacking out again, like earlier when he'd found himself sheltering under the hedge. Trying to put the morning's events into place was like piecing a jigsaw together. His head was fuzzy, his bones ached, his neck and shoulder were sore from carrying the coiled rope, and he'd not found the bull either. George Weaver wouldn't be best pleased, but he was past caring. All he had left to pray for, was that Loveday wouldn't be home.

Pushing the back door open, he called out Loveday's name. It echoed around the cottage. He called again. Loveday. A beautiful

Cornish name, for a beautiful Cornish maid.

They'd met at the village school when they were five years old and had been friends ever since. She used to follow him everywhere, like a lost lamb. Lost Loveday, the teachers nicknamed her.

She was a strange soul, even back then. They married when Loveday reached eighteen, in the chapel up on the headland. She had looked like a princess. He could picture her as clear as anything, as though it had happened yesterday. Her dress had been made of cream lace, handed down from her ma, and her ma before her. And woven into her luscious auburn hair, she'd worn a garland of wildflowers and berries.

That's how he wanted to remember her.

Life had been good, until he signed up to fight for King and Country. He knew he was lucky, to come back home alive, while others were still out there fighting. He didn't care that he'd lost his arm, he didn't care if he'd lost both of them. But he did care deeply, that he'd appeared to have lost his mind. Without it, he was nothing. How could Loveday still love him? How would he manage to be a good father? That's if they were ever lucky enough to have a cheel of their own. As it was, he struggled to be a mediocre husband.

He was afraid of the way he loved her. How he really needed her. How lonely he was. He didn't understand. Any of it. But he couldn't tell her. God knows he'd tried hard enough.

He called out her name one last time, her name lingering on his lips.

George appeared from upstairs meowing, rubbing himself up against Will's legs, purring, hoping to be fed. After rummaging for a good while in the pantry, he found some offcuts of ham under some cloth and put them on a plate for him. He wouldn't be needing it, so he might as well give George his share. Then he dragged a chair across the kitchen, until it was directly underneath the iron hook in the ceiling beam. Unravelling the rope from his shoulder, he tied a slip knot and attached the rope to the hook. His head was hurting really bad now, even worse than when he'd had a skinful…but it wouldn't be for much longer. However, there was one last thing he had to do.

Finding a pencil and some paper in the kitchen dresser, he scribbled Loveday a note.

Loveday
I am so sorry
Will xx

Loveday would never forget that day for as long as she lived. By the time she'd left Mrs Cromp's it was dark, and an eager wind had gathered speed, whistling through the trees and anything else it could rush and rustle through.

Opening the back door. Seeing Will, hanging from the iron hook, the chair on its side. George meowing. The note. The smell of death that would stay with her forever.

How she held on to the unborn cheel inside of her, how she made it back to Myrtle Cromp's cottage, she would never know.

The funeral was a quiet affair. The sun shone as though it had never risen before. Strong and fierce, in a cloudless blue sky, despite only being the middle of January. Mabel, Daisy, George and Maggie were there. Bobbie Trevelyan, along with a few others, paid their respects. Even Myrtle Cromp and Gribble Gummo, who appeared to have come back to Trunrowan just for the funeral, laid flowers at the chapel door, although they did not stay for the service. Reverend Jones could not have made the service any more special, given the circumstances. And after the service, as Loveday looked out from the graveyard across the estuary and out to sea, she saw a line of drifter boats, bobbing up and down, their sails at half mast.

Later that evening there was a small gathering in The Ferryboat Inn, as Will would have wanted, although Loveday didn't stay for long. It was time to move on. She had things to attend to. There was no way she could stay in Rowan Cottage after what she'd seen, but she would do her best to keep on the cottage for their cheel in the future. How, she didn't know, but for now, she had to concentrate on ensuring that their unborn child was brought into the world safely.

As Loveday walked away from the pub, she held her stomach, knowing that part of Will still lived on and instinctively felt for the silver coin that nestled in the dip of her neck. It was warm and gave her hope, love and the courage to fight on. Just as Will had intended it to when he'd sent it to her from the battlefields.

Present day

After a bumpy ride to Truro in the back of the ambulance, Kitty had given birth to Loveday May Gridley, in the hospital delivery suite…just.

It had all happened so quickly, and she was left feeling completely overwhelmed. She still couldn't believe she'd actually given birth to a real little person.

Loveday had been born with a head full of dark hair and, as all babies had initially, dark blue eyes. She was all Daddy. There didn't appear to be an ounce of herself in the wondrousness that gazed back at her.

Lizzie had visited her frequently while she was in hospital, sitting by the side of her bed, feeding her cake and the occasional obligatory grape. Filling her in with all the information about Will and the cottage. Kitty was more than grateful to Morwenna Cromp for helping Will's spirit to finally pass over. Listening to the tale of why Will had haunted the cottage in the first place saddened her deeply, but she got it. She now understood why, and she hoped he had been reunited with his Loveday and the daughter he never knew.

She'd felt it was the right thing to do, to name their child Loveday. In fairness, after what she'd been through, Ben would've let her name her anything! It was a nod to the past, and the future, embracing their new Cornish life. Giving their child, born in Cornwall, a Cornish name which meant; *Dear, loved and precious*. Its traditional meaning, relating to a love day, set aside for reconciliation and the settling of disputes. How apt.

XXX

Kitty was finally discharged from hospital four days after Loveday had been born. She was excited to eventually be going home and starting a new life, all of them together. As she walked up the shingle path and looked at the whitewashed stone cottage that stood in front of her, she thought how solid and strong it looked, still standing after two hundred years or more. This was her home, Ben's home, and now Loveday's. This was Creek Cottage, once known as Rowan Cottage.

And so life settled back to normality, whatever that was. There were no more strange feelings or floorboards creaking. No madness, no craziness, nothing but an overwhelming sense of love that seemed to seep through the stone walls and envelop itself around them as they embraced the future together.

Twelve months later

'Have you seen Loveday's green wool cardigan, Ben?' Kitty asked, moving toys, blankets and various fluffy animals that had now overtaken the cottage.

Ben was enjoying some Loveday time, bouncing her up and down on his knee and pulling faces at her, making her giggle.

Kitty watched them both, laughing and blowing bubbles. He had all the fun, not a care in the world, while there she was frantically trying to remember where she'd put Loveday's cardigan. What had her life come to? There was once a time when she'd been responsible for patients and making sure they didn't die, now…it was all about the wool, and not the type she often thought her head was full of.

'Found it! Right, let's head off. Have you got everything?' Kitty put the cardigan into her bag and grabbed Loveday's hat.

'Which way are we going?' Ben asked, adjusting the baby backpack.

'Pete said to follow the path alongside the woodland, then once we see the chapel, just follow our nose. His words, not mine. Can't be too difficult and it's a lovely day, so we can take our time. I've packed sandwiches and a flask.'

'Da-da,' Loveday said, pointing at the door.

'Ha! No, I'm Da-da, that's a door, but I get what you mean. Right, off we go then!'

Kitty followed behind them, down the garden path and into the cove. She really didn't think she could feel much happier, but today there was something she needed to do…

It was a steep climb to the headland, one she'd done before, once. But they'd never visited the chapel. She wasn't sure why. Neither of them were particularly religious but when they finally reached the small but beautifully presented stone chapel they weren't disappointed.

Inside it was understated and serene. There were two huge bunches of wild flowers adorning either side of the altar that someone had obviously taken great care in arranging. They looked beautiful. At the back of the church was a plaque on the wall that denoted the names of villagers who'd lost their lives in the Great storm of 1905, but surprisingly there were no names of soldiers, either from the Great War or the Second World War.

'Shall we have a wander outside in the graveyard?' Ben suggested. And, as they walked around the small graveyard, careful not to stand on any graves, they finally came across a headstone that held the inscription they had been looking for. They both stood in front of the headstone in silence, while Kitty placed a bunch of sweet peas from the garden onto the grave, and Loveday pointed to a robin that had perched on top of the headstone.

'Bir – Bir.'

'That's right, Loveday. It's a bird called a robin.'

'Bir – Bir,' she repeated.

They both read the inscription while Loveday chattered.

HERE LIETH WILLIAM NANCE
B. 1888 D. 1917
LOYAL SERVANT
SLEEP DEAR HUSBAND, SLEEP, THY WORK IS
DONE, THY TOIL IS O'ER, THY CROWN IS WON.
HOW SWEET TO REST ON THAT BLEST SHORE,
WHERE PAIN AND SORROW ARE NO MORE.

Added at a later date was a further inscription.

BELOVED WIFE
LOVEDAY NANCE
B. 1890 D. 1961

And a final, more recent one.

LAMORNA NANCE
B. 1917 D. 2007
FINALLY REUNITED WITH HER FAMILY.
R.I.P.

Kitty reached into her bag for the small hand trowel she'd packed. Carefully, she knelt at the grave and began to uncover some of the soil until she was satisfied enough had been moved. She then placed the silver king's shilling, which she'd rethreaded onto a piece of vibrant purple velvet ribbon, into the soil. She hoped no one would chastise her for digging into the soil of the grave. She stood up and brushed off her hands on her trousers and took Loveday's hand while they watched Ben. Methodically and in silence, Ben covered over the king's shilling with the disturbed soil and patted it down, replacing the sweet peas over the top.

'Shall we say a prayer or something?' Ben suggested.

'I found this in the garden shed a while back when I was clearing it out, amongst all the letters and papers. It's a book of poems. Do you think we could read one together?' Kitty opened the book and showed Ben the poem she had chosen, its watermarked and fragile page fluttering in the gentle breeze.

'It's a poem by Rupert Brooke, called *The Soldier*.'

'Yes, let's read it together before it's taken on the wind.'

> *If I should die, think only this of me:*
> *That there's some corner of a foreign field*
> *That is for ever England. There shall be*
> *In that rich earth a richer dust concealed;*
> *A dust whom England bore, shaped, made aware,*
> *Gave, once, her flowers to love, her ways to roam;*
> *A body of England's, breathing English air,*
> *Washed by the rivers, blest by suns of home.*
>
> *And think, this heart, all evil shed away,*
> *A pulse in the eternal mind, no less*
> *Gives somewhere back the thoughts by England given;*
> *Her sights and sounds; dreams happy as her day;*
> *And laughter, learnt of friends; and gentleness,*
> *In hearts at peace, under an English heaven.*

And when the last word had been spoken Kitty wiped the tears from her eyes.

They would never know why this had happened to them, but they did know that life was precious. There would come a day when they too would die. But, for now, life was for living.

POSTSCRIPT

Things have moved on, in terms of understanding PTSD, in particular since the days of the Great War (1914-1918). There are now many charities and bodies of help out there today that did not exist when Will came back from war. Below are a few that can offer advice and assistance.

http://www.ptsdresolution.org
http://www.rock2recovery.co.uk
http://www.samaritans.org
https://www.helpforheroes.org.uk/get-support/
mental-health-and-wellbeing/

AUTHOR'S NOTES TO
AID THE READER

Trunrowan – A fictional village in Cornwall.

Cheel – Child.

Pisky/Piskies – Fairy folk/spirits.

Madron (Eglos Madern) – Village in West Cornwall.

Standing stones – Stones set vertically in the ground dating from the Neolithic/Bronze age.

Men-an-Tol – Small formation of standing stones, 3 miles NW of Madron.

Crick stone – Local name for the Men-an-Tol.

Cunning folk – Also known as folk healers, wise women, pellars and white witches.

Spriggan – A mischievous and thievish legendary creature from Cornish faery lore.

Hun – British Army slang for Germans (WW1).

Furlough – Leave of absence, in particular granted to those in military service.

Trelawny – Cornish patriotic song. The anthem was adopted by the 7th Battalion of the Duke of Cornwall's Light Infantry (WW1). Also known as 'The Song of the Western Men'.

King's shilling – A shilling in WW1 was the basic wage of a soldier. To take the King's Shilling was a 'handshake' before signing an official contract, as well as some soldiers being given a tangible one shilling coin.

Tiddy – Potato.

Harvest Moon – The full moon that falls closest to the autumn equinox.

Cold Moon – The first full moon in December.

Droll Teller – A Cornish travelling story-teller.

Guise dancing – Traditionally a West Cornwall tradition, usually celebrated around the 12 days of Christmas. The guise dancers wear masks to hide their identity. They dance, sing and play music and can be very mischievous.

Hevva cake – A Cornish cake that is derived from the pilchard industry. Sometimes known as heavy cake.

Maid – Girl/Woman.

Breel – Mackerel.

Lugger/Drifter – Traditional fishing boats (sailing), mainly for catching pilchards & herring.

Lathered – Drunk.

Teasy – Grumpy.

No Man's Land – A term associated with WW1/The Great War; an area of land between two enemy trench systems.

Bleddy – Cornish for bloody.

Wasson – Hello, Good morning/evening, What's going on?

Lightning Source UK Ltd.
Milton Keynes UK
UKHW010635120822
407216UK00002B/347